NO SUCH CREATURE

GILES BLUNT

NO SUCH CREATURE

RANDOM HOUSE CANADA

www.randomhouse.ca

Random House Canada and colophon are trademarks.

LIBRARY AND ARCHIVES CANADA CATALOGUING IN PUBLICATION

Blunt, Giles
    No such creature / Giles Blunt.

ISBN 978-0-679-31431-8

    I. Title.

PS8553.L867N6 2008   C813'.54   C2008-901663-7

Design by Leah Springate

Printed in the United States of America

10 9 8 7 6 5 4 3 2 1

For Janna

NO SUCH CREATURE

ONE

ON A COOL NIGHT IN LATE JUNE the traffic on Highway 101 was not heavy—not for a Saturday night, anyway—and moved along at a steady clip, people cruising out to restaurants or movies or to spend the evening with friends.

There was one car travelling north from the city—a midnight blue Lexus. An old man was driving, his considerable belly pressed up against the steering wheel, and the passenger seat was only partially filled by a blade-thin boy who looked to be in his late teens.

As the Lexus rounded a curve, it broke away from the rest of the traffic and veered across an entire lane. A sharp left, and then it bounced into the parking lot of a gas station and made a swift circle so that it came around again, nose pointed toward the highway.

Inside the car, the boy took his hand from the dash, where it had been bracing him against becoming a highway statistic, and said, "Would you mind telling me what that was all about?"

"Final wardrobe check."

"We already did that, Max. Why do we have to do it over again?"

"It's your hide I'm looking out for, Owen, me lad. You know I never give a thought to myself—I've been accused of it many times. 'Max,' the doctor said to me—cardiologist, I hasten to point out, knows a thing or two about this sorrowful organ we call the human heart. 'Max,' he said, 'the fact is you are suffering from magnacarditis. Your heart's too big. An albatross borne down by giant wings. You care too much for other people, and it's driving you to an early grave.'"

"The only thing getting bigger on you," the boy said, "is your gut, and if you had a decent doctor—not that I believe you ever went to see a doctor—he'd tell you to cut back on the Guinness and the single malts, not to mention the hamburgers, the milk-shakes and the shepherd's pie."

"It pains me to hear such cynicism from one so young." Max placed a hand over his heart as if to protect that overworked organ. "The world is a barren, comfortless place when a seventeen-year-old—"

"Eighteen."

"—when an eighteen-year-old addresses his mentor this way—insulting the sage and learned man who's raised him up as his own and taught him everything he knows."

"I know lots of stuff you didn't teach me. The capitals of Africa, the rivers of South America, how to calculate the area of an irregular surface."

"Trivia," Max said. "Tell it to Roscoe. But you wound me, boy." He tapped a plump finger on his heart and sighed. "I'm a gentle creature, beset by a heartless teenager, no doubt an incipient gangbanger. You, of course, are a warlike American, whereas I remain your humble Warwickshire yeoman, and ever shall."

"I'd like to visit Warwick one day. I'd love to hear from some-body other than you what you were like as a kid. I have a feeling they'll be telling a very different story about Max Maxwell over there."

"Nonsense. They would recall a heroic figure, just as you see me today."

The boy examined himself in the rear-view mirror. "Okay, so how do I look?"

Max squinted at him, ginger eyebrows furrowing. "Terrifying. Perfect young Republican."

They had decided on a dark wig and vigorous curls for Owen, and neatly trimmed sideburns. A gorgeous black Armani jacket and pants were set off by an expensive white T-shirt that showed off his fat-free abdominals. Owen's first draft of the look had been red hair, freckles and polka-dot bow tie, but Max overruled him: too on-the-nose, he called it, a parody. And besides, it was important to make optimal use of Owen's heartthrob potential. The curls did give the boy's profile a touch of the Greek god, not that Owen believed that heartthrob business for one minute.

"You don't think the hair's too curly?"

"It's perfect. Gives you a bit of the Kennedy—to which even the most granite-hearted Republican is not immune. And me?" Max smoothed his ginger moustache. Even up close it looked completely natural.

"I'd say you were a real bastard. Kind of guy who owns several mines and seriously mistreats his workers."

"Thank you."

"Hey, Max, I bought you a little present."

"No time, boy, no time." Max started the car again. "We must get a wiggle on."

"Hang on. You're gonna love this." Owen pulled it from an inside pocket and held it out.

"A cellphone?" Max furrowed his new ginger brows. "Why in the name of heaven would we need another cellphone?"

"We don't. Try to make a call from your cell."

Max gunned the motor, eyeing the traffic whizzing by. "Owen, time is of the essence."

"We've got plenty of time. Try to make a call."

Muttering, Max extracted his cellphone and dialed Owen's number. "Nothing happening," he said. "Completely dead." He showed the tiny blank screen to Owen.

"Exactly," Owen said. "Because what I have here is not a cellphone. It's a cellphone *jammer*. Good for up to five hundred yards."

"You actually found one?" Max said. "Sweet boy, you are my very Ariel."

Owen put on a thin, reedy voice—he was good at voices, and this one made him sound like a tiny alien. "*All hail, great master!*

I come to answer thy best pleasure, be it to fly, to swim, to dive into the fire!"

Max laughed. "You're a good lad, Owen. Truly, it's not every boy who's cut out for a life of crime."

The old man slid the gear shift into drive and the Lexus eased back onto a highway peopled with innocent civilians.

TWO

THE HOME OF MARGOT PEABODY WAS LIT UP like a Chinese lantern, all four storeys of it, a beacon to the rich, the Republican and the reprobate. It was an ornate wooden structure located in the most exclusive segment of Belvedere, purchased by pulp and paper magnate Cyrus Peabody (now defunct) some ten years previously for a comparative song. Expensive automobiles gleamed in a semicircle of driveway, their uniformed drivers absorbed in the sports pages.

Owen's usual stage fright kicked up a notch.

"We're gonna be coming right back out," Max said to the teenager directing traffic. His accent was now American, a touch of the East Coast in it, but not much. "Put us somewhere we can make a fast getaway."

"Sure thing, sir. Just park it over there under that tree. I won't let anyone block you."

"First class, kid." Max handed him a rolled-up bill. "First class."

At the door they were met by an Asian houseboy in white livery. His hair was so slick, his skin so flawless, he looked as if he had escaped from a waxworks.

"Good evening, sir. What name shall I say?"

"Carter and Christopher Gould, but it's hardly worth the bother," Max said, "we can't stay."

In the vast cathedral of space before them, men in dinner jackets mingled with well-tended women too thin for their hairdos. Owen looked up at the beautiful redwood beams supporting a ceiling that had to be at least forty feet high, but Max had taught him never to comment on such things, to act as if he took luxury and service for granted. Under massive skylights, a redwood mezzanine ran around the entire great hall.

The butterflies in Owen's stomach took flight up into his chest. But he loved this moment, this sense of balancing on the edge of the high dive, poised to plunge into triumph or disaster. It would be a hard thing to leave behind.

"Turn around, kid," Max said to the houseboy. "Just let me use your shoulder, I'll write a cheque right now and we'll be out of your hair."

The houseboy obligingly turned, tilting his head slightly, and Max whipped out a chequebook.

"This state has had a Republican government for nearly eight years and I want to make sure it stays that way. Twenty thousand should help. If it was legal to give more, I'd do it in a shot. Carter, your turn."

Owen pulled out a chequebook and wrote out a similar figure, signing it Carter P. Gould with a flourish.

"Now, where do we drop these?"

"In the large bottle by the stairs, sir, but I must tell Ms. Peabody you're here."

"Relax, kid, put your feet up. Margot!"

Max waved to a woman just emerging from the crowd in an ivory summer dress tied at the waist. The sandals laced elaborately round her ankles hinted at ancient Greece, besotted fauns and massive hedge funds.

"How lovely to see you," she said with a smile that gave no hint they had never met. Max was always meticulous about his research, and had assured Owen that Margot Peabody was renowned for a spectacular collection of jewellery. It was not much in evidence tonight: a single strand of pearls, perfect milky spheres, circled her throat. "Come and have a drink on the lawn. I'm sure you'll find scads of people you know."

"Sorry, Margot. Can't stay. Gotta be in the capital first thing in the morning." He waggled the cheque at her and popped it into the bottle.

"Oh, stay for one drink, I insist. I'm trying to remember where it was we met."

"Hah! You've got me there. The Leonardo drawings?"

"The Getty! Of course, of course! And is this your son?"

"Nephew. Carter Gould—doesn't like to use the numerals. Grumpy teenager, way they all are."

"A handsome teenager nevertheless." She reached out a hand that was pure gristle. He gave it a brief squeeze. "Are you really such a grump?" she asked.

"Not at all, ma'am," Owen said. "Pleasure to meet you." He inserted his cheque into the mouth of the bottle and tapped it home.

"You're both too, too kind. Now follow me."

She led them through the crowd toward a pair of French doors. Owen noted earrings, necklaces, brooches, watches; your honest, God-fearing Republicans were not averse to a little ostentation. What's the point of owning diamonds if you never wear them?

Under a snow-white canopy out back, a cover band was doing an earnest version of "Born in the U.S.A.," the singer sounding in imminent danger of aneurysm. Sausalito glittered across the black water, and off to the south the arc of the Bay Bridge. In the dark of the waterfront, the house seemed to blaze and shimmer.

Ms. Peabody led them to the bar and made sure they got their drinks—gin and tonic for Max, Coke for Owen. She introduced Owen to a busty debutante who shook his hand and smiled shyly. He tried to engage her in conversation, but she blushed and looked at her feet.

"To be perfectly honest," Margot Peabody said to Max, "I don't think we're in much danger of losing in November, but we do want to be on the safe side, don't we."

"Absolutely," Max said. "Have to generate a healthy investment climate, get those returns growing again."

"Well, yes. And property values."

"Excuse me," Owen said, "back in a minute." He headed into the house at a clip that suggested serious discomfort.

"Poor kid," Max said. "Ever since the accident he's had the bladder of a little girl."

"Accident?"

"High-strung filly. Took a nasty tumble."

Ms. Peabody spread that gristly hand, fanlike, over her heart. "A riding accident! He's lucky he didn't end up paralyzed, or in a coma."

"He was wearing the regulation helmet, thank God."

"He was playing polo? There's nowhere near here, is there?"

"Cirencester, U.K. Charity match. Three princes there that afternoon, and I guarantee you not one of *their* horses balked. I was ready to blow a gasket, but you know you can't say anything to a royal—raise an international stink. They did send a nice card, I'll give 'em that."

"The least they could do, under the circumstances. You probably could have sued them."

"Nah," Max said. "Polo's a tough game. Have to expect to get knocked around a little."

"How delightfully macho," his hostess said, and gave a musical laugh.

Inside, Owen bounded up the front stairs two at a time.

"Sir! Sir!" the houseboy called after him, "there are plenty of restrooms down here."

Owen found a sumptuous bathroom halfway along the hall. He stepped in and checked himself out in multiple mirrors. The black Armani looked great, he had to admit, and the new curls seemed to be working wonders with the female element. He flushed the toilet and set the tap running in the sink so the bathroom would sound occupied, then shut the door from the outside.

At the end of the hall a pair of double doors was closed. Under Max's tutelage he had developed an instinct for such things.

If you want to rob a Republican, your best time is suppertime, Max had taught him. They always have company, the place is full of strangers, and every alarm is exactly where you want it: off.

Five minutes, he wouldn't need more.

The master bedroom was all rustic wood and white fabric, but Owen made straight for the dressing room, a compact chamber redolent with aromas of cedar, Guerlain and shoe leather, and got it right on the first guess: the set of library steps gave her away. He reached up into the space between the ceiling and the top shelf and pulled out a high-quality wooden chest secured with a paltry lock that he snapped in less than two seconds.

Inside, there was a diamond brooch that had to be worth thirty or forty grand, an exquisite jade cameo, and a gold and ruby bracelet. But the real showstopper was the pair of emerald earrings, emeralds being more valuable even than diamonds. Both gems looked free of inclusions and were at least twelve carats, the light and clear green of a cat's eye. Hundred and twenty grand on a bad day.

Owen lifted the tray out of the chest. Underneath, he found two fat packets of hundred-dollar bills. He had no idea why Margot Peabody would be stashing approximately thirty grand in her jewellery box, but he certainly wasn't about to complain.

"God, I love this job," he said softly. He stuffed his pockets, closed the doors, and returned to the bathroom to shut off the water.

When he emerged, a somewhat off-kilter babe in a shimmery blue dress was having trouble making it up the last few stairs, pressing a cellphone to her ear with one hand and clutching a martini in the other. She snapped the phone shut, eyeing Owen.

"What are you doing up here?" she said, an edge in her voice.

"Bathroom."

"There are bathrooms downstairs," she said, slurring a little.

"They were occupied."

"Yeah?" She looked him up and down, taking her time about it. She was pretty in a hard way; her frown looked like it might be permanent. "Who are you? Why haven't we met?"

Owen put out a hand. "Carter Gould. Who are you?"

"Melinda Peabody. Unfortunately."

"Why unfortunately?"

She waved a limp hand. "Long story. How old are you, anyway? I'm twenty-five." She looked ten years older.

"I'm eighteen," Owen said. "Just turned."

"Too young. Which is too bad, because you're so cute you're making me dizzy." She steadied herself against the wall.

"That must be the martini," Owen said. "I better be getting back downstairs." Max would be wondering where the hell he was. A missed cue could ruin the whole show.

"No, really," Melinda said. "People must tell you that all the time, right? That you're totally fucking devastating?"

"Never," Owen said. "This is the first time."

"Liar. Get out of here before I jump you." She flung open the bathroom door, nearly toppling herself, and shut it behind her.

Owen stopped at the mezzanine on the way down. The band was taking a break, and Margot Peabody was herding everyone into the great hall below, where a bulky bear of a man in a tux was seated at a grand piano. Max looked up at Owen, and Owen pulled out the jammer and flipped it open. He pushed the On button and held it to his ear as if answering a call. Then he scowled at it and put it back into his pocket.

When she had got the crowd quiet, Ms. Peabody told them they were in for a terrific surprise. "We are honoured to have a very special guest with us tonight, one who needs no introduction, seeing how she's come here straight from the stage of New York's Lincoln Center. Ladies and gentlemen, I give you Evelyn del Rio."

Max was always hauling Owen off to the theatre—he'd seen more productions of *Hamlet* than he cared to think about—but he had never been to an opera. Even so, he knew who Evelyn del Rio was. He was disappointed that she was not fat. She was a trim blonde woman in a plain black skirt with a sparkly top that drew attention to her chest. When the applause died down, she nodded at the piano bear and he began to play a set of dark, dour chords. Over these the famous voice came hovering, floating at first, and then sweeping upward into the ceiling, sending a thrill up Owen's spine. It was something, a voice of pure silver at such proximity; he'd never heard anything like it. One of the great things about robbing the rich was you got to see some first-class entertainment.

It was a sad aria, not too long, and when it was over, the audience couldn't stop grinning and applauding. Melinda Peabody had made her way back downstairs and was off in a corner, stabbing repeatedly at her cellphone and frowning. Owen looked around. Max's caterers, as he called them, were in place at the two exits. They wore livery much like the houseboy's and stood with folded arms, looking serious and professional.

Before the applause had ended, Max stepped into a spot right below Owen and raised his hands. Owen's adrenalin shot up several levels, his heart hammering.

"Well, that was stupendous, wasn't it?" Max said to the crowd. "Beautiful music, beautifully rendered. But, before we go any further, I also have an announcement to make, and I want you to promise not to get upset. It's the kind of thing people can get hysterical about, so let me tell you up front that such a reaction is totally unnecessary. You are here to part with money, after all. And so this gathering is being robbed. That's right, you heard me—robbed."

The great hall seemed to darken, although the lights stayed on. There were murmurs and catches of breath and questioning, worried looks.

"Rest assured that I myself, not to mention the able assistants you see at various points around the room, are fully—by which I mean lethally—armed. Still—"

A couple of men started to speak up, but Max silenced them by pulling out a .38 Special, which he did not point at anybody. He didn't have to.

"Still," he continued, "there is no reason in the world why this has to be a totally negative experience. I urge you—strongly urge you—to simply drop your valuables into the sack we'll be bringing around. Watches, brooches, necklaces, jewellery of any kind. We're not brutes—wedding rings are not required unless extraordinarily valuable—worth, say, over five thousand."

"Bullshit," someone said. Owen didn't see who it was; he was more worried about a small, lean man moving slowly, almost imperceptibly toward Max from behind. Owen unhooked the elegant velvet rope that reached upward to the skylights all the way from the lower floor. He took a pair of leather gloves from his pocket, put them on, and slowly slid down the rope to the floor below, planting himself firmly between Max and the approaching man. Pure Errol Flynn.

"Don't even think about it," he said, and the man went still.

Max handed Owen a sack emblazoned with a red Republican elephant. Owen began going to each of the women in turn, holding it open.

"No tricks, mister," Max said to the man, still in his East Coast accent. "The usual rules will be strictly enforced. Nobody moves, nobody leaves. This'll only take a few minutes."

The lean man was now edging toward a door.

"Don't spoil it for everybody," Max said to him, gesturing with the gun. "This is very much a money-or-your-life situation."

"Try and stop me."

Roscoe, one of Max's caterers, reared up to his full height, which was considerable, and the man veered toward a different exit. Pookie, Roscoe's colleague, stepped forward. The man kept coming. Pookie reached for his weapon, but Max fired first, a single shot into the ceiling that made an enormous noise. The smokeless blanks they always used were even louder than the real thing, and made Owen jump every time.

The man stopped and turned back to face them, very pale.

"The next one won't be a warning."

"Look," Evelyn del Rio said, "I think everybody needs to calm down. Especially you, sir."

"Your humble servant, madam," Max said with a bow. "Consider me becalmed."

"If we're going to be robbed anyway," she added, "we should at least have some music. Giorgio?"

"You expect me to play?" said the bear. He seemed more shook up than his diva.

"What else are we going to do?" she said. "I'm damned if I'm going to crumple up and cry."

"Marvellous," Max said. "And I know that a woman who sings like you has just got to be a magnificent dancer. I beseech you, Giorgio—a waltz."

The bear shook his head, but turned back to the keyboard and started to play. Owen recognized the tune, though he couldn't have named it.

Max put his gun away and took Evelyn del Rio's hand. As Owen stepped from guest to guest accepting "donations," Max twirled around the floor with the soprano, who looked as cool as ivory.

"The ring, too," Owen said to the girl in front of him. She was about twelve—a red-haired vision in Calvin Klein who started to cry and handed it over.

"It's just a ring," Owen said. "A material object. There's no reason to get so worked up."

"My daddy gave me that ring," she said, a Southern girl, maybe Arkansas, "'fore he died. It was my momma's engagement ring."

"Well, why isn't your mother wearing it, then?"

"Because she's dead too, you snake."

Owen took her hot little fist and opened it, placed the sparkling ring into her palm, and folded her fingers over it. "You don't know me well enough to call me that," he said.

Max was still spinning around the floor with Evelyn del Rio. There was an abstracted air on his face that worried Owen. Lately the old man had been having spells of vagueness—usually not more than a few minutes—during which he forgot where he was and what he was doing. Max should have been collecting loot in a second bag, thus doubling their speed, but instead he was dancing with an opera star. Not good.

A couple of the men glared as if they would take him apart, but the rest were exceedingly co-operative. One of the things that had surprised Owen when he had first become involved in the lively pursuit of robbery was that men were generally as terrified as women. They didn't cry and carry on, but they trembled a lot. He wished they wouldn't; he wished they understood how truly safe they were, provided they didn't try anything.

"I suppose you want credit cards too," said one fellow—he had a lot of freckles. He looked like the type of guy you'd enjoy tossing a Frisbee with.

"Just cash and jewellery," Owen told him. "But thank you for asking."

"Fuck you."

"Settle down, man. It'll all be over soon, and you'll have a great story to tell your grandchildren."

Another two minutes and it was done. Owen signalled to Max, but Max was still lost in his dancing, a blissful smile on his face. Pookie had to bull his way through the crowd and take Max by the elbow to get him back down to earth. Max bowed deeply and kissed Evelyn del Rio's hand.

———

They took the Lexus at a stately pace along Shore Road, until Pookie said, "Turn here, turn here." They drove around a mock Tudor house, which was empty and up for sale, and abandoned the Lexus behind it. They jogged down to the private jetty, where Pookie and Roscoe had moored the motorboat which, like the Lexus, they had stolen earlier in the evening. They heard sirens and saw police lights flashing on Shore Road, but by then they were plowing across the bay toward the lights of San Francisco.

It was cold on the water. Owen pulled the lapels of his dinner jacket together against the wind. The boat was a mid-size outboard, a seventy-five horse on the back. Pookie and Roscoe were up front, since they knew where they were going. Max was in the rear, shouting over the racket of the motor.

"Evelyn del Rio," he yelled, once again in his own English accent. "What grace is seated on her brow! I'll tell you, lad, if I was ever to completely lose my mind and marry, Evelyn del Rio is the woman for me. What poise! What self-possession!"

"She hated you," Owen yelled back. "I saw her face! She was wishing you were dead the whole time!"

"A palpable lie! She was cool as a waterfall. Fresh as a crystal stream!"

Pookie swerved the boat into a deserted city maintenance wharf. They tied up, and climbed into the Taurus he had rented. Here they all removed their various wigs and moustaches and dropped them into a garbage bag.

"Evelyn del Rio," Max sighed, wiping the last of the glue from his eyebrows. "I feel love's keen arrow. Evelyn del Rio and Magnus Maxwell. We'd be the envy of the world."

"You old lecher," Pookie said. He had been disguised with a dark wig, thick eyebrows and a too-long moustache that made him resemble a Wild West sheriff. But now he was the old Pookie, with his baby face, pale blue eyes and alopecia so thorough that he was entirely devoid of eyebrows, indeed of hair of any kind. "You're so insensitive, you can't even tell when a woman is harbouring negative thoughts against you."

"I was robbing her, Pookie. Of course she was harbouring negative thoughts. But she would have warmed to me over time," Max said, "even granite warms in sunlight. She would have come to appreciate my intelligence and sense of humour."

"Hah!" Pookie said. "Good one."

"Pay the thug," Max said to Owen. "It's this kind of negative thinking that keeps you down, Pookie. Cynicism is the flag of despair."

Owen handed over ten hundred-dollar bills and Pookie counted them slowly. He had a big, gaudy pinky ring on his right hand—a death's head with fake ruby eyes that flashed in the street light. Like Roscoe, Pookie was not a partner, he was strictly freelance: a fee was agreed upon up front and that was what he received, no matter how the job went. But he worked with Max and Owen every year.

"How'd you do upstairs?" Pookie asked.

"Not bad," Owen said. "Pretty good, in fact." There was no point lying about it. Thieves were obsessive about reading up on their crimes. Pookie would hear about the jewels in a day or two.

"You mean I'm underpaid again, right?"

"Pookie," Max said, "think of all the times we've paid you your exorbitant fee even when we came up empty. I've paid you for jobs where I lost thousands. Those occasions found you oddly mute."

Pookie, like many criminals somewhat childish, stuck out his tongue.

"Which country gave the world the Panama hat?" Roscoe said out of the blue. He was a trivia addict, and you couldn't spend more than ten minutes with him without being questioned on points of geography, history or entertainment. He was six-four and built like a linebacker, but his only true passion in life, as far as Owen could determine, was *Jeopardy*.

"Panama?" Owen said, counting out another thousand.

"Ecuador," Pookie said.

"Ecuador is correct," Roscoe said solemnly.

"Had some business in Ecuador once," Max said. "Sullen little country. No sense of humour."

"I thought the jammer worked well tonight," Owen said.

"It's not the worst idea," Pookie said. "But those sirens still came up awful fast."

"Yeah," Owen said. "I guess we should still collect all the cellphones."

Roscoe folded his money into his pocket. "Smooth job, I thought."

"Our shows are always smooth," Owen said. "It's called preparation."

"Preparation," Max agreed, "and a friendly, respectful attitude. Respect the other man and he'll respect you, it's as simple as that."

"Most people don't recognize being robbed as a mark of respect," Pookie said. "You were too busy dancing your fat ass off to—"

"Fat! The bald bandit dares to call me fat! I am goodly portioned. I am what in better times was referred to as a fine figure of a man."

"If you believe that," Pookie said, "you're living on your own small planet."

"He *is* a small planet," Owen said, and they both laughed.

"*Haw-haw-haw*," Max mimicked them. "*Haw-haw-haw*. O thou monster ignorance. I tell you, aside from courtesy in action, it's being willing to spend money to earn money that makes a successful thief."

"His Munificence speaks," Roscoe said.

Owen was impressed that Roscoe knew the word, but Roscoe Lukacs knew lots of things you wouldn't expect from a criminal.

"O base Hungarian," Max said, raising a plump forefinger. "How many men do you know who will hire goons like yourselves simply to stand in front of the exits and look menacing? I'm out of pocket, I tell you. I won't see a dime out of the whole venture. I'll have to pull another job to buy my way out of this one."

This brought a chorus of derision that even Max couldn't shout down.

A few minutes later, Pookie dropped Max and Owen at the entrance to a public parking lot. There they got into their own car, another Taurus, and drove themselves to the Redwood Trailer Park, lot 61, and parked beside an enormous and aged Winnebago. Max had won it years ago in a poker game, and they had referred to it affectionately ever since as the Rocket— though less affectionately now that the price of fuelling it had become extortionate.

They were surrounded by acres of trailers—trailers of every manifestation, from the kind that fold out into semi-tents to massive, wheeled bungalows. But few could boast the dog-eared grandeur of the Rocket. It was the size of a semi, deep blue with bands of stainless steel in blinding diagonals, a giant Adidas running shoe. Thirty-five feet long, eight and a half wide, give or take. Inside, *Star Trek*–size leather seats faced the windshield. Behind these, the interior stretched in a glory of gold and tan. A couch was fitted to one side, and across from this a set of stairs led to a roof deck that could be furnished with chaise longues, table, umbrella and even a few plants, should they ever stay in one place long enough to warrant it.

The Rocket also boasted a Hitachi hi-def TV with built-in satellite, deep-pile carpeting of marmalade colour, a fold-up kitchen table, a fridge, washer-dryer, and a cozy wooden dining booth across from a set of bunk beds. Owen always slept on the top bunk; Max slept in splendour on a queen-size bed in the bedroom at the rear of the coach.

This was how they travelled every summer across America, towing the car behind them like a faithful goat. At the end of the trip, car and trailer went into storage on whatever coast they happened to finish.

Owen dumped the swag onto the dining table to survey the take. They had netted roughly six thousand in cash from downstairs, maybe sixty thousand in jewels. Owen's upstairs haul was thirty grand in cash—"My personal best!" he said, waving the packets at Max—and about $200,000 in jewels, but they would not receive anything close to that from their fence, the discount on stolen merchandise being severe. Max looked all set to pout until Owen pulled the emerald earrings out of his pocket.

"Oh, my." Max held one up to the light. "Can't even put a price on these beauties. Never seen their like." He examined the setting. "You see each of these tiny diamonds? These are not chips, my son—no, no, no. Each one of these is perfectly cut, perfectly identical. This is work of brilliant, painstaking craftsmanship. It makes my heart glow to look on 'em."

"Too bad they're going to be so hard to fence," Owen pointed out.

"Thou sayest right, lad. Setting's utterly unique, and therefore recognizable. Split these dazzlers up, they lose eighty percent of their value. Shame."

"Still, great show tonight. How about my entrance? I finally get why you showed me all those pirate movies."

"A touch over the mark, lad. Spectacle over substance."

"*I'm* over the mark? We could have been out of there twice as fast if you hadn't got lost in dreamland."

"Rubbish. I was sharp as a laser."

"Max, it looked like you forgot where you were."

"Bollocks. I engineered another exceptional show—worthy of the Pontiff himself."

They took off their evening wear and changed into more casual clothes. Their dinner jackets went onto hangers and into dry cleaning plastic. Max was a stickler for keeping kit in good shape, particularly wigs. The black curls and the ginger rug went onto Styrofoam heads and then into boxes. Max's cover, should he be required to produce one, was wig salesman and distributor, and he'd already visited several customers. San Francisco was home to some of his biggest accounts: theatre troupes, gay cabarets and college drama classes.

"If the Pontiff's so damn brilliant," Owen said, hanging up his white T-shirt, "how come he's in prison and we're out here on the road?"

"He's not in prison anymore. I told you, they've put him in hospital, where he's probably going to die."

"You didn't answer my question."

"Why did he end up in the brig? Very simple. An ill-chosen associate made a colossal blunder. Gun goes off, and a security guard ends up dead. Not John-Paul's fault. But what a string of successes the man had! Wells Fargo, Chemical Bank, Lufthansa—no one can touch him. And character! The Pontiff is your quintessential gentleman of the road. No friend of his ever went hungry while he had a dime in his pocket. Looked after families when his brothers went up to Oxford. A great soul, that man, a great soul."

Owen combed his hair, naturally brown, and inspected his face for any remaining traces of spirit gum. "I don't know about you, but I was ready for dinner about an hour ago."

Max turned to him from the mirror, tweed jacket, khaki pants, polo shirt. "How do I look?" he said. "Old money?"

"Old perv is more like it."

"Nonsense. I'm a splendid specimen of manhood." He slapped his belly. "Not bad for sixty-four."

"Sixty-four!"

"Doubting your loving uncle yet again. *Tsk, tsk.* Suspicion is the habit of a guilty mind. Causes ulcers, cancer, all manner of plague and carbuncle. A healthy mind is free and open, willing to be informed."

"Max?"

"What, boy?"

"Can we please go eat?"

THREE

"It's four o'clock," the Elvis clock said, *"and I'm all shook up."* It was a passable imitation of the King's voice, but it still gave Zig Zigler the creeps. Apparently his partner Clem didn't like it either, because he threw his apple core at it and cursed when he missed.

Their acquaintance Melvin Togg was into Elvis in a big way. He had vinyl copies of all the King's albums on a beautiful shelving unit built around his stereo. The shelves and the stereo were the only things in this grunge pit of an apartment that didn't make you want to hang yourself. First off, it was a basement joint, hardly any light squeezing through its two windows. Second off, it was in one of the noisiest neighbourhoods in Las Vegas, jet planes blasting overhead every five minutes. Third off, the ceiling was low, meaning that if you actually employed the hot plate for any cooking you'd be inhaling your curry or whatever for the next month. Not to mention bathroom smells.

"Melvin," Zig said, "how can you live in a pathetic little hole like this? Don't you got any self-esteem?"

"It isn't that bad, man. Rent's real low."

"Vegas ain't New York, pal. You could do a lot better."

"I got room for all my stuff. I know one day I'll need a bigger place, but this fulfills my needs right now."

"That would be your need for Elvis crap?" Clem said, picking up an Elvis mug from the row that lined one shelf.

Zig looked around at the Elvis calendar stuck to the fridge, surrounded by a halo of Elvis magnets, and the life-size Elvis doll, if that was the right word, that stood in the place of honour under the window. "Say, what do they make these out of, any-way?" Zig asked, tapping the doll with a knuckle.

"I don't know. Zig, could you take the tape off me now? I don't like this."

"I've never actually seen one before. I mean, I've seen one, it just wasn't an Elvis. It was a Bogart."

"Yeah, I seen them too. But, you know, I prefer Elvis."

"No shit," Clem said.

"Tell me something, Melvin," Zig said. "You still pulling that fake investigator shit?"

"Not just investigator. Food inspector. Water department. I got a bunch of 'em."

"That's something might interest me. You could possibly pur-chase some of my goodwill with one of those."

"Blanks are in the top drawer. You gotta put in the proper-size photo and get it laminated and stamped."

"Where do I do that?" Zig said, taking a couple of blanks.

"Ben Ditmar. He's got all sorts of seals: city, state, you name it."

"Ben Ditmar?" Clem said. "He's okay. I beat the shit out of him once."

"What's this here?" Zig said.

"Autograph letter."

Zig peered closely at the item on the wall. Actually, it was two items. A nice picture of Elvis—not one of the ones you see everywhere—looking thoughtful and relaxed, sitting on a couch with an old beat-up guitar. Beside it was a letter on Elvis letter-head, not Graceland, typewritten to somebody named "Mr. Schmelling," thanking him for his help resolving a real estate issue. It was signed, "Sincerely, Elvis Presley."

"This looks real," Zig said. "I mean, to my untrained eye and all."

"Zig, could you take this tape off me now?" Melvin said. "It's totally not necessary."

"I may take this home with me," Zig said. "Depending."

"Sure, man, you can take it. It's worth a few hundred at least. But let's untape my hands now, huh? This ain't the way to discuss business."

"Melvin, there's only one question you have to answer: where is the take from the Discount Diamond job? Just tell me that and you're free as a bird."

"I told you, man. I didn't have nothing to do with that."

Zig didn't answer. He opened up a pocket in his shoulder bag. It was hard to get a grip on the little zipper, wearing the latex gloves, but finally he managed to pull out a clear plastic bag that had a drawstring. It had actually taken a couple of days to come up with exactly the kind of bag he was looking for, and he'd finally found it at a shoe store. The salesman was happy to give him a couple of extras. Just the thing for when you're packing a suitcase, the guy had said.

Zig fitted the bag over Melvin's head, not pulling the drawstring.

"Aw, no, Zig, take it off, man. No joke, man, take it off." Melvin's voice was muffled by the bag. "Fuck this, man, get it off me."

"Take your time there, Melvin. Think it over. Simple question, simple answer."

"I ain't got nothing to do with no Discount Diamond job."

"Don't lie to us," Clem said. "Honesty's your best policy here."

"I ain't got nothing to do with it. Fuck, man. Take this thing off me. Please, man."

"You know," Zig said, "I can actually read your mind right now? I can actually hear what you're thinking, Mel. You're thinking, if I tell this asshole where the stuff is at, Conrad Moss is gonna kill me in some extremely painful fashion, so what's to gain?"

Melvin shook his head vehemently. Zig wasn't sure if that was in denial or in desperation to shake the bag off. You could hardly make out his features behind the condensation. In any case, what Zig said was perfectly true. If Conrad Moss was indeed the guy behind the Discount Diamond job, he would certainly kill Melvin for talking about it.

"I'm not going to ask again," Zig said. "Last chance."

"Okay. Okay. I'll tell you. Take the bag off, man, please."

"Tell us first," Clem said. "Then we take the bag off."

"No, man. Take the bag off first."

"See ya, Melvin." Zig slung his satchel over his shoulder and headed toward the door.

"Lock 'n' Leave Mini-Storage. Lock 'n' Leave Mini-Storage."

Zig paused at the door, hand on the knob. "You got a key?"

"No, man. No way. Conrad keeps the key. Only Conrad."

"What's the locker number?"

"I don't know, man. I forget, I forget! Come on, man. Take this fucking bag off!"

"Tell us the locker number."

"Fuck, man, I don't know. Oh, Christ, man, please."

"What was that?"

"Seven-oh-four, man. Try locker seven-oh-four. I'm not sure. Bag, man. Bag. Please."

Zig looked at him for a moment, debating. Then he looked over at Clem, who shrugged. Zig really didn't want to make a second trip back to this dump. He went back and tightened the drawstring around Melvin's neck.

Eight-thirty in the morning and here they were at Fisherman's Wharf, Max gripping his second coffee of the day and looking as bewildered as Max ever looked.

"Seasides like me not," he muttered, barely audible above the slap of waves and the wind whipping in off the bay. "Look, even the gulls have lost their mirth," he said, pointing at a row of scruffy birds on the back of a bench.

Max was wearing a windbreaker with *Stuyvesant Town* stencilled on the back, and a Merrill Lynch baseball cap. No one could possibly mistake him for the man who had robbed the Margot Peabody fundraiser the night before. This morning he looked like a soccer dad, which, to give him his due, until rather recently he actually was. He used to show up at Owen's games, wearing that cap and jacket, and bellow encouragement from the sidelines. The unsettling thing was, he bellowed encouragement to whoever happened to control the ball. He just liked to see goals, he didn't mind which team scored them.

"I want to win!" Owen had cried. "My friends think you're crazy! The coach hates you!"

"A goal is a wonderful thing," Max said. "It doesn't become a better thing just because your team scored it."

Eventually Owen quit sports just to avoid the humiliation, but Max never threw clothes away, no matter how old and worn, so here he was in full regalia. Lately, Owen had been asking himself if Max is ever out of costume.

Not that he was asking himself any questions at the moment. He was reading from some pages he had downloaded off the Internet. The papers were curling in the waterfront damp, and he had to grip them tightly against the wind.

"Tell me again, my starry-eyed son, why we are going to this place at six o'clock in the morning."

"It's eight-thirty. They say to go early or it gets too crowded and you can't enjoy the visit."

"And why are we visiting a prison in the first place?"

"Oh, come on, Max. You saw the Clint Eastwood movie."

"Yes, but he was leaving the place, which is what any sensible person does with a prison. No sane person, or even mad person whose medications are in order, goes *to* a prison."

"It's a *disused* prison, Max. A decommissioned prison."

"But look at it."

Max gestured with his paper cup toward the island. Gulls, apparently now awake, circled its lighthouse and the forlorn buildings that looked as if they might slide off the rock into the lethal currents of San Francisco Bay. Even from this distance Owen could feel it putting an indefinable pressure on his heart.

"You'll enjoy it once we're there," he said, not that Max had any choice. This was their deal on their summer road trips: Max chose the shows, but Owen chose the sights they saw in their off-hours.

He read the prison history aloud to Max as they crossed over in the ferry. There were perhaps two dozen people on board, some paging through guidebooks, others snapping pictures. As they approached, Owen opened his backpack and took out his own camera. He took several shots, showing the best ones to Max on the stamp-size digital screen, but Max just harrumphed and looked away.

Owen manoeuvred them over to the ferry's exit so that they could be first off. "It says be sure to go up to the cellblocks first," he explained, "before everyone crowds in and spoils the atmosphere."

"It's not possible to spoil the atmosphere of a cellblock."

It was a steep climb, and Owen herded Max along as if he were an irritable old camel. When they got to the top, Max sat down heavily on a bench, red in the face and puffing.

"Wow, look at the city," Owen said, snapping another picture. "It looks great with the sun hitting it."

But Max was staring in front of them. "What manner of fiend would lock a human being up on a godforsaken rock like this?"

"These were not minor criminals," Owen said. "These were hit men. Multiple murderers."

"Not likely to be improved by sea air and a sound regimen, then."

Max's mood didn't improve when they visited cellblock D, which was once reserved for the worst of the worst. Toilets in the solitary confinement cells were holes in the floor. In some of these, the light had been kept on twenty-four hours a day. In others, there was no light at all.

Max cheered up when they got to cellblock B, which had housed Frank Morris, who, along with two fellow prisoners, managed to pull off the only successful escape in Alcatraz's history. He and his colleagues had chiselled away at the cement around an air vent, using tools such as a metal spoon soldered with silver they had melted down from a dime, and an electric drill created out of a vacuum cleaner motor stolen from the prison shop. They covered their exit by placing papier mâché heads in their beds. The heads were now on display on the bunks.

"What ghastly wigs," Max said. "Must have made them out of old paintbrushes. Now, may we please leave? What kind of nephew hauls his gentle old uncle off to prison on a bright sunny day?"

By now the rest of the ferry-load of visitors had made their way up to the cellblocks. The place was taking on a Disneyland feel.

"Just one last stop," Owen said.

It was in block C, his downloaded material informed them, that a psychic visiting the prison had been disturbed by a "disruptive spirit" named Butcher. Deep in the night, long ago, inmates had awoken to the sound of a prisoner yelling for help, screaming that a wild creature with red eyes was trying to kill him. The next day, it turned out, one Abie Maldowitz had died in his bed, apparently suffocated. He had been a hit man for the mob, and his nickname had been "The Butcher."

Cellblock C was as dank a ruin as the rest of the place.

"Get me out of this house, Benvolio," Max said, "or I shall faint. Truly, Owen. The exit. Now."

They had to walk against the incoming crowds to get out. The sun had taken the chill out of the air, but the wind was still howling around the prison, and their windbreakers flapped like pennants. They walked past the ruin of the warden's house, past the gardens that the guards' wives had planted, long overgrown, and sat on a large flat rock facing the water.

Max immediately decided that he should have used the washroom and lumbered back toward the prison, leaving Owen staring at the gulls, the whitecaps and the enormous freighters in the bay. He had something important he had been waiting to tell Max. Something Max was not going to want to hear. He had thought the ferry ride and the sea air might provide a good occasion, but Alcatraz was having an unsettling effect on his guardian, and now did not seem an opportune moment. He was beginning to wonder why Max was taking so long when a voice called out behind him.

"Excuse me, I think I've found something of yours."

Owen turned to see Max being led down the hill toward him by a chubby young man in a yellow pullover.

"They need more signs," Max said. "All these bloody brambles look the same."

"Seemed a little disoriented," the young man said in a quieter voice.

"That happens sometimes," Owen said. "Thanks for bringing him back."

"Let's have no more prisons," Max said when the man was gone. "Sightseeing may be your department, but I'm putting in a formal request."

"Max, how can we keep putting on shows if you forget where you are half the time?"

"Rubbish. Just got turned around, that's all."

"I don't know. There were a couple of moments I thought you zoned out when you were dancing with Evelyn del Rio."

"I was having fun. You remember fun, don't you?"

"You're worrying me these days, Max."

Max did a King Kong imitation, drumming on his chest and hooting. "Fit as a fiddle," he said, "and ready to roll. Las Vegas, Tucson, Dallas—not to mention Savannah, Georgia—the Max and Owen show is going to bring down the house!"

FOUR

ZIG HATED THE SMELL OF HORSESHIT, and he could detect it from a long way away. At first he couldn't understand why a self-storage outfit would smell like manure. But the moment he and Clem had stepped off the huge freight elevator, he'd figured it out; you could tell by the shape of the units.

"Jesus," Clem said. "Why's it smell like horseshit in here?"

"Used to be a riding academy," Zig said. "Remember there was a sign coming north off the Strip?"

"Why you gonna put a riding academy in the middle of Las fucking Vegas?"

"I don't know, Clem. Why do certain assholes have to smell like a fucking distillery all the time?"

"I had an Irish coffee. What's the big deal?"

They walked along the corridors of units, each one numbered and padlocked, until eventually they found 704. A security camera halfway down the corridor stared at them with a baleful purple gaze.

"Stu better be taking care of the kid on the front desk," Zig said.

"He will. He was gonna start a big argument about missing items and insurance and threaten lawsuits, the whole bit. Kid won't be looking at no camera. Anyway, that's why we got ball caps."

"He better be good, this guy."

"Stu's good. Known him for years."

"I haven't."

Zig took the bolt cutters out of the duffle bag and sent the lock crashing to the floor. When they stepped inside the locker, the smell of horseshit was a lot stronger.

"Fuck me," Zig said. "Fucking Melvin."

Except for some loose plastic bags and pellets of Styrofoam, the locker was empty.

"I knew we shoulda kept that guy alive for a while."

Zig turned on Clem. "Oh, yeah? You knew it, huh? You're so fucking clairvoyant? I suppose that's why you said something at the time, right? That's why you said, 'Hey, Zig, maybe we better keep him alive till we make sure he's telling the truth.'"

"Okay, okay, you're right. You're right. I shoulda said something."

Zig kicked the locker wall with the heel of his boot, making a dent.

He cursed himself silently as they headed back to the elevator. It should have been obvious that no one would store the proceeds from a jewellery heist in a place like this. A smart thief would put them in a safe somewhere, just like a jeweller. He'd been half expecting to find a safe inside the locker, which would have posed a problem, for sure, but he could see in retrospect why that didn't make sense.

"I am sick and fucking tired," he said, "of learning from mistakes."

"I know what you mean, boss."

"Next time'll be different."

"Way different." Clem punched the elevator button.

"Next time we detain the guy someplace safe, someplace where speed is not required. We're gonna be way more thorough. And we're gonna make sure we got our hands on the goods before we do anything else. Melvin just panicked and made shit up."

"I think you're right," Clem said. "He wanted that bag off in a big way."

As the elevator rattled them back toward street level, the barnyard smells began to diminish. Zig kicked the door. Fucking Melvin.

———

It was Max and Owen's practice to take back roads wherever possible. They sought out the old U.S. highways that had been superseded by the interstates. Partly this was a security measure—the old highways were less frequently patrolled than the interstates—but mostly it was for pleasure. Max always scheduled their shows so that there was no hurry, and he liked to see the small towns and the countryside. Otherwise, he said, you might as well leave the Rocket at home and take a bloody plane.

Consequently, it took them fourteen hours to drive from San Francisco to Las Vegas, taking US 93 down through Nevada. Along the way they listened to dialect CDs, practising accents as they drove. Max was particularly insistent on Australian at the moment. When they weren't doing that, he liked to find the smallest radio stations to hear the local news and ads. "When Walker's Shoes are what you wear, it's almost like you're walking on air." And he enjoyed hearing the "so-called Christians," as he called them, foaming at the mouth over homosexuals, liberals and other degenerates.

Sitting beside him all day, Owen tried to think up a good way to tell him his news. After the next town, he would think, then maybe after the next gas station. So far he hadn't managed to work up the courage.

Max was at the wheel as they approached Vegas, and even though he was exhausted and yearning for his bunk, Owen felt as if they were landing on a distant planet. As the sun set, the sky turned lilac, then mauve, and in the dry desert twilight the lights of the city became visible when they were still a hundred miles away.

"It looks like an idea," Max said. "Not even an idea—a notion—soon to become an idea."

"You should've been a poet, Max."

"I am a poet. Every poet's a thief. Poets break into your mind and heart, and their verses are so many shards of glass they leave scattered around."

"Except people like poets. They don't like thieves."

"They don't like poets either. Any poet who dies rich is either a charlatan or a songwriter."

"Shakespeare got rich. He owned the biggest house in Stratford, you told me."

"Will Shakespeare, aside from being my hero, my angel, was a one-man corporation: actor, manager and playwright. He was also a dab hand with real estate. In my heyday I knew everything there was to know about the great Will."

"I still don't understand how you could give up acting. You must have been great."

"Sadly, the world thought otherwise. There was a time, though—oh, there was a time. I wish you could have seen my Hamlet. The Old Vic—the Old Wreck we used to call it. I got to play that slippery little Dane for three months running before the most discerning audience in the Western world." Max swept a hand grandly across the speeding desert. "Standing ovations every night. Dozens of letters I got. Dozens! Gielgud wrote me the most charming note. I thought to myself, 'Max, your ship has come in. You're going to be a second Olivier."

"I can't believe you never made it," Owen said.

"Neither can I, my lad. Neither can I. You put your heart and soul into something, devote your life to it, you think success must surely come. But ambition is a one-armed bandit. The world spits out success just often enough to keep us mortal fools yanking that lever. But nothing came of it. No film offers, no great parts. It was as if there'd been no Hamlet, no letters, no standing ovations. As if it had been erased from the entire world's memory banks, except my own."

"It's totally unfair."

"Well, I made mistakes. Thought I could do anything. Took on roles I never should have considered. Turned down others that, in hindsight, might have been better bets. Offended a few people here and there."

"No, Max. You?"

"It's not funny, boy. It ate me up. I wanted it so badly. Perhaps I wanted it too badly. Tried too hard. Certainly a couple of critics took me to task for chewing the scenery. I learned from that. But possibly I learned too late."

"Well, you've put on enough performances since," Owen said, trying to cheer him up. "You've put on a lot of shows."

"So I have, boy. So I have. It was either that or spend the rest of my life heaving sandbags backstage. That's what they had me do! After a few years I was so desperate to stay in the theatre, I actually did it—on the sly, of course. Then the stagehands' union got wind of it and had me cashiered, and that's when I turned to my life of travel and romance. Note it well, lad: classical training will never see you wrong. Not that I'd want to see you become an actor—perish the thought."

Owen had visited Las Vegas before, back when he was twelve years old, the first long trip he had ever taken with his uncle. That time, before the Rocket and before Owen was included in Max's shows, they had stayed at Circus Circus, a children's paradise, and Owen had loved every minute of it.

After they got settled in the trailer park, they took the car downtown to the El Cortez for dinner.

"Why did you pick this place?" Max said when they sat down to eat. "A sudden fit of thrift?"

"Bugsy Siegel used to own it," Owen said. "It's my theme this year. Criminal history. That's why we had Alcatraz, and that's why we're having dinner at the El Cortez."

"Poor Bugsy. Ended up with more holes in him than Saint Sebastian. You're a peculiar boy, Owen, have I told you that today?"

"Well, look who brought me up."

"Bollocks. I get to choose where we have dessert."

———

Max chose Sir Slots-a-Lot's Kitchen, just off the Strip. It was reasonably priced, served down-home cooking, and offered several rows of slot machines in case a diner should feel the urge to shed money between courses. It was decorated with suits of armour that had been shipped to Vegas all the way from a Hollywood movie set.

They ordered chocolate sundaes, with brandy for Max and a Coke for Owen. As they waited for the food to arrive, they stared dumbly at the array of television screens, all tuned to *Celebrity Poker*. The room rang with the intermittent *ka-ching* of the slots.

"Chocolate sundaes," said Max, who had the sweet tooth of a ten-year-old. "Food of the gods."

Owen couldn't finish his.

"Why so down in the mouth, old chum? We put on a great show the other night, and you sit there like a death's head."

"I got accepted into Juilliard's drama program."

Max regarded him, spoon in mid-air. The blue eyes were bright and alert, but he suddenly looked very old.

"I'm gonna go, Max. I want to start my own life."

Owen couldn't meet Max's gaze. He had to look away at the televised hands stacking their chips, gripping their fans of cards. Moans of disappointment wafted over from the slot machines.

"Don't study theatre, boy," Max said. "You'll just end up another bloody waiter."

"I have a good shot at it, Max. They loved my audition."

Max sat back, rolled his shoulders bearlike against the booth, and leaned forward again as far as his bulk would permit. He spoke in what was for him a pretty soft voice. "Look at us, Owen. We're free and easy. We have excitement, money, friends! Most boys your age would kill for this life."

"It's been fun," Owen said. "It really has. We've had some great times. But I need to move on. I've saved a lot from our

road trips, and there's that money from Mom and Dad to cover
the rest. Hey, listen, my marks were so good the school's offered
to pay half my tuition."

"Of course. And who was it made you study? Who stood over
you like a learned Colossus?"

"You did, Max. I could never have done it without you."

"And not just the studies, mind. Do you have any conception
of the life I saved you from? Modesty forbids I should raise the
issue, but you force me. Think about it, boy. Do you have any
idea where it was you were headed?"

Owen's tenth birthday is the best birthday ever. He is an only
child, and his parents—both British by birth, both physicians in
a family practice in Norwalk, Connecticut—tend to go overboard
on birthdays. In addition to his presents, which include a tele-
scope, several books and five complete seasons of *Doctor Who*
on DVD, they've driven down to New York City in the Volvo to
see *The Lion King* on Broadway.

After the show, they stroll through the crowds and the noise
and traffic, the ruby flashes and multicoloured pinwheels of
Broadway's light show, and make their way to Serendipity. New
York seems to Owen the most brilliant creation in the universe—
it *is* a universe, where everything is gaudy, loud, musical and fun.
When Serendipity's house specialty of frozen hot chocolate is set
before him, Owen feels like a king himself.

He loved the musical, and can't stop talking about it. To his parents' amusement he breaks into an excellent reprise of "The
Madness of King Scar," singing at the table *I'm revered, I am
reviled, I'm idolized, I am despised, I'm keeping calm, I'm going wild!*

His parents beam at him across the table.

"Owen," his mother says, "do you even know what 'reviled'
means?"

"Nope. It sounds good, though."

"Ten years old and already a ham," says his dad. His wiry black beard made his smile a vivid flash.

Owen glows under their praise, and resumes spelunking in the depths of his frozen hot chocolate, which performs the culinary miracle of being simultaneously hot and cold.

That night, as they drive back home in the dark, he falls in love with the vast glittering bridges, the Fifty-ninth Street and the Triborough.

"Hey, Dad. Do they make models of those bridges?"

"I don't know, Owen. They might."

"Would they have lights on them?"

"I don't know. Why don't we look them up on the Net?"

"That would be so cool. I'd build one right across my bed and sleep under it."

His mother turns around in the front seat. "Someone's imagination is working overtime tonight. Did you have a good birthday?"

"The best. Best, best ever."

"That's good, sweetie."

By the time they get to the relative darkness of the Merritt Parkway, Owen is sacked out across the back seat. The road surface is glassy calm after the constant chop of the Bronx, the curves slow.

He can't have slept for more than a few minutes—Norwalk is only about eighteen miles up the Merritt—before he is awakened by sirens. He's too sleepy to sit up, or even to open his eyes, but he can hear them getting closer, and his parents' disembodied voices.

"Police," his mother says. "My God, there's someone moving awfully fast back there."

The sirens get louder. A sudden roar and then the car swerves. Owen sits up, gripping the back of the driver's seat.

"God, that was a near thing," his father says, real agitation in his voice. "Idiot barrelling along on the inside lane."

Horns honk up ahead. The sirens gain on them from behind.

"It's a police chase," his mother says. "Can we get in the other lane?"

"Unfortunately, everybody else has the same idea."

"Owen, sit back, sweetie. Is your seat belt on?"

Owen sits back and adjusts the shoulder strap across his chest. A police car goes blaring by on their left, red light flashing.

"Good Lord," he hears his father say.

Then an oncoming car veers into their lane. His mother's scream is the last thing Owen hears.

Eight years later his memory of specific details following the catastrophe is thin. He woke in hospital with no memory of the cars' actual impact. He tried to call for his mother but couldn't speak; there was a tube in his throat. Where were his parents? Why weren't they here beside the bed? He wanted them to come right away and take him home. A young nurse came in and saw he was awake. She checked his chart and called for a doctor.

When the doctor came in, he removed the tube in Owen's throat and held out a glass of water with a straw in it. Owen took a sip and asked for his mother and father. The doctor wanted to examine him first. He asked him a lot of questions, shone a light in his pupils, and tested his reflexes. When Owen asked again for his mother and father, the nurse said she would have to ask someone else. She and the doctor left together.

They were gone so long that he thought they must have called his mom and dad at home and they would now be driving to the hospital. His room was filled with cards and stuffed animals from classmates. He realized he must have been unconscious for a few days; his parents would have had to go home. Owen was not a boy who cried easily, but tears now flowed from his eyes and down his cheeks. He turned on his side, bruises protesting, and sobbed.

Finally an older woman came in, not dressed like a nurse. He realized later that she must have been the hospital social worker. She had a soothing voice, and the face of a beneficent moon surrounded by a penumbra of platinum hair. Mrs. Callow. She told him he'd been sleeping for three days.

"The first thing I want you to know, Owen, is you're not alone. Have you noticed all your cards and presents?"

"Where's my mom? I thought someone was going to get her."

Mrs. Callow reached out and smoothed his hair. "Don't forget, Owen, there are lots of people on staff here who care about you and want only the best for you. People who work in other departments, other floors, they're all asking after you. I think you're going to find you're kind of special around here."

"My mom and dad are coming, though, right? You called them, right?"

"Things may look pretty bleak sometimes," Mrs. Callow went on, "but Owen, we're going to do everything we can to help. We're going to find a way to ensure your happiness, I promise. You're my number one priority, young man, and I'm going to go all out for you. But," she added with a social worker's rhetorical flourish, "I'm going to need your help with that—can you do that, Owen?"

"I want my mom." Owen couldn't stop himself, he didn't want to cry in front of a stranger, but the spigot opened and the tears gushed out again.

"I need to tell you something, Owen. Something very sad."

"I don't like it here. I want to go home." He was bawling like a newborn now. He'd never felt anything like this before, unless it had been in a nightmare, some nameless voracious thing devouring him. He had no idea what this moon-faced woman was about to tell him, but he knew it wouldn't be good. "I want to go home," he wailed again.

"I know, sweetheart," Mrs. Callow said, and took his hands in her warm palms, "but unfortunately that's the sad thing I have to tell you."

Owen was absolutely, unequivocally alone. It wasn't as if he had relatives in the area, or even in the country; he didn't have any relatives at all. His mother had lost both her parents when she was in her early twenties. His paternal grandmother had been a drunk who died in a psychiatric hospital of Korsakoff's syndrome, and his grandfather had recently died of Parkinson's. Like himself, both his parents had been only children, and so he was without aunts and uncles.

The state had to intervene and make him a temporary ward until such time as a suitable home might be found. The order of such business begins with a receiving home, usually run by a good-hearted, inexhaustible couple who are on call seven days a week to take in children they have never met. A child may stay overnight or as long as a few weeks.

If suitable relatives are not forthcoming, and the child is not a major behavioural problem, he or she will then be moved to a foster home. This is intended to be for the longer term—ideally until the child is returned to his natural home or adopted into a loving family. This is not generally expected to happen with children over the age of seven or eight, but the social agencies try to be optimistic.

A difficult child faces a bleaker future of group homes and detention centres, but that was not likely in the cards for a good-natured boy like Owen Maxwell.

Various friends and neighbours came forward in the early days—Owen didn't lack for friends—but none of their families proved suitable to the Department of Children and Families. Either they could not make the required long-term commitment or they had children too close in age, which would be likely to cause conflict. Owen was lucky in one way: both his parents had been covered by munificent life insurance policies. In some cases the applicants to foster Owen may well have been motivated by something other than altruism.

He would never forget the cold clench in his stomach when Mrs. Callow first took him to the receiving home. It was a natty little house of red brick in a corner of Norwalk with which he was completely unfamiliar. Mr. and Mrs. Platt were both jolly ovoids with carroty red hair, as if a pair of Toby jugs had leapt from the shelf and incarnated themselves for the sole purpose of greeting newly orphaned boys.

Mrs. Platt showed him where the bathroom was, explaining the house rules, which were Byzantine, and showed him to the IKEA-crisp chamber he would be sharing with a buzz-cut urchin some two years his senior nicknamed, appropriately, Buzz. Buzz had claimed the top bunk upon arrival some days previously and warned Owen on his first night that if he tried to storm that fastness he would be repelled "by any means necessary." Those were his actual words.

Outside the borders of his own bunk, Buzz had no concept of privacy, or of its corollary, private property. Within the first three nights Owen lost a Harry Potter book, a Game Boy and a much-loved baseball mitt. Buzz was a versatile sportsman, and one of his favourite pastimes was a game he called Goober. The rules were not complex. When the rest of the household was supposedly dreaming, Buzz would roll back the top end of his mattress, affording him a perfect if somewhat segmented view of Owen, lying awake in grief and loneliness.

"Watch this," Buzz said one night, and with a solemn expression he released a viscous blob of saliva from between pursed lips. It elongated, drooped toward the transfixed Owen, and was then reeled back up by a sudden intake of Buzz's breath. "The trick," Buzz explained, "is to see how low I can get it to go without actually hitting you."

"Kind of a one-sided game," Owen pointed out. "What am I supposed to do—spit upward and see if it'll reach you?"

"No, doofus. You're supposed to not move a muscle, no matter how close it gets. It's a test of nerve."

"I don't want to play."

"Too bad, 'cause here it comes." Another hideous blob drooped toward him.

"If that hits me," Owen said, "I will kill you."

Buzz made an insincere attempt to recall his missile and it hit Owen squarely in the forehead. His reaction was instantaneous. He booted the springs above him with all his strength, causing Buzz to carom off the ceiling and plummet to the floor. The noise was stupendous, and brought Mr. and Mrs. Platt clattering into the room. Accusations were hurled, evidence weighed, and a rapid judgment reached: the boys would alternate bunks every other day until they learned civility. The experience left Owen with a lifelong aversion to bottom bunks.

Terror and loss were with him day and night, and yet Owen behaved with the utmost calm and politeness to his social worker and foster parents. But every night, when Buzz was asleep, he wept, clutching his pillow to his face in a hot, soggy mass.

After a few days in the land of Buzz, Owen was taken to visit a prospective foster home. Melanie Prine, his social worker from the Department of Children and Families, drove him for miles and miles outside of Norwalk, so that he really had no idea where he was. She was pretty, and yet he couldn't bear to look at her. To him she consisted entirely of the ten red fingernails that gripped the steering wheel and the chirpy voice telling him about the Tunkles, his prospective foster parents, but his heart was too thick with grief to take anything in. Owen, strapped into the passenger seat as the ever-bleaker countryside rolled by, felt a heavy numbness travelling upward from his ankles until it encased his whole body.

The Tunkles were waiting on the front porch. Melanie Prine gave them a cheery wave as they drove up, five scarlet fingernails flashing in the sun. They were nice enough, and their house was a nice-enough house. Owen could see that it was a comfortable place, a house where people could live with each other, but it was not *his* house. He did not live here. He did not know anyone here.

The family had an older daughter of sixteen, a blonde girl who said hi and then vanished, and a still older son who was away at college. Melanie Prine abandoned Owen there for the afternoon, leaving the Tunkles to try to interest him in farm life. He was shown to his room, a nice-enough room to be sure, but not his. Just as the bathroom was not his bathroom, the kitchen not his kitchen, the basement not his basement, the front yard with its single stunted maple not his yard. It was as if everyone was playing a game: Let's pretend this is normal. Let's pretend we know each other. Let's pretend we care.

With each minute that ticked by, Owen was exiled deeper into an inner Siberia. The worst moments were when Mr. Tunkle, a bony little man whose skin looked parched and stiff as if he'd been salted and left to dry in the sun, took him by the hand (a hand rough as a plank) to show him the pigs, the chickens, the fields, the cows. Owen had never seen anything so dreary.

Norwalk is not a big city, but it is not a small town and it is most definitely not the country. To Owen, farms were something you drove by to get somewhere interesting—a river, an aquarium, a museum, a campground, an airport. You didn't stop at farms. The sunlight beat down on the place in a way he had never experienced in shady Norwalk. The chickens were repulsive, the cows somnolent, the pigs appalling. Owen was not afraid of manual labour; he had enjoyed helping his father fix things around the house, and he earned pocket money shovelling snow and raking leaves. But the idea that he would be expected to spend time with these creatures made his heart shrivel.

He would be required to change schools, the nearest neighbour was a mile away, and he would probably never see his friends again.

"Well, what did you think of the Tunkles?" Melanie Prine asked when they were on the way back to the receiving home.

Her fingernails had dimmed to carmine in the late afternoon light.

Owen couldn't answer.

"They're nice, don't you think?"

"They're okay."

"And isn't that farmhouse incredible?"

"I don't want to live there."

"So much to do out here, don't you think?"

"I don't want to live there."

"Open space everywhere. Lots of fresh air. Did you see they've even got a swimming hole?"

"I don't want to live there."

Five of the ten red fingernails lifted off from the steering wheel and travelled toward him as Miss Prine tried to comfort him with a touch on his shoulder. It was the briefest feathery touch, but it burst something inside Owen's chest and he convulsed with tears.

"No one expects you to like it right away, Owen."

"I don't want to live there," he said again, all but choking on each word.

"You're not used to the country, I know. But a farm is an ideal place to grow up. So much to do. And it's fun looking after the animals, don't you think?"

"I want to live in my own home," he said miserably. "Why can't I just stay at home?"

"Owen, your parents aren't there anymore. There's no one to look after you."

"But you said there's money, right? Insurance money? Why can't we pay a babysitter and I'll just stay in my house? I don't have to have new parents. I don't want new parents. Would you want new parents?"

"No, Owen, I wouldn't. Nobody wants to lose their parents. You've been very unlucky. But we have to find you another family to live with, and the Tunkles are good parents and they have room."

"But I don't want to live there."

Owen was sent to the Tunkles the following day. He spent a painful weekend supposedly adapting to the routines of the farm, and when Monday rolled around he took the bus to his new school and sat silently throughout his classes. He made no effort to acknowledge his new classmates, and when his teacher called on him, he had nothing to say, he had heard nothing. He was focused strictly on the final bell, waiting hour after hour, minute after minute, for it to ring. When finally it did ring, he went nowhere near the bus stop. He walked into town and back to his old neighbourhood.

He had never seen his house with all the curtains closed. It sat blind and mute on the corner where it had always been. No car in the drive, of course, but then there never was when he got home from school. He still had his key, and let himself in.

It was a little stuffy, a little dusty, but it smelled the same. It smelled of his house, the way no other house would ever smell. And nothing had changed. All the furniture was there. The coats were still hanging in the vestibule—his mother's, his father's, his own—above a chaotic jumble of footwear. The merest objects filled him not just with pain, but with awe: his father's enormous running shoes, the wellingtons his mother wore in the garden. He went and sat on the couch in the living room, facing the television. His reflection on the dim screen, thin and distorted, looked back at him.

He had never seen the house so dark, not during the day. He fell sideways into the cushions and cried, but it didn't help. After a while he went to the kitchen and pulled a bottle of Snapple from the fridge. All the same food was there. Nothing had been done yet, by whoever had come in to close the curtains. The electricity was on, and the water.

The message light was blinking by the phone, but he didn't want to see who had called.

His plan was this: He would live in this house by himself. He would continue going to school as if nothing had happened. If he could get that insurance money, he would hire someone to cook and clean and look after the house while he was at school. He pictured a fat, cheerful woman who would bake lots of pies. Miss Prine would be impressed; she would see that he could get along without a mother and father.

But for now he had to keep quiet. He couldn't open the curtains, and he was afraid even to turn on lights. The cops would burst in, thinking there was a burglary in progress. He brought a jar of peanut butter and some crackers into the living room and ate in front of the TV. For dessert he had a granola bar.

His parents had not brought him up to be religious, but he found, looking around at the empty chairs where his parents used to sit, with their books still open beside them, that he was thinking about God. What possible reason could God have to snatch his parents from this house, this town, this planet, and leave him behind? He would have to be a mean God. How would He explain it to his parents, wherever they might be now, who surely must be missing him too?

He woke up when the lights came on sometime later. Miss Prine stood over him, along with a policeman and an older man in a sober grey suit. He had an English accent just like his parents, and he looked a lot like the pictures of his grandfather.

"Owen?" Miss Prine said softly. "I think I have some good news for you. This is your great-uncle, Uncle Max."

This jocular, highly verbal and theatrical tonnage of humanity managed to wade his way through the swamp of child welfare regulations, and to win over the support of Miss Prine in particular. It turned out he was the brother of Owen's paternal grandfather, whom this strange apparition referred to as "Tommy." He had a battered satchel full of family photographs that he showed Owen and Miss Prine during their first, supervised office visit.

Many of them were the same images his parents had kept in musty old albums, but there were others he had never seen before: Max and Tommy as young men in cricket whites, Max and his father as a boy on a Brighton pier, Max in the crowd at Owen's parents' wedding in London. He told Owen a couple of amusing stories involving his father as a boy—the time he got stuck in the mulberry tree, the time he blew up his train set using his chemistry set, the time he ran away from home and asked to live with Uncle Max.

"Bit of a sticky situation, that one," he said. "Tommy was quite miffed that I'd taken the boy in. But what could I do? He was on my front porch with a little suitcase. Anyway, it was only for a weekend. Tommy and I had a rather bitter falling-out eventually— not over that. This was much later. Real estate deal went bad and we ended up losing pots of money. Anyway, that's why me and this handsome young lad have never met. Didn't even realize I had family in the country until I read the terrible news."

The DCF checked Max's background. He had been the first of the family to move to the States, settling into Manhattan years previously, where he ran a thriving theatrical supply business with a specialty in wigs. Since there were two countries involved, the paperwork took a considerable amount of time.

A bargain was worked out whereby Owen would stay with the Tunkles while he got to know Max better through more visits. Max drove up regularly from New York. At first they were supervised by Miss Prine—lunches at coffee shops and the like. But then Max was allowed to take Owen on day trips to the city: the Central Park zoo, the boat pond, the Museum of Natural History, the Staten Island Ferry.

When Miss Prine saw how well he and the boy got along, she became Max's champion at the agency and in court. Eventually Owen was placed with him as a temporary ward, taking up residence in the extra bedroom of his Stuyvesant Town apartment. The initial adjustment period was rocky but brief, and soon the boy began to thrive. He got used to Max and Manhattan both, and he loved the long trips Max took him on, which, as far as he knew to this day, were crime free.

After two years Max asked him if he would like to make their arrangement permanent. "You and me against the world, lad. Taking on all comers. Thick and thin. You don't have to call me Dad, you can call me Max, Uncle Max, Sir Max, Lord High Max, whatever variation strikes your fancy, what say you, sir?"

Owen replied with an unhesitating and resounding yes.

So here they are years later in Sir Slots-a-Lot Kitchen in Las Vegas, Nevada, Owen trying to explain that he isn't ungrateful, he just wants something different for his life than robbing dinner parties. Something his mother and father would have been proud of.

"Ten years old, both parents dead—tragic, heartbreaking, positively Dickensian. You were headed for a series of foster homes, maybe a group home, maybe a locked facility, who knows? You'd've probably got molested and beaten and crushed and ruined and ended up a serial killer or next thing to, drooling away your final years on death row."

"Well, look at me now," Owen said, stirring the melted puddle of his sundae. "I'm a criminal."

"Tush, boy." Max leaned across the table and gave his best stage whisper. "You are a gentle criminal, a saintly criminal, a Saint Francis of the highway. You lead a completely non-violent existence. You harm no one, just as I taught you. Your life is good, I engineered it for you, and now you repay me by deciding to take up the sorry occupation that tore me up and spat me out." Max sat back. The banquette wobbled ominously.

"Max, I appreciate everything you've done for me. You gave me a home—sort of."

"Sort of! I know not sort of! I put a roof over your head, made sure you got a good education, taught you right from wrong. No, no, let's have no sort-ofs. Why can't you study something useful? Locksmithing. Martial arts. Computer security."

"Max, you loved acting. You still love acting."

"The skill, not the profession. If you try to do it for a living, it will break your heart. I don't want to see that happen."

Owen spoke softly. "I don't want to be looking over my shoulder for the rest of my life, or wondering where the next job is going to come from. And anyway, Max, I think it's time for you to retire."

Max shoved his dish forward and dabbed at his mouth with his napkin.

"I know you don't want to hear it," Owen went on, "but this line of work, it isn't for old—older guys. You're getting tired, you're forgetting things. Yesterday you forgot where you were, for Pete's sake. Sooner or later you're going to make some horrible mistake, and I don't want to see you go back to jail. I don't want to go to jail either."

"*Pah*. Seven years of hell, that was, seven years of hell. I will never go back inside. Never, never, never, never, never." Max gripped Owen's forearm as if he were taking his blood pressure. "Who are you to tell me my powers are in decline? Where are these glaring lapses, these colossal blunders? You're only trying to justify running off to Juilliard so you can become a waiter, a cab driver."

"Max, you're not listening to me. It's not just you're getting too old. This life is getting to you. You're not sleeping anymore."

"I sleep like a baby."

"You're forgetting things, you're having nightmares, half the time you're not even all there. You're a threat to your own safety."

"Rubbish."

"Max, please don't be hurt. It's just that I—"

Owen was saved from further speech by the arrival of a man wearing baggy shorts and a blinding Hawaiian shirt, carrying a mug of beer in both hands as if it were some kind of isotope.

"Max, you old mofo," the man said. "You have room at your table for a respectable working stiff?"

"Yes, and even for you," Max said, patting the seat beside him. "Owen, allow me to introduce Charlie Zigler, known to all and sundry as Zig. Old acquaintance from Oxford." Oxford was Max's word for prison, in this case a certain locked institution in Ossining, New York.

Zig put down his beer glass to shake hands. He was a compact, nervy man who blinked a lot. It gave him a look that was both curious and startled, a raccoon rudely awakened.

"Who's the kid?"

"I don't even know this boy," Max said. "Never seen him before in my life. He just came up and asked me for money."

Owen introduced himself. "I'm his nephew."

"Uh-oh," Zig said with a wink. "You must have bruised your old uncle's ego somehow. How you keeping, Max?"

"Couldn't be better. And you? Last time I saw you, you had grandiose plans to usurp William H. Gates, third of that name, in the pantheon of computer gods."

"Exactly right," Zig said, blinking. "Took a 'puter repair course at a community college. Paid for itself after two weeks. Ask me anything."

"How do I replace the PRAM battery in my PowerBook?" Owen said.

"No idea," Zig said, and let fly with a laugh that sent pressure waves slamming into Owen's eardrums.

"Don't even talk to him," Max said to Zig. "You'll give him the illusion he's human."

"Poor old Max. Say, you still pulling those lame-ass dinnertime gigs, or did you finally retire?"

"Suddenly the whole world is breathless for my resignation. I suppose you want me to carve my own coffin and lie down in it too, you hideous dwarf."

"Maybe you should move into an honest trade like myself."

"I'm a travelling salesman—a friend to the bald, the gay, the theatrical. What could be more honest? Anyway, what do you care what I do, where I live, or whether I retire?"

"There's some badass dudes out there, my friend. I wouldn't want to see the Subtractors get hold of you."

"The Subtractors," Owen said. "I always thought they were a myth."

"They exist," Zig said. "And believe me, you don't want to get on the wrong side of those guys."

"Urban legend," Max said. "No such creature."

"Legend, huh?" Zig drank down half his beer. With each gulp his Adam's apple bounced higher and higher up his gullet as if it might ring a bell and win a prize. "Lemme tell you about this urban legend, kid." His face loomed forward across the table, blinking and foam-flecked. "The Subtractors is a group of individuals, a secret organization, call them. No one knows who they are, only what they do. And what they do is not pleasant. They prey upon thieves, see? They hear about a tasty job going down, they get their hands on one of the likely crew, and they, I don't know how else to put it, they subtract parts of his body until he reveals where the score is tucked away. Bolt cutters are their tool of choice, although they have been known to use straight razors, exacto knives, whatever's handy."

"That's sick," Owen said.

"Scares hell out of me." Zig jerked his head toward Max. "Gramps never mentioned them to you?"

"Naturally not. I keep rumour, superstition and falsehood off the curriculum."

"The Subtractors exist, kid. And if Pa Clampett here was a decent father figure, he would have warned you about them."

"Sounds like something out of a Tarantino movie," Owen said.

"Doesn't it?" Max said. "The distinct tang of fiction."

"You don't believe me?" Zig said to Owen.

Owen shrugged.

Blinking ferociously, Zig opened the buttons of his shirt, top to bottom, eyes fixed on Owen, a smirk on his face. He pulled open his shirt.

"Whoa," Owen said, and looked away.

Zig turned to Max, displaying his chest like a stripper.

"Hmm," Max said. "And they didn't return them when they were finished?"

"That's all you got to say?" Zig said. "Urban legend? No such animal? If that's the case, where the fuck are my nipples?"

"Do I need to remind you," Max said, gesturing at Sir Slots-a-Lot's shining armour, the maces and lances, "that we are in a restaurant?"

"Just don't tell me the Subtractors don't exist," Zig said, buttoning up. "Happened three years ago. Me and a couple of colleagues got into the customs house in San Francisco. Had a tip on some icons that were being held there. Next thing I know . . ."

"Your tits were in the wringer."

"Razor, actually."

Owen was still having trouble catching his breath. "Did you tell them where the stuff was?"

"Course I did. What do you think I am? Superman?"

"I would have told them after the first one," Max said. "In fact, I would have told them *before* the first one. I would have handed them a map and a key."

"Unfortunately, the Subtractors don't work that way. They had 'em off and in a jar before I could say jack shit. They hadda show they were serious, see? I had five more seconds to tell 'em or I'd be sitting here singing soprano."

"I don't imagine your colleagues were too pleased."

"No, I imagine not. Lucky for me, in the process of helping themselves to our score the Subtractors killed both of 'em. Paper put the number of bullet holes at thirty each."

"That *was* lucky," Max said. "Have you thought about cosmetic surgery?"

"I don't know," Zig said with a shrug. "Kind of a conversation piece."

Later, on their way back to the Rocket, Max told Owen to be sure and keep away from Zig if he should bump into him anywhere else in town. Despite his surface friendliness, the man was a violent pig, a rapist, and possessed of nothing resembling a conscience.

"If he's so awful, why were you so friendly to him?"

"That, my boy, is one of the cruelties of incarceration. One must choose one's friends from a very murky pool."

FIVE

IT STARTED OVER A DISAGREEMENT concerning a pack of cigarettes—a half-empty pack of Marlboro Lights—but it quickly escalated to the point where Zig was banging the guy's head on the floor.

Being a berserker, an unknown quantity capable of exploding over the smallest of provocations, had worked well for Zig up to that point. It had worked for him in the juvenile detention facilities where he spent most of his teenage years; it had worked for him in his time at Rikers; and it had even worked reasonably well for most of his ten years (sexual assault, aggravated assault, attempted murder) at Sing Sing.

He was a decent talker, and he had sunny periods during which he was able to nurture relationships that almost approximated friendships, but always, sooner or later, he would explode and someone would end up in hospital, and it was never Zig, despite his deficiencies in height, weight and reach.

Until the cigarette thing. Unfortunately, the head he was banging on the cement floor of the TV room—a privilege he had earned during one of his sunny periods—belonged to one Teddy Kern, favourite punk of no other than Khalid Mossbacher. Khalid Mossbacher, until his incarceration for murder and conspiracy, had been a hip-hop star famous for his abs and biceps.

It was only a matter of time. The messages started arriving well before Kern was out of hospital: messages yelled down the wing after lights out, messages that arrived with Zig's food. He even began to hear messages in the clanking of the prison's old radiators, though he hadn't the first clue about Morse code.

Khalid going to pop you—that was the mildest note he received. Others were more exuberant: *Khalid going to dismantle you. Khalid is going to torch your ass.*

He thought about faking cardiac pain. At best, that would get him into hospital for a few days. But when it was over, he would still have to return to the wing to face the righteous wrath of Khalid Mossbacher. The only way Zig was going to survive was to get transferred to another wing, and the only way you got transferred was if there was a credible risk of grievous injury or murder. His predicament certainly met that standard. But the catch was, if you snitched about your problem, the risk of getting murdered increased tenfold.

So Zig didn't say a word to anyone. Within a week he had scored cocaine from one source, a razor blade from another. One night, when the whole prison seemed to be asleep, he made the cocaine into a paste and rubbed it into himself at the crucial points. He sat himself on the floor and, with his back to the door, tied himself to the bars. He cut off first one nipple, then the other, slipped his free arm back into his bindings, and let loose some hellish shrieking.

Worst part of it was, the cocaine paste didn't work all that well.

Guards came running, the wing was locked down, and Zig was wheeled off to the prison hospital. In the circumstances, his claim that his life was under imminent threat was deemed credible, and he was transferred to another wing where he was not known. Max's wing.

It was while recuperating in hospital that Zig came up with his money-making idea. He'd had lots of money-making ideas over the years, but incarceration tended to dampen entrepreneurship, and somehow they had never come to anything. The Subtractors had long been the stuff of criminal legend; Zig had been hearing about them since he was twelve. Since their victims were thieves, they could hardly report matters to the police.

You'd expect there would be lots of thieves hobbling around missing toes and fingers and what have you, but somehow, despite his long association with the profession, Zig had never run into any of these victims. And yet everyone claimed to know someone who had been kidnapped, maimed, and let go, and most criminals believed the gang existed.

Now, as Zig contemplated the missing nipples under his bandages, he began to see possibilities in the Subtractors' business model. He knew hundreds of thieves and robbers; he even knew their MOs. All he had to do was keep up on the crime news—dead easy in this Internet age—and do a little guesswork. The rest was simple.

So, shortly after his release from Sing Sing four years previously, he had set about bringing the Subtractors into actual existence. The fear factor was definitely in his favour, and he was in an excellent position to amp it up, given his own peculiar mutilation. He told himself he had no intention of turning into a sadist. You don't want to lose your humanity, after all. It was simply a business model. He formed a loose association of assistants to put his scheme into action, and the Subtractors myth became his biggest asset.

From the outside, the Desert Moon funeral parlour looked like a drive-through bank. In fact, that wasn't a half-bad idea, Zig thought as he went inside. You could have the coffin low in a window, loved one on display, and people could just drive by, stop for a second, and take off.

The interior offered the usual collection of hushed rooms and pastel fabrics. Melvin Togg was laid out in viewing room three. Besides Melvin himself there was only one lone occupant, a woman sitting on a long, low couch beneath a soothing abstract.

Zig went and stood over the casket, head bowed. Melvin looked peaceful, and quite a bit healthier than he had in life, the mortician's art tastefully applied. A tiny guitar with *Graceland* scrolled around it was pinned to Melvin's lapel, a rosary entwined in his fingers. The cuffs of his burial suit covered his wrists and any microscopic evidence of duct tape that might have remained, not that any would.

It hadn't taken Melvin long to lose consciousness, but Zig had to be sure, and he and Clem had waited quite a while after the bag stopped puffing in and out before venturing over. They had untaped his wrists and ankles from the chair, putting the tape into their pockets. Then they had carried Melvin over to his bed and laid him down on it, still with the bag over his face. Zig washed his wrists with rubbing alcohol to remove any trace of the tape.

Melvin's Elvis clock had startled them as they were leaving.

"*Man, am I beat,*" the King said. "*It's six o'clock.*"

Zig went over to the woman. "Charlie Zigler," he said. "Would you be Melvin's wife?"

"No, no. Melvin wasn't married," the woman said. "I'm his sister. Monica Davies."

"Very sorry for your loss."

"Thank you."

"Melvin was a good guy. I didn't know him very well, but I liked him, same as most people."

The woman smiled faintly.

"I was shocked when I heard he'd, you know . . ."

"Committed suicide? How would you even hear such a thing? It wasn't in the paper."

"No, I know. But people talk. And they're all saying the same thing: no one saw it coming. Melvin seemed pretty chipper, pretty gung-ho, right up to the end. You know the way he was."

The woman nodded, dipping her head once.

"I probably should have seen it, though. I'm kicking myself about that."

It took a moment for this to register. When Ms. Davies

looked up at him, it was with a frown of puzzlement. "But you said you hardly knew him."

"I know. That's what makes it so weird. In retrospect, I mean."

Zig reached into his satchel and handed her a parcel loosely wrapped in brown paper. She slipped off the rubber bands and unfolded the paper, contemplating the framed rectangle in her hands.

"It's from Elvis," she said.

"Uh-huh. Isn't that amazing? Melvin come over to my place one afternoon last week and give it to me. I was kinda surprised at the time, because I knew he was a real Elvis fan. And I couldn't figure out why he wanted to give it to me."

Monica Davies seemed frozen in that hunched-over position. Not a muscle moved. A tear detached itself from her eyelash and splashed onto the picture. She rubbed it away with a neatly painted index finger.

"Like I say," Zig said, "Melvin hardly knew me, but he give me this thing. I was surprised, but I didn't think too much about it until I heard the news. Then it kinda made sense. They say people give away things that are precious to them, you know. Anyway, I thought I'd come here and give it to his wife or family or whatever."

"You're very kind," she said, and wept a little into a Kleenex.

"I'm just sorry I didn't realize what it meant at the time. I coulda done something maybe."

"How could you know?" she said softly. "What does anybody know about anybody?"

For the entire next day Max was sullen as only Max could be. Here they were strolling the brightest, gaudiest blocks in the world—neon cowboys, a Manhattan skyline, the temple of Luxor—and Max was ignoring it, muttering to himself like a gargantuan baby. Owen kept trying to interest him in the criminal

history of Las Vegas, the colourful, murderous life of Bugsy
Siegel, but Max would not snap out of it.

That night in his bunk, Owen could hear Max talking to himself in the Rocket's master bedroom. He reached for a paperback in an effort to ignore him: *The Magus,* a novel with which
he was flat-out in love. Owen was soon absorbed in the story.

"I have of late, and wherefore I know not, lost all my mirth . . ."

Max was reciting loudly enough to make sure Owen could
hear.

". . . forgone all custom of exercise. And indeed it goes so
heavily with my disposition that this goodly frame the earth
seems to me a sterile promontory."

Yeah, yeah, keep it up, Max. I know you're upset.

Owen fitted the buds of his iPod into his ears. This little
gizmo was the legacy of a raid they had pulled on a dinner party
in the Hamptons a couple of years ago. It wasn't one of the
video models, but it was still a little gem. Owen dialed up a pod-
cast of flutey New Age stuff, supposedly for meditation but perfect for reading. By the time he had finished the story of
Conchis and the Nazis and switched out his light, all was silent
in Denmark, the curtain having apparently come down on
Hamlet and his depression. Owen drifted off to the whirr of the
Rocket's air conditioner and the traffic on the distant Strip.

He was awakened sometime during the night by a cry ringing
in his ears—loud enough that his heart was jacked up and his
eyes wide open. He lay still, hearing nothing but the rattle from
the AC. Then another shout.

Max and his nightmares. A burst of incoherent cries got Owen
out of bed and into his bathrobe. He opened the bedroom door.

"Max?"

Max was cowering against the head of the bed, striped pyjamas soaked in sweat, his face pressed into a pillow balanced on
his knees.

"Max?"

"Wuh-hah!" He thrashed at the air with one hand, clutching the pillow with the other. A quiver shook his massive frame.

Owen went over and laid a hand on his shoulder.

Max heaved with a great intake of breath and lifted his head from the pillow. His eyes opened, glazed and bloodshot.

"The Butcher," he said hoarsely. "The Butcher was here. Right here. In my room. In this very room."

"The Alcatraz guy?"

"S'blood, boy. I could have reached out and touched his cleaver. Fuh! Sitting in that chair, talking to me."

Max leaned toward his night table, straining mightily, and hoisted his water glass. An interlude of gulps and slurps.

"Blood up to his elbows. Both hands. Blood over his face. Like he'd been swimming in it. And he says to me, 'Welcome home, Maxie. I think we're going to get along fine.'"

"It was just a nightmare."

"No! I tell you he was in this room. Alive as you or me."

"Max, you had a nightmare."

"He reeked of prison. I wouldn't survive if I had to go back inside, boy. I frankly prefer death, d'you hear?"

"Max, take it easy. You're not going to prison."

"Boy, listen to me." He clasped Owen's hand between two hot paws. "I've not been the perfect father, God knows. But I've done my best to bring you up like my own. Asked nothing in return. Nothing big, anyway—well, nothing too big. But now I am, I do, I must. Look me in the face, boy."

The old eyes were red and watery and full of fear.

"D'you love me, kid?"

Owen couldn't believe his ears; he wanted to flee. "Uh, yeah, Max. Of course I do."

"I need you to promise me something. I need you to promise me that, no matter what happens, you will never let me go back to prison."

"Max, how can I promise that? You know the old rule: if you—"

"If you can't do the time, don't do the crime. Not a rule I've ever lived by. My rule is, if you're going to get caught, not. That's why I'm the most conservative thief the country has ever seen. But if something should happen—God forbid—if something should go wrong and I'm facing a prison sentence again, I want you to promise to get me out of it."

"Max, I'm not gonna machine-gun ten cops to get you out of jail."

"I'm not talking about anyone else, I'm talking about me. Just think of it as putting the dog down."

"Max, you always taught me to keep things non-violent. Now you expect me to shoot you?"

"All right, maybe you don't do it yourself. You could hire someone. No one's ever going to suspect you."

Had it not been the middle of the night, and had Max looked even slightly less terrified and vulnerable, Owen might have put up further resistance, but as it was he found himself agreeing, regretting it even as he did so. "All right, yes. I promise. I won't let you go to prison."

"Swear it?"

"I swear."

"That's my boy. Now haste thee to thy bed."

SIX

"Time for you to hit the road, Charlene."

Zig was propped up on the pillows, watching her cute little fifteen-year-old butt waving in the air. She was down at the end of the bed totally absorbed in Zig's collection of graphic novels—not reading them, just grooving on the drawings and exclaiming every five seconds.

"That is so cool," she would say, and flip another page.

"I got stuff to do this afternoon," Zig said.

"This is so beautiful," Charlene said, pronouncing it *beauty-full.*

Zig could have stared at her butt all day, except for the fact that they'd already done it twice. Amazing what the kids of today would do for free drugs. Although clearly he had misjudged his proportions. There was a real art to getting it just right.

He used to prefer his females totally unconscious, courtesy of Rohypnol or some variant. In fact, he had done serious time for a couple of those. But these days he preferred them, well, compliant and relaxed but not comatose. He'd been in the mood for a bit of fun, so he and Charlene, a kid he'd picked up near Covenant House, had been playing Ex, Dex and Sex, as he liked to put it. The Ex had worn off, but the Dex was obviously still working because she was speed-focused on his damn comics.

She said *beauty-full* once more and that did it. Zig got out of bed and put on his pants. He picked up the girl's clothes from the floor and threw them at her in a ball. She looked up, giggling.

"You got thirty seconds to get dressed and get out of here."

She looked back down at the book. Zig snatched it out of her hands.

"Hey!"

"I said beat it. Now get the fuck out."

"There's no need to get nasty about it."

"You don't know what nasty means. Keep talking and you'll find out."

Stu Quaig sipped his beer and tried to ignore the television behind the Five Card's bar. He wasn't interested in poker, mostly because he'd never won a poker game in his life, and he didn't understand the current fascination with the game. He tried not to be too obvious about staring at himself in the bar mirror, but he could see his reflection between the Glenlivet and Johnnie Walker and he definitely needed a haircut. He seemed to enjoy a peak period of two weeks where his hair looked its best, and then all of a sudden he looked shaggy and pathetic and it was time to head back to the salon.

Clem Boxley was staring at the poker game as if at any minute money might fall out of the TV screen onto the bar. Stu was still on his first beer of the night, while Clem was rapidly disposing of his second margarita. Clem could line them up and drink them down, but it didn't do anything positive for his interpersonal skills. He was congenial, even chummy, after one or two, but once he got onto three, four or more, chummy could turn gloomy could turn hostile and then there was no telling what kind of mayhem he would raise.

Clem held up his empty glass for the cute little bartender to see. Number three coming up.

Stu glanced at the mirror where half the lounge was reflected and saw Zig coming in.

"Boss is here," he said.

Clem turned to greet Zig with extravagant heartiness, but Zig just ordered a beer and got right down to business.

"Old guy named Max Maxwell I met in stir. Shoulda retired a long time ago, but he's in town and I think he's still in the game. In fact, I think he's feeling pretty flush."

"Why?" Stu said. "He's throwing money around?"

"He's too smart for that. But I can read this guy and he's in the chips. In fact, I think he may be behind this." He held up a couple of pages downloaded from the *San Francisco Chronicle,* headlined THE DIVA AND THE THIEF. "An old guy and a kid pulled this off and got away with some serious bling, not to mention cash. I think it coulda been my old friend Max and his nephew."

"I know Max," Stu said. "Did a job for him years ago."

"Shit," Zig said. "Is he going to recognize you?"

"Doubt it. Not unless he gets close."

"Well, don't let him. I bumped into him and his so-called nephew earlier at Slots-a-Lot and followed him. Turns out he's staying at a fucking trailer park. Unfortunately, I don't know which trailer is theirs—I didn't have a card to get through the gate. But I want you guys to keep an eye on him. And I mean a close eye."

"What kinda guy brings a kid to Las Vegas?" Clem said. "How can you have a good time in Sin City if you got, like, offspring with you?"

"Maybe he really is his nephew, who knows," Zig said. "He was okay for a teenager. Very polite."

"Gives me hope for the world," Stu said, and took a sip of his Corona. He'd asked for it with no lime, but the bartender had stuck a lime in it anyway. In Stu's experience girls never made good bartenders.

Clem raised his hand to get her attention. "Bar mistress!"

Zig grabbed Clem's wrist. "You don't need another drink. What you need to do, the both of you, is keep an eye on the trailer park, starting at, like, dawn. Follow Max and this kid and see who his associates are. If this is a working vacation he's on, and you can bet your ass it is, he's gonna be staffed up. I want to know who's with him and what they're up to."

"How we gonna know what they look like?" Clem said.

"Stu's met Max, dipstick. The kid will be with him."

Max was reading aloud in the back of the limo. They had made the papers—even the Las Vegas papers—thanks to the celebrity of Evelyn del Rio.

"'He was completely charming,' Ms. del Rio said. 'Or at least, as charming as a man can be while he's robbing you. Yes, I was terrified at first, but it became clear very quickly that they weren't going to hurt anybody, they just wanted their loot and out.'

"'The loot and out,'" Max repeated. "I couldn't have put it better myself."

A voice addressed them from the front of the limo in a strong Indian accent. "You are utterly bewitched by this woman," Pookie said. For some reason he had it in his head that all limo drivers hail from the Punjab.

"Just drive, Pookie. Please don't act."

Max was dressed in baggy khaki pants, sandals and a pale pink polo shirt. He wore a baseball cap on his head that said *Las Vegas,* and he had covered the exposed skin of his arms and face with makeup that turned him lobster red, over which he had added little curls of "peeled skin." An ancient Aer Lingus travel bag was slung across one shoulder. Owen had never seen him look so bad.

Not that Owen was doing much better. His hair was red tonight, his face and arms freckled. He had yellowed his teeth, and even blacked out one bicuspid as if it were the casualty of a bar brawl. For pants he had selected extremely baggy shorts with elaborate pockets that went badly with his battered pair of green high-tops. The Guinness T-shirt was new, and its deep black made Owen's skin look extra pale.

The MGM Grand of course contained a casino, and casino security staff are the masters of facial recognition software, so in addition to the wardrobe Max had expended a good deal of effort adjusting their brows, noses and jawlines. They wouldn't stand up to the full sun, but would be convincing under artificial light.

"Right to the door, if you please, driver," Max said with a Dublin lilt. "Don't go droppin' us a country mile downstream."

"Yes, sir, of course, sir," said Pookie the Punjabi. "Many plenty good."

"Pookie," Max said in his normal voice, "just be your normal, rude, untutored self and all will be well."

"You are being the boss, sir. But enlighten me, please—who is this odd-looking carrot-top?"

Owen laughed.

Pookie turned onto the Strip and slipped into a school of limos cruising the shoals of coral and ruby lights.

"Don't let's lose our fizzy stuff," said Irish Owen, handing a two-hundred-dollar bottle of champagne to Max. It was a good prop for a show like this; plus, there was always the chance that you might end up actually drinking it.

Pookie pulled up in front of the Grand and opened the door for them. Max and Owen headed for the entrance, Owen weaving a little, Max extremely upright in the manner of the self-conscious drunk. A svelte youth over-decorated with gold braid opened the door for them.

They had the elevator to themselves.

"Tell me again why we're doing this," Owen said.

"I've always been in it for the money, myself."

"But why a break-in? Always before it's been the dinnertime thing. Now here we are, it's the middle of the night, and we're breaking into someone's hotel room? Besides which, she's not even a Republican. She campaigned for Obama."

"Don't be so conservative, laddie. One must evolve or die."

"This is not good, Max. You know it."

"Relax, boyo. I've done the research. Her fancy-man actor and her bodyguard are going to be at the concert."

They got off on the twentieth floor. The corridors had the solemn hush of a good hotel, with thick pile carpeting that ran halfway up the walls. Although there were no security cameras, Max maintained his stately gait all the way down the corridor.

Except for the champagne, they were travelling light. As Max put it, you could explain being on the wrong floor, but you couldn't explain bolt cutters. At the end of the corridor they took a stairwell down four flights.

Their destination was the corner suite on sixteen. This was where Max's research in all those issues of *Rolling Stone*, *Variety*, *Hotelier*, *Town & Country*, *Hollywood Reporter*, *Premiere*, *People* and *Hospitality* paid off. He had determined that Angela Lake would be staying in suite 1601 for the full two weeks of her engagement at the Grand. Her last set was due to finish at two a.m.

They listened at the door for a full minute, but there was no sound of voices, television, running water—nothing.

Max, who was a champion pickpocket, had liberated a card key from a manager earlier that afternoon. Now he slipped it into the slot and the lock clicked open. Owen sensed impending disaster.

They entered a living room. The hotel billed itself as a non-smoking environment, but there was a strong smell of nicotine in the air—the acrid after-smell that clings to clothing, as of someone who had just come in after stepping outside for a smoke.

Owen tugged at Max's sleeve, but Max just scowled at him and moved farther into the room. The curtains were open, and ambient light from nearby buildings was enough to cast his bulky shadow low on the wall.

Between the living room and bedroom lay a dressing room and bathroom. Goodies were lined up on the dressers like a midnight snack set out for Santa Claus: two watches, a sparkling necklace and a fat wad of cash in a money clip. With one swift motion Max swept it all into the Aer Lingus bag.

Owen checked the closet safe; it was open and empty. He was just turning back when a voice said, "Get out of here. Now."

"Nora?" Max said, not even looking. "Darlin', that's a considerable frog you've got in your throat."

The man stood just inside the bedroom doorway. He was about forty, with close-cropped hair and dark circles under his eyes. Owen recognized him instantly. This was bad. This was not supposed to happen.

"I'm telling you again," Tony Tedesco said, "get out of here."

Tedesco was the kind of actor producers cast as the cop's badass partner, the tough bastard who turns out to have a heart of gold. More recently he had been taking smaller parts in independent films.

"Jeannie Mac," Max said, holding the pass card up to his face, studying it like a jeweller, "how for the love of Pete did our key work?" He took a step toward Tedesco. "I've no doubt yourself could use a drop about now. Please accept the bubbles as a token of—well, like a consolation, sort of."

Max set the bottle down on the dresser and started toward the door.

"Hold it right there, pal. How about I call the manager and you explain all this to him?"

"Tony Tedesco," Owen said, snapping his fingers. "The very man. I've seen you in tons of fillums. *Highwire*? *Detective Blue*? Absolutely grand you were. I'm bettin' you studied under some real coppers, because you had the look, you had the manner, you had the whole thing down perfect. Bruce Willis is bollocks next to you."

"All right, Seamus," Max said. "Let's be off now and not inconvenience yer man any more than we already have."

Tedesco snatched up the phone.

"Now, now, sir," Max said. "Don't be after phoning the authorities."

"Why should it bother you?" Tedesco said. "You're just in the wrong room, right? Honest mistake, right? And that's your room key? I'm sure management will understand."

"We'll be off, then," Owen said. "Take care, Mr. Tedesco. Sorry to disturb you."

He tugged Max's sleeve. Max shook him away and grabbed the champagne bottle. Before Owen could stop him, Max had swung the bottle full into the actor's head. Tedesco slumped sideways and slithered to the floor.

"Jesus Christ," Owen said, dropping the accent. "Jesus Christ."

He knelt beside the actor, feeling his pulse. He was alive, but his jaw was crooked and blood flowed from his mouth onto the carpet.

"Leave him," Max said in his normal voice. "Pookie will be waiting."

Owen went to the bathroom and soaked a face cloth in cold water. "It's not good to be unconscious too long," he said. "You can end up in a coma."

"Why don't we call security while we're at it?"

Owen pressed the cold face cloth against Tedesco's forehead and the actor began to stir. Owen grabbed a cushion off the couch and placed it under him.

"Sorry for the misunderstandin'," he said, back in character. "Didn't mean to hurt no one."

Tedesco groaned louder and his eyes fluttered open.

When they were in the elevator, Max said, "If you want to be Florence Nightingale, why don't you go to a bloody nursing school."

"You broke his jaw, Max." Owen could hear the quaver in his own voice. "I've never even seen you get physical before, and you break the guy's jaw. You broke some teeth. He'll be lucky if he isn't disfigured. And he's an actor, Max. How could you do that to an actor?"

"It was him or us, lad. Him or us. I prefer us."

The elevator door opened and they strolled into the lobby. The entire staff seemed to be on cellphones or engaged with computer screens and didn't even look at them.

Pookie was in the limo halfway up the block, reading a Harry Potter novel.

"Quick," Max said. "Get us out of here."

Pookie spoke up, still the cheery Indian. "You have been enjoying a pleasant evening, I trust, sir?"

"Just drive, will you?" Max said.

"You have been imbibing some alcoholic beverage, I am thinking. You are no longer transporting your bottle of champers and your mood is noticeably darker. Have you been forcing alcohol on the young fellow, too? He is looking ghostly pale, is he not?"

"Pookie, for God's sake move it."

In the back seat, Max and Owen removed their wigs and other makeup, Max scratching at bits of glue on his eyebrows. The smell of rubbing alcohol filled the car. Sirens grew louder in the distance, but there were always sirens in Las Vegas. They struggled out of their costumes and into the casual stuff that was waiting for them in an open suitcase.

By the time Pookie dropped them off at the El Cortez parking lot—for security reasons, neither he nor Roscoe knew about the Rocket—they were once again the old British wig salesman and his nephew.

They paid Pookie and said good night.

"*Namaste,*" he said. "I am wishing you peace and joy always."

"Pretty good haul," Max said.

"You didn't have to hit him," Owen said.

Max was checking his face in the bathroom mirror, looking

for any makeup he had missed. "Tony the Thug was going to either jump us or get us thrown in the slammer, and I wasn't about to let that happen. I don't see why you're so jellified about it. We're thieves, boy, we dance with danger. Part of the fun."

"Fun? Suddenly out of the blue you smash a guy's jaw? An *actor?*"

"Tedesco is a well-known right-wing lunatic. I do not consider him a colleague. You'd be feeling a whole lot worse if we were sitting in jail now."

"Max," Owen said, "let's please get out of this business before something terrible happens."

"Get out any time you like, me lad. I'm in for the long haul."

Max headed for the galley. It was their custom, after pulling a job, to have a snack before going to bed, but Owen got changed in the bathroom and climbed into his bunk.

"What's this, lad? Going to bed without your midnight snack?"

"I'm not hungry."

"Nonsense. You hardly ate any supper. You'll waste away."

Owen turned out his light, wanting to put an end to the day.

The Rocket filled with smells of toast and the melted cheese in Max's inevitable midnight omelette. Owen turned his back and stared at the wall.

SEVEN

OWEN AWOKE THE NEXT MORNING TO A SOFT RAPPING on the side of his bunk. It took him a moment to remember where he was—the Rocket, Las Vegas, Tony Tedesco's jaw.

Max's face was alarmingly close, his expression an almost comical rendering of sheepishness.

"Breakfast is served, boy."

"I'll be there in a sec."

"A chorus line of pancakes awaits."

"Great."

But Max's face stayed right there, worried and sad and—it had to be recognized—probably acting.

"Uh, boy," he began, then turned politely aside while a series of throat clearings and prim little coughs was performed. "Boy, about last night . . ." Max went to the window opposite and opened the curtains, staring out at the vista of another Winnebago. He was wearing his Hyatt bathrobe. "You were right to speak sharply to me, boy. Your old uncle misbehaved, and—"

"I'll say."

"No, no, let me finish. You can't go cutting a man off mid-apology. What I wanted to say was, I'm sorry."

"It's Tony Tedesco you have to apologize to. He's probably in the hospital."

Max raised his hand for silence. "I regret you were witness to mayhem. I was taken by a force-ten hurricane of panic. Utterly blew me over. So I lashed out." He made a harmless-looking jab at the air, a kitten pawing a string.

"Sure didn't look like panic," Owen said. "For one thing, we weren't in any danger. If we had just run right then, there's no way hotel security would have caught us. We'd have been in the limo before they even got up to the room."

"That's why I'm apologizing, you clot—oops." Max covered his mouth with his hand lest another insult escape. "Come and eat before it gets cold."

Zig came out to the table carrying a latte in one hand and a cookie in a small paper bag in the other. He set the coffee down fast.

"Man, that's hot. I think they got like a nuclear coffee maker back there or something."

"Secret of Starbucks' success," Stu said. "Nuclear espresso machines."

"Where's Clem?"

"Went to get something in the mall. Here he comes."

Clem came up the escalator. His sunglasses were Ray-Bans, but they were just a touch crooked. He was carrying a magazine.

"Where the fuck you been?" Zig said.

"Magazine store," Clem said, offended. "Got the new *Woodworker*. I got a subscription at home, but I didn't want to wait. They got a feature on gun racks."

"Magazine store? Then how come you reek of alcohol?"

"One drink, I swear. Shot of Johnnie Walker."

He sat down heavily on the metal chair and pulled closer to the table, making a horrible scraping noise on the floor.

"It's eleven o'clock in the morning," Zig said. "Already you're drinking. I want you to stop right now, you got that? From now on you drink like a normal human being or I'm gonna kick your ass, you got it?"

"Yeah, yeah."

"Don't say yeah, yeah. I asked you if you got it."

"Yes, Zig. I got it."

"All right, what's the scoop? What'd you find out?"

"I gotta get a coffee first."

"No you don't. Just tell me what you found out."

"The fuck, man. You guys got coffee." Clem started to get up but, seeing Zig's look, sat back down. "All right. Your fat man has got two associates that we've seen so far. Three if you count the kid."

"I don't count the kid. Who are they?"

"Roscoe Lukacs and Terry Pook—bald guy. People call him Pookie."

"I met Pookie on the job I did with Maxwell," Stu said. "Good driver. Seemed like he was a steady guy, you know, reliable. That was a long time ago. Haven't seen him since."

"What about the other guy?"

"Lukacs used to work with Jonny Knapp few years back. Totally minor player. Strictly freelance. Lives in Seattle, where he does something in real estate—manages a couple of buildings."

"So why's he working with a guy like Max?"

"Why am I working with a guy like you?" Stu said, and Zig glared at him. "He likes to steal shit."

"You figure out which trailer they're in?"

"Yeah, we did. And it ain't a trailer, it's a Trailersaurus. Biggest damn Winnebago you ever saw."

That night, Max insisted that Owen get dressed to the nines before they went out to dinner. When he saw Luigi's Restaurant, he was glad he had put on the Armani. The casual opulence of the place made him feel like a movie star enjoying a night out incognito. Max was resplendent in summer-weight Zegna. He looked like a European film producer.

Having Pookie and Roscoe along would be "good for *esprit de corps*," he had explained to Owen as they drove over from the trailer park. "They're loyal little bastards," he had said with some affection, "and they are underpaid. I like to make up for it once in a while."

"Why don't you just pay them more?"

"Honestly, Sunshine, you are such an infant."

It was obvious to Owen that one of the reasons Max liked to have Pookie along was that Pookie just out-and-out worshipped him. Tonight he was trying out a cowboy accent.

"Pookie, speak normally," Max said. "Really, sometimes you are insupportable."

Roscoe was staring out the window, coloured light flowing over his long, angular features. Without even turning to the others, he said, "Christopher Jones was captain of what vessel?"

"O base Hungarian," Max said. "Spare us the trivia just once?"

"The *Pinta*," Owen said.

"That was Columbus," Pookie said. "The man distinctly said Christopher Jones. Who the hell is Christopher Jones?"

"Christopher Jones," Max said, "as all you pathetically igno-rant Yanks should know, was captain of the *Mayflower*."

"*Mayflower* is correct," Roscoe intoned. "We have a winner."

They all went quiet when their waitress arrived—not out of politeness, but just because she was that kind of beautiful. She handed out their menus, and then Max surprised everyone by asking her to wait a moment.

"Everybody," he said, "I want you to meet Sabrina, child of an old, old friend of mine. My dear, there are a thousand Maxwells in the phone book but only one Magnus Max. Surely you remem-ber? Used to visit you when you were still playing with dolls."

"I'm sorry," she said, "I can't say I do. You knew my parents? How'd you know where to find me?"

"Your father has had people looking out for you here and there, and I've done my own modest research. I asked Luigi to make sure we were seated in your section."

Max introduced everyone at the table. When he came to Owen, Owen found himself blushing for no reason whatsoever, other than the fact that Sabrina was flat-out gorgeous. Her dark hair was pulled back into a twist, exposing a perfect neck. The effect was erotically prim, and Owen found himself imagining her with her hair spilling over her shoulders. Her eyes were green and caught the light in a way that reminded him of certain purloined items back at the Rocket.

"I still miss your mum," Max said. "Sweet lady. I used to love to visit just to bask in her beauty. You're the very image of her."

"I am not," Sabrina said. "She was way more elegant than I'll ever be."

Max raised a hand to forestall argument. "My dear, the two halves of a cleft apple are not more like. Now, before we move on to food, we shall require an extremely cold bottle of Dom Pérignon. Have to get the best," he added with a nod toward Roscoe and Pookie. "I'm trying to buy their loyalty."

"Do you think it'll work?" Sabrina said.

"It will fail miserably," Max said. "But I shall be happy as a clam nevertheless."

Sabrina smiled and it was as if the power had just been restored after a blackout. Owen had to fix his gaze on the tablecloth to avoid gaping at her. Pookie and Roscoe were entranced as well, though Roscoe registered this by fiercely gripping his menu, and Pookie by drumming his fingers on the tablecloth, skull-and-crossbones ring flashing.

"Sabrina," Max informed the table when she was gone, "is no other than the daughter of John-Paul Bertrand, otherwise known as the Pontiff. The thief's thief, and a gentleman of the first order. Promised him the day he was hauled off to Oxford that I would look in on her whenever I could. Make sure she was okay."

"Looks okay to me," Roscoe said.

Pookie ran through the menu, warning the others of cholesterol here and triglycerides there. He became more fanatical on the subject each year.

Sabrina returned with the champagne and Owen felt her beauty pass through him in waves of benign radiation.

"A timely arrival, my sprite," Max said to her. "We are gnawed by the tooth of hunger."

The champagne was followed by a bottle of Amarone, and then another. Owen burnt his tongue on his spinach ravioli and had to keep cooling his mouth with sips of wine.

Max noisily devoured a huge plate of osso bucco. "Nothing like a first-class meal," he said, swilling the last of the Amarone in his glass. "Makes all seem right with the world."

"What word do the Amish use," Roscoe inquired, "to refer to anyone outside their community?"

"Auslander," Pookie said.

"Amish—Not," from Owen.

"Must we?" Max said.

Roscoe looked around the table, solemn as a horse. "English."

"I'm so glad we cleared that up," Max said. He launched into a war story about Peter O'Toole, making the others laugh. He became bossy over dessert, ordering tiramisu for everyone. Owen wished they could have ordered separately, just to keep Sabrina lingering at their table.

Later, the older people had brandies and espressos.

"I gotta say, that Sabrina is one good-looking girl," Pookie said.

"She doth indeed teach the torches to burn bright."

"I think the kid here is smitten," Pookie said, pointing across the table at Owen. "He's looking a little dreamy."

"It's just the wine," Owen said, and excused himself to go to the washroom.

On his way back to the table he passed close by Sabrina, who was waiting at the end of the bar for a round of drinks.

"You having a good time?" she asked him.

"This may be the best restaurant I've ever been to," he said, hoping desperately to come up with something witty to say and failing.

"That's nice to hear."

She turned her attention back to the bartender, and Owen made his way back to the table.

They lingered over their brandy, the trivia questions popping back and forth and Max spouting quotations. Owen barely listened. He kept analyzing his brief exchange with Sabrina with the intensity of a code-breaker. He knew there probably was no code, that she was just being polite. In any case, by the time they left, the busboys were putting chairs upside down on stripped tables and Sabrina was gone.

"So why didn't we bring Stu along?" Clem wanted to know.

Zig didn't answer. He hated being cooped up in a car with Clem, who suffered mightily from low frustration tolerance, ADD, claustrophobia and all the other disorders formerly known as ants in the pants. Clem was not one to suffer in silence.

"Boss? Did you hear me? I asked you why didn't we bring Stu along?"

"Maybe I don't trust him yet."

"Stu's a stand-up guy," Clem said. "You think I'm gonna recommend some jerk-off's gonna waste your time?"

"I'll trust him when I feel like trusting him."

Clem reached for the radio dial.

"Don't."

Clem sat back again. There were only a handful of cars left in the restaurant lot. Three hours now they'd been sitting here watching people coming out of Luigi's looking pleased with themselves. Clem was getting more and more hyper, obviously, but Zig didn't mind sitting it out. He was sure Max was behind the San Francisco job. Old guy, young guy, two associates. And he'd heard Max's theories about dinnertime robbery back in Ossining.

"Finally," Clem said.

"Looks like they've been into the vino pretty good."

"Bald guy's Pookie. Other guy's Roscoe."

The kid had to practically lever Max into their car, the old guy was so busy holding forth. He boomed and blustered and cackled, even as the kid was getting into the driver's side. The other two got into separate cars.

"Three cars, three Tauruses," Clem said. "Musta got a volume discount."

"Staying in separate places too, I bet," Zig said. "That's smart."

"So which one we gonna take down?"

"I like Baldy."

"A fine evening," Max said when they were moving. "Sumptuous meal. Good service. See, lad, these are the good things the diligent life will bring your way. The rewards of application far outweigh talent. The productive man wants for nothing."

"Last week you said there was no meritocracy."

"Oh, plague me not with your last week this and your previously that."

"You're always contradicting yourself."

"Last week I was talking of the theatre. Not real life."

"Hey, look!"

They were stopped at a traffic light. In the parking lot beside them a man was screaming at a girl. Owen rolled down his window.

"Ask yourself this question, missy," the man yelled. "Just ask yourself what kind of woman do you want to be? Do you want to be the good woman, whose worth is above rubies? Or do you want to be some no-account whore of Babylon?" The man grabbed her wrist and pulled her to him.

"Do my eyes deceive me," Max said, "or is that not Sabrina?"

The man slapped her across the face, and the report echoed off the surrounding buildings.

Owen was out of the car before he even thought about it.

The man had her by the hair and was slapping her repeatedly across the face.

Owen was wishing he knew a few Jet Li moves.

Sabrina twisted this way and that, trying to escape. The man yanked her closer, and spoke as if to the multitude.

"'The loose woman is bitter as wormwood, sharp as a two-edged sword.' Is that the kind of woman you want to be? I am not gonna sit by and watch it happen, Sabrina."

Owen launched himself from ten feet away and hit the man mid-chest—too high to knock him over, with the result that Owen fell to the ground. .

"Get away from me, boy, or I will bust your sorry ass, and that's a promise."

"Bill," Sabrina said through gritted teeth, "I am not your property."

"And you don't owe me nothin', I suppose. Did I or did I not get you out of one heap of trouble?" The man gave her hair another yank.

"Ow! Yes!"

"Did I or did I not share with you all my worldly goods?"

"Leave her alone," Owen said, picking himself up. He wished the parking lot wasn't so deserted. Nothing around but empty cars and stacks of junked parking meters.

"Let me go," Sabrina said. "You bastard, let me go."

"Did I or did I not take you down to Cancún?" The man called Bill clutched Sabrina's hair with one hand. "Boy, take care that ye come not between a man and his wife. That phrase mean anything to you?"

"I'm not your wife." Sabrina kicked at his shin ineffectively.

"Doesn't matter if she's your wife, girlfriend or sister," Owen said. "You don't get to hit her."

"Boy, you'd best get shed of the idea you can do anything about it."

Owen kicked him hard in the behind.

The man let go of the girl and faced him. He was short, almost square, with a considerable paunch but arms that looked like he could press three hundred easy.

"You go wait in the car," Owen said to Sabrina. "We'll take you home."

"Home? Who do you think she lives with, peckerwood?"

"Don't mess with him," Sabrina said to Owen. "Really. You're making a mistake."

"Oh, he's already made it," the man said. "This boy's neck-deep in the mistake hole."

A swift jab caught Owen's cheek and it felt like a train hitting him. He went down on one knee, praying that Max would run this T-Rex over.

"You want more of the same, just get up, Yankee Doodle."

Owen got to his feet and hurled himself at the man, trying to get in close enough to avoid those fists. A right hook glanced off his ear. Using the one kick he had learned from a judo website, Owen swept the man's legs out from under him and sent him sprawling. He jumped on him, but the guy flipped him off as easily as a bull.

Before Owen could organize himself, three jabs sent him staggering backward. He raised his arms in defence, but a haymaker caught him in the ear, spinning him around. A right hook, and Owen felt the inside of his cheek split and blood flow into his throat. He was on his knees with no memory of how he got there. A blurry Max seemed to be moving in the blurry background. Please, he prayed, fire a blank or something.

"Stay down," Sabrina said. "Just stay down."

"Leave her alone," Owen tried to say, but the words came out in red bubbles.

"Looky here, boy, you are in no position to give orders or even make suggestions. Take the girl's advice and stay down."

Owen hauled himself to his feet, the cars in the lot wheeling around him. He took a swing, but the man just dipped his head to one side and Owen nearly fell.

"Boy, you don't learn, do you?"

A fist caught Owen in the stomach and lifted him off his feet. He went down hard, stones and glass biting into his skin. Sabrina was yelling, the guy was yelling, the world wobbled on its axis. It was probably only ten seconds, but it felt like ten minutes before he managed to pull in a lungful of air. Tears blurred his vision.

He raised himself to his knees and promptly threw up.

"Leave him alone, Bill," the girl was saying. "He's half your size. He was just trying to help."

"Kid, do yourself a favour and stay down."

I'm on my feet, Owen realized. Jesus H. Christ, I'm on my feet again.

"For cryin' out loud, kid. You gotta be dumber than mud."

Owen jabbed and missed. He was already falling, so the answering punch missed his cheek and caught him in the forehead. He hit the pavement hard.

He tried to get up again, swaying badly. The man, double-wide chunk of beef that he was, looked dismayed. Max loomed up behind him. Where did he get hold of that parking meter, Owen was wondering as it came whistling around and caught the guy smack in the side of the head. He went down like an imploded building.

"Hit my boy, you pre-hominid? While I live, no one hurts my boy and gets away with it."

Max checked to make sure the man was still breathing, then bundled Owen and Sabrina into the back seat of the car.

"The heart of a lion," he said as he plunged into the traffic. "My boy has the heart of the lion. Couldn't have been more heroic myself."

"You shouldn't have got involved," Sabrina said.

"Nonsense, my dear. Rage must be withstood."

"You don't know Bill. He's a maniac. He won't give up until he finds you."

EIGHT

ZIG DROVE TO A MOTEL 6 ON THE OUTSKIRTS OF TOWN. He liked it for the isolated location, and also because it was made up of separate cabins rather than one long strip of rooms. You could have your privacy while you worked and not worry too much about noise.

He had rented the last cabin in the row, the farthest from the highway. All the other cars were gone, the cabins dark, the occupants answering the call to donate money to casinos.

"Guy's not making a sound," Clem said.

"The miracle of pharmaceuticals," Zig said.

"Yeah, but aren't we gonna want him compos mentis?"

"It's short-acting. He'll be fine."

Zig backed the car to the door of the cabin: the chances of being seen were minimal.

The bald guy was lying on his side in the trunk, groaning faintly.

"Take his feet," Zig said.

They got him inside and lowered him into the bathtub, his bald head under the tap. Zig snapped a manacle onto his wrist, the other end onto the drainpipe under the sink. He turned on the cold water in the tub.

"Hey, Baldy. Wakey, wakey."

The guy coughed and tried to sit up, banging his head on the tap.

"Oopsa-daisy," Zig said. "Don't wanna damage the cue ball there."

"The fuck's going on," the guy said. His speech was slurred, the sedative boosting the alcohol he'd no doubt consumed at Luigi's.

"My name's Sub. And this is Tractor."

"I don't wanna know your names. I don't even want to see your faces."

"Too late now."

Pookie squinted at the manacle on his wrist. He straightened his arm so that the chain went taut. "The fuck?"

"Sub-Tractor," Zig said. "Ring any bells?"

Zig could see the first tiny flame of fear igniting behind the fog in the guy's eyes.

"Don't worry. We'll have you out of here in no time," Clem said, and Zig gave him the look. "Provided you tell us what we need to know."

"About what? You think I work in a bank or something? I don't know nothing about nothing."

"We'll be the judge of that," Zig said. He picked up the bolt cutters and held them over the tub. "You ever play This Little Piggy?"

"Fuck you, let me outta here." He yanked hard at the manacle, taking it into his other hand and really pulling.

"Take his shoes off, Clem."

Clem reached for a foot, but Pookie started kicking and thrashing. Clearly, a bigger dose was indicated. Clem finally clutched his far foot and stood up so Pookie couldn't kick at him with the other. He was really panicking now, twisting frantically back and forth, jerking this way and that. Manacles for the feet next time, Zig decided. He probably should have figured that out ahead of time, but he wasn't going to get down on himself for learning on the job.

"Knock it off, Baldy," Zig said. He stood up and stomped at the guy's head, not too hard. Still, it made a noise against the tub. "We're not going to do anything to you, if you co-operate."

"Jesus Christ, I told you, I don't know anything."

"Don't answer yet. I want you to think long and hard about how you can help me with my problem."

"What fucking problem?" Pookie closed one eye against the water dripping into his face.

"My problem is that Max Maxwell was behind the San Francisco job, and I need to know where he put the take."

Pookie shook water out of his eyes, blinking. "You're asking the wrong guy. Max pays me cash. I don't know anything about the take. I don't even know how much it is."

"You'll have plenty of opportunity to revise your answers." Zig opened and closed the bolt cutters right in front of Pookie's face. "Just think about these and This Little Piggy."

The guy opened his mouth and sat up a bit. He looked like he was going to say something, but then he winced as if he had really bad gas pains and turned his head to one side. He slid back down the tub and lay still.

"That's fucked up," Clem said.

"Turn the tap on again."

Clem turned on the cold so it splashed all over Pookie's face, but he still didn't move. "Man, guy's really out."

Zig leaned over the tub and pressed the point of the bolt cutters against Pookie's throat. "Hey, Baldy. Pay attention."

Zig pressed harder. The guy didn't move.

Clem looked up at him. "You think he's dead?"

Zig took Pookie by the lapels and pulled him up to a sitting position, then shook him hard, but his head just lolled against his chest.

"Wake up, you bastard." Zig shook him again. He held him out at arm's length, a look of disgust creasing his features. "Fuck."

He let him drop, and Pookie's head connected with the tap in a way that looked extremely dead.

"Jesus," Clem said. "How can you plan for something like this?"

Zig looked at him. "I don't suppose you would happen to know CPR?"

———

Owen woke up, drifted off, and woke again to Sabrina pressing a cold compress to his forehead. He could hear Max talking to someone—the television, of course. Sabrina didn't say much. When she saw he was awake, she placed a face cloth full of ice into his hand and pressed it up against his ear.

She had the Rocket's first aid kit open on her lap and must have been using up the entire supply of disinfectant, because it hurt like hell.

"Gah," Owen said. "If I look anything like I feel . . ."

"You don't look bad," she said. "But he did kind of mash up your ear a little. I'm sure it'll shrink again."

"I really need to rinse my mouth out."

"Can you get up?"

She stood aside as he pushed himself to a sitting position. Nausea swirled around him, but he managed to totter to the bathroom. He rinsed his mouth, spitting streaks of red into the tiny sink.

By the time he emerged, he was feeling a little better. His stomach hurt, his head was throbbing, but at least the nausea was ebbing. Sabrina was sitting on the edge of the dining banquette, the first aid kit now closed on her lap and her hands folded neatly on top of it.

"God, you're beautiful," Owen said. It just came out.

"Oh, boy. Someone's head is still out of order."

Owen lowered himself to the bunk again. It was just a foam mattress over a wooden platform, which he could now feel attacking his bruises.

"Galahad awakes," Max called. "How is thy head?"

"Hurts. Everything hurts."

"Well, you have an angel of mercy tending you. It can hardly be hellish."

Sabrina leaned forward. "Is he always like that?"

"Like what?"

"So theatrical."

"Always. Oh, my head hurts."

He lay back on the bed. Sabrina sat on the edge and took his shoes off. It felt strange but far from unpleasant. Even in his pain he was thrilled by her proximity.

"Thanks for cleaning up my face," he said.

"No, no. I should be thanking you. You were so relentless! You just wouldn't quit."

"I just wanted him to stop slapping you. Are you okay?"

She smiled, and Owen felt something open up inside him, as if a lock had turned. "You're the one who got hurt," she said. "And Bill, of course."

"Max hit him with something, didn't he."

"A parking meter. There was a pile of them at the corner of the lot. Talk about theatrical."

"Who was that guy, anyway?" Owen said. "He sounded like some kind of preacher."

Sabrina shook her head. "He works for a hotel security outfit. He got born again a few years ago and he takes his Bible pretty seriously."

"I'll say. Is he your husband?"

She laughed, and it was a sound he wanted to hear again as soon as possible. "Husband? God, no." Sabrina helped him rearrange his pillow. "Bill is, um, obsessive, I guess you'd say. He helped me out when I was in a—a very bad way, and ever since then he's been convinced we were made for each other. He's not always like you saw him."

"But he hits you."

"That was just the second time. I told him the first time, if he did it again, I'd leave and he'd never see me again. He can actually be very sweet sometimes, very thoughtful. He kind of made himself indispensable. At least it seemed that way. Bill has lots of good qualities—he's generous, kind-hearted."

"He's also bat-shit crazy."

"Well, if I'd known what I was getting into . . ."

"How'd you meet a guy like that in the first place?"

"I was working in this bar near the Strip, making hardly any money. My landlord was booting me out of my basement apartment because he sold his house. Bill was a regular in this bar—he'd come in twice a week for a beer and a shot of Canadian Club, and he was always very friendly but, you know, nothing more than that.

"Then one day he asked me how I was doing, and I just totally lost it. And he was great. A real rock, you know? He offered to help me find a place to live, and when he saw how tiny and grubby the places were—the ones I could afford—he said, 'No way. I've got room at my house. You come and stay with me.' No, don't look like that. I knew I could trust him. So I moved in with him—it was just supposed to be for a few days, but before I knew it, three months had gone by—nearly four now. He's never made the slightest move on me, not seriously anyway. I guess he tried to hold my hand a couple of times. But when things started looking up for me, ho boy."

"He got possessive?"

"He always wants to walk me to work, or go with me when I go anywhere. When I get off shift, he's outside the restaurant. Every time I pick up my cellphone, there's a message from him, even though I'm staying at his place. 'Sabrina, I miss you.' 'Just want you to know I'm thinking of you.' Stuff like that. It might be romantic under other circumstances, but, I mean, he's twice my age and we have exactly zero in common."

"So, why'd you stay?"

"I was broke. The new job at Luigi's pays really well, but I was totally in debt. And besides, he wasn't a serious pain until just the last couple of weeks. Now, if he sees me talking to any man—any man at all—he gets crazy jealous. I've never so much as kissed him, and he's insane with jealousy. Like tonight. He was waiting for me at the bar in the restaurant and, I don't know, he didn't like the way I smiled at you or something. And when I got off work, he was waiting outside and I knew it was gonna be trouble, and that's pretty much when you came along."

"You going to stay in Las Vegas?"

She shook her head. He loved the way she did it, pursing her lips, closing her eyes, and then that little side-to-side movement that made her hair, now that it was untied, swirl against her shoulders.

"I don't really know where I'm going or what I'm doing."

"That's hard to believe," Owen said. "You look like someone who knows exactly what she's doing."

"I was studying design—jewellery mostly—at the Pratt Institute in Brooklyn, but I can't really afford it. My father's been in prison forever, as I guess you know, and the student loans are going to cripple me for life. I'm not sure it's worth finishing. I thought I'd make a killing as a croupier, but that's actually a hard job to get, and let's just say my family background didn't help."

"What are you going to do now—I mean about Bill?"

"I don't know. I can't stay at his place anymore, obviously. I can't even go to work or he'll find me. I was going to leave Vegas in a couple of weeks anyway. It's kind of depressing being in a town where everyone's losing money."

"We're heading to Tucson tomorrow. Why don't you come with us?"

"What would I do in Tucson?"

"Well, you won't get beaten up, for one thing. And I guarantee no one's going to quote the Bible."

"Just Shakespeare." That smile again.

"Come on. You'll have a good time. We always do."

"Well, if you think it's all right. It might be a good way to put some space between me and Bill before I head back to New York."

"Oh, I'm old, I'm old!" Max had turned off the television and was struggling, with much groaning, to rise from the sofa. "What doth gravity from his bed at midnight?" He shuffled toward them in a pair of white slippers bearing a Hilton monogram. "How now, boy? Feeling better?"

"Hey, Max, is it okay if Sabrina grabs a ride with us to Tucson?"

"Aha! The angel takes flight! My dear, I'm a mean old man—selfish, hideous, and somewhat given to excess—but I've never yet said no to a beautiful woman. You're fleeing the Caliban of the parking lot?"

"I have to. But there's no reason why you should help me. You've already done enough."

"Nonsense. We have a brief appointment in the morning. You can pick up your goods and chattels, such as you require, and we'll be three for the road. Right, boy?"

"Right."

"Day or two later, we'll be continuing on to El Paso. Perhaps you'd like to come along and visit your papa?"

"Uh, no. I doubt that I'll be visiting my father."

"What? But the man's in hospital now. They finally let him out of his cell."

"You and I have different opinions about my father. And, sorry, but I think mine is probably better informed. Can we just leave it at that?"

"*Tsk.* A melancholy thing, family discord." Max looked from Sabrina to Owen and back again. "I trust that in time your conscience will be your guide. And so, weary with toil, I haste me to my bed." He lumbered toward his bedroom, pausing at the door. "On matters of gender, nakedness, sexual congress and all manner of behaviour falling under the general category of lust, Owen, I shall be brief: you are to remain a gentleman at all times."

Owen rolled his eyes, which made his head throb even more than it already was.

"Hey, listen," he said when Max had closed the door. "Let me take the top bunk. That's where I always sleep. Otherwise, we'll have to change the sheets."

"Don't you move. Just tell me where they are."

But Owen forced himself to sit up, climb to the top bunk, then lie down again, pretending the whole time not to be in agony.

Sabrina switched off the light. When she began to undress, Owen turned his back to her, another painful and by no means fast operation. Still, he couldn't help hearing, item by item: the drop of her sneakers, the zipper of her jeans. Then her weight on the bed frame as she got into the lower bunk. But soon the exhaustion that follows a flood of adrenalin washed conscious-ness away and he plummeted into dreamless sleep.

Max had all his life been one of those blessed individuals who have the knack of being able to drift off anywhere, any time. He was as comfortable in the Rocket's queen-size bed as if he had been born in it. But now he lay on his back, staring at the ceil-ing and listening to the persistent *crump, crump, crump* of some dimwit's subwoofer a few trailers away. He thought of the upcoming show, going over in his head the various roles he, Owen, Pookie and Roscoe would play.

Then time left him for a while—he had no idea for how long—and when he came to himself again, he was assaulted by the acrid smell of cigar smoke. Some droop-lip trailer trash, no doubt clad in overalls and baseball cap, was sneaking a midnight smoke out-side the Rocket. And then a noise, a rustling sound. A newspaper?

He sat up, goggle-eyed.

There was a man sitting in the corner of his tiny bedroom reading the *Los Angeles Times*. Curlicues of smoke and the crown of a fedora were visible above the headline: TRUMAN VETOES TAFT–HARTLEY.

"Who the hell are you?" Max managed to say. Smoke was stinging his eyes and throat. The man paid him no attention, hidden behind his paper. "What do you want?"

A rustle of paper as the *Times* was lowered. The man's features were hidden in the shadow of his hat brim. He sat forward, bringing his face into the light. His left eye was no more than a blood-filled socket, the lower half of his face a mask of gore.

"They got me, Max. I was having a great time, but they got me."

"What are you talking about?" Max's lower lip trembled so that he could barely form the words. "Who got you?"

"New York. Who else?"

Max gathered the bedclothes around his chest. He hadn't been this frightened since prison.

"You're Bugsy Siegel."

"Bugsy." The man puffed hard on his cigar so that the tip glowed neon red. "I've killed guys for calling me that."

"But you're dead."

The man shrugged. His suit was big in the shoulders, a wide chalk-stripe riddled with bullet holes from which wisps of smoke were coiling. His face minus the blood and with both eyes in place would have been handsome. A part of Max's brain registered that this was not Bugsy Siegel but Warren Beatty *playing* Bugsy Siegel.

The gangster raised a finger to his face. "Got me in the bridge of the nose. Right through the newspaper." He held the *Times* and blew a thin plume of smoke through the .45-calibre hole. "Force of the thing blew my eye out. Stings, too."

Bugsy got up and came around the side of the bed, reeking of blood and cigar.

"No." Max cowered against the bedboard. "Get away from me."

"I only came to warn you."

"Stay away." When the apparition didn't move, Max added, "Warn me of what?"

"Same thing's going to happen to you."

"No, no. I won't let it. Now get away. Get away from me. Please."

"Here." The thing held out its hand. "Take it as a reminder."

"Get away, I tell you. I don't want it."

"It'll help you see it coming."

"I don't want it, blast you."

"Take it!"

The voice would not be denied. Max's hand travelled of its own accord out from under the bedclothes, palm up. Into it, the creature pressed a flesh-hot eyeball.

Max screamed and tried to throw it away, but it refused to leave his hand. He screamed and screamed and covered his head with his blanket and curled himself into a damp ball. He remained that way for some time, listening for the sound of the newspaper, but there was nothing. Eventually he heard worried voices. He lowered the blanket just enough to look into the alarmed faces of Owen and Sabrina.

NINE

You would never have guessed that the man who was standing before the grill, flipping pancakes and whistling a tune from Gilbert and Sullivan, was the same man who had been quivering in his bedclothes scant hours before. But that was Max. Owen had never met anyone else who could change so completely from one mood to another, often mixing despair and sunshine in the confines of a single hour. Now he was pouring pancake batter into artful shapes—Marilyn Monroe, Mickey Mouse, a tapir (or so he claimed)—and chatting away as if he had passed a peaceful night of sweet dreams.

After breakfast, Sabrina called several hospitals until she established that William P. Bullard, hotel security agent and man of God, had been admitted to one of them with a concussion. Then Max and Owen dropped her at his neat little bungalow so that she could pack her things. The front lawn of cedar chips was surrounded by a very solid-looking white picket fence, and this was set off by a lawn jockey, also painted white, who proffered a welcoming lantern in the brilliant Nevada sun. Promising to retrieve her shortly, they went to meet Pookie and Roscoe at the Desert Inn coffee shop.

Roscoe was seated at a table for four by the window, a cup of black coffee steaming beside him. He was absorbed in a dog-eared paperback of *Ripley's Believe It or Not.*

"It contains nine trillion gallons of water," he said as they sat down. "And it's the largest man-made lake in the world."

"Lake Mead," Owen said. "I read it online when we were planning the trip."

"Lake Mead is correct," Roscoe said. "You look like you got hit by a truck."

"The lad takes after his guide and mentor," Max said. "Last night, defending a damsel in distress, he repeatedly attacked a pious baboon."

"Yeah? Kicked his ass, I hope."

Owen shook his head. "He was pounding the crap out of me until Max knocked him out with a parking meter."

"Unusual choice," Roscoe said.

Max threw his arm around Owen. "A veritable lion, this lad. Takes after his uncle. Where is Pookie?"

Roscoe shrugged.

"It's not like him to be late."

The waitress came over and they ordered coffee. She was a skinny, friendly woman who asked them where they were from. It turned out that her enthusiasm for New York, Broadway in particular, was boundless, dwarfing her excitement about the weather and *American Idol,* which was also considerable.

"I don't like this," Max said when she was gone. "Pookie has many defects, but tardiness is not among them. Give him a call."

Roscoe pulled out his prepaid cellphone and dialed. After a moment he said, "Not answering. I'll leave a message." Then, into the phone, "Hurry up. We're waiting."

The coffee came and Max explained the upcoming show to Roscoe. Roscoe asked some questions, and by the time they were finished their coffee Pookie was forty-five minutes late.

"I don't like it," Max said again. "If it was you, O base Hungarian, I wouldn't give it another thought. I would assume you were playing a high-stakes game of trivia somewhere. But Pookie? Something's wrong."

"You want me to go check on him?" Roscoe said.

"No, no. You get on the road to Tucson. We'll roust the errant Pookie and meet up with you there."

Roscoe left soon after. He was travelling separately from Pookie anyway—a security precaution Max insisted on.

Owen drove them a couple of blocks up the Strip to the Disney-style castle complete with multicoloured turrets that was the Excalibur. The castle itself was tiny compared to the vast fortifications of the hotel that surrounded it, an establishment of some four thousand rooms.

"You go in first," Max said, "and I'll watch your back."

"What are you being so paranoid for?"

"Pookie is behaving out of character. When a man behaves out of character, it's a portent. We go in separately and we come out separately. I'll meet you on the fourth floor in five minutes."

Five minutes later they were outside room 4418, and they were in luck because the door was propped wide open by a housekeeping cart.

"I don't like it."

"Max, stop saying that." Owen rapped on the door. "Pookie?"

They stepped inside, surprising an old Chinese woman in black and white housekeeping livery, who came bustling out of the bathroom. "He not here," she said. "Nobody here. I clean."

"Did you already make the bed?" Max asked.

"Why make bed? Nobody sleep in it. See? Chocolate still on pillow."

"This is bad," Max said, his bardic turn of phrase deserting him for once.

"Please," the maid said. "Not your room, you must leave." She made flicking gestures at them with a damp rag, and they backed out into the hall.

"We should check his car," Owen said.

That was easier said than done in the vast parking garage. They marched round and round the dim concrete bunker looking for Pookie's vehicle, muttering to each other over false positives and near misses.

"At least we know it's a Taurus," Owen said.

"Exactly. And why do we always rent Tauruses? Because they're the commonest car on the road. Hard to notice, hard to pick out."

"Yeah, but we know it's got California plates and an Enterprise label."

After another half-hour's plodding, they found it parked in the shadow of an elevator shaft. Close inspection revealed the doors to be unlocked.

"Pookie would never leave it like that," Owen said.

He opened the driver's door and peered inside. There was nothing else that looked out of place. The radio was intact, CDs were splayed on the passenger seat, the Luigi's parking stub was still on the dash. No blood or signs of struggle.

"Car looks fine," Owen said, closing the door.

"That doesn't." Max pointed to the concrete floor. With the toe of his shoe he nudged the remains of a broken hypodermic.

TEN

ALL THE WAY SOUTH ON 93, sunlight streamed into the Rocket so that they had to have the air conditioning up full. The dashboard showed an exterior reading of ninety-eight degrees Fahrenheit; inside, it was a comfortable seventy-two.

Sabrina sat quietly in the seat behind Owen, staring out at the passing desert. Owen couldn't stop thinking about Pookie. One reason Max used him over and over again was that he was completely reliable. If Pookie said he was going to be somewhere at a certain time, he would be there, simple as that. The crushed hypodermic may have been totally unrelated to his disappearance, but it didn't bode well. Owen hated to think that he might be hurt somewhere. One of the drawbacks of the criminal life is that it makes it difficult to call the cops even when you need to.

Max had found an AM station that played music from the forties and fifties—Owen had never heard so many clarinets in his life—but then the announcer recounted every last detail of the Vegas Stars game and Max switched it off.

"Tell me, O Lady of the Back Seat," he said. "What path in life do you plan to tread?"

Sabrina sat forward a little. "I can't really afford any plans. Twenty years old and no sense of direction—pretty pathetic, huh? My *fantasy* is to buy a hot little Mustang and zoom around wherever I want. As for reality, school's out of the question—for now, anyway—prison hasn't done a lot for the family finances. What about you, Owen?"

"I'm starting at Juilliard this fall," Owen said with a nervous glance at Max.

"Sheer folly," Max said.

"I want to try acting."

Sabrina smiled. "Oh, yeah? Get famous?"

Owen shrugged. "I've been in the drama club every year since grade school. I think I might like it."

Max muttered something unintelligible and leaned on the horn for no reason. The sun was high now. The cactus and the tumbleweed cast no shadows, and there was nothing moving except their vast, chugging Rocket.

After many reddish mountains and ochre plains, they slowed in a convergence of holiday traffic heading through Boulder City.

"Looks like the suburb to end all suburbs," Sabrina said.

"It was built by the government to house the people who worked on the dam," Owen said.

As the name implied, the mountains here were like heaps of boulders, as if some super alien race had touched down on earth and left behind colossal cairns. They passed through a rocky no man's land in a stately procession of vehicles. Then an octagonal visitors centre sprouted out of the rocks, encased in towers and wires that clung to the mountain at all angles. A weird profusion of generators and transformers followed, surrounded by metal fences and bales of razor wire. The sky was brilliant blue, but everything else, whether natural or man-made, was grey.

They rounded a bend and a vista opened up around them. On one side, Lake Mead, on the other, nothing as far as the eye could see.

"Where's this bloody dam?" Max said.

"We're on it," Owen said. "We're driving across it right this minute."

"I don't believe this," Sabrina said. "We're in the middle of the desert and there are people water-skiing."

It was true. The lake was dotted with sailboats, motorboats and Sea-Doos. Parasails flew across the sun, sending thin shadows skimming over the water.

"Do you want to stop?" Owen said.

"Bloody tourist trap," Max said. "I'm against it."

"Me too," Sabrina said. "Too much traffic."

Several miles later, they pulled into a service centre that was itself the size of a small city—a collection of fast-food joints, video arcades, gift stores, newsagents, the entire thing overrun by obese adults with too many children. Owen and Sabrina got out to stretch their legs, while Max manoeuvred the Rocket through the gas pumps. The sun was hot, but not unpleasant; neither of them was sweating.

"Max is crazy about the Pontiff," Owen said. "I mean your dad. He's always saying what a great guy he is."

"Sure. Meaning he was a laugh to be around. Generous. Funny. Full of ideas. He was all that . . ." She frowned a little, staring at the ground as they walked under a row of trees at the edge of the parking lot. "He was good to me, too, took me places, taught me stuff. He built me the most beautiful doll house you ever saw—all the little lights went on in every room. He was great—usually—when he was home.

"But he was hardly ever home. And depending how his work was going, we'd be in a great house with a swimming pool for three months, and then we'd get booted out and have to live in a tiny apartment. That happened so many times I lost track."

Owen was about to say something sympathetic, but he didn't want to interrupt. It seemed, once she got started on the subject of her father, Sabrina couldn't stop.

"It was so hard on my mother. She totally loved the guy. She wanted him home. She wanted him around, you know? But no. He always had some big plan for another score and he'd be gone for weeks at a time. She never knew when he was coming back, and when he did come back, half the time it meant we had to move again.

"Sometimes he asked us to be his alibi. I hated doing that. And I hated him being gone. When he came back, I would find ways to misbehave—I realize now it was because I was so angry with him—and he would lose his temper and the house would turn into this deep freeze.

"And of course he wasn't just away on jobs. He got caught a bunch of times, you know—so he wasn't exactly a criminal mastermind, no matter what Max thinks. I can't tell you how many times I was woken up in the middle of the night by cops kicking the door in and tearing the place apart. And you know what? It doesn't feel great when you're eight or ten or twelve years old to see your father hauled away in handcuffs. We begged him to stop, but he couldn't leave it alone. Always had to pull one last score. Which would be one thing if he was the only one to pay the price, but, you know, others happen to be involved."

Owen found himself getting angry at the Pontiff on Sabrina's behalf. "Sounds like it was pretty hard on you," he said.

"It was harder on my mother. When he got sentenced to ten years this last time, she just fell apart. She lost all interest in her job—she was a teacher for special-needs kids—and stayed home all the time watching TV. Stopped looking after herself, stopped cleaning the house. Then one day Dad's lawyer called to let her know they'd tacked another two years onto his sentence for some scam he'd been running from prison. That was it. A week later she took an overdose of sleeping pills and never woke up."

They were sitting on a picnic table out of the sun, watching Max, who was now attacking the Rocket's tires with an air hose that was too short.

Owen touched Sabrina's shoulder, feeling the heat of her skin through the fabric of her top. "I'm sorry you went through that," he said. "How old were you?"

"Sixteen. Luckily, my best friend's family really liked me. They took me in, and I finished high school living with them. That was pure luck, though. If it hadn't have been for them, I don't know what would have happened to me. I could have gone to live with my aunt in Dallas—but I didn't want to leave all my friends."

Max was approaching now, all belly and sunglasses and a jaunty hat with chinstraps that he'd picked up in the Australian outback decades ago. He was rarely able to resist the call of candy stores, and his pockets bulged with chocolate bars and licorice.

"Gas prices," he said, "are going to put me out of business. I ask you, how's an honest man supposed to make a living?"

"You managed to find the candy store, I see," Owen said.

"Take two," Max said, proffering Kit Kats. "I'm nothing if not a good provider."

Clem piloted the Prius through the gate with tremendous care, as if he were docking a spacecraft. The Vegas lights blinked and swirled off to the south, but it was quiet out here. Not surprising, since the area had been condemned several years back, owing to its being the former site of a chemical plant. There were danger signs posted all over. Clem waited while Stu closed the chain-link gate.

Stu climbed in and said, "Car's so quiet I thought you were switched off."

"Gotta love hybrids," Clem said. "Did you know blind people have actually asked Toyota to make them noisier so they don't have to worry about getting run over with no warning?"

"Yeah, I read something about that."

Clem killed the lights and they glided forward.

"Hear that?" Clem said. "Thing's a stealthmobile. Plus you're doing good for the environment."

The terrain turned jagged and they bounced for a while over broken tarmac and potholes, bits of metal and broken glass.

Acres of wasteland, lit by two high lights hundreds of yards apart. They stopped in the darkest area, halfway between them.

"Grab a shovel," Clem said.

For the next forty-five minutes they assaulted the mixture of clay and sandy soil that lay beneath the rubble.

"Easy work, he says. Good money, he says. You can't lose," Stu said, his voice heaving with the rhythm of his shovel.

"You're not complaining, are you?" Clem said. "I can't stand whiners."

"This the sort of job you get a lot?"

"Not that often. Once in a while."

"Well, listen, Clem. I didn't sign on for killing anybody. I'm not interested in a murder rap, thank you very much."

"The people we deal with, I guarantee you, are not fine upstanding citizens."

"I don't care what they are. I'm just saying."

Clem jammed his shovel into the ground and looked at him. "I'm doing you a favour bringing you along on this, cupcake. Zig don't exactly trust you yet, but I do. I wanna be able to tell him you're solid."

Stu kept shovelling. "Fine, man. I'm not complaining."

"This is deep enough."

They opened the trunk of the Prius.

"Garbage bags," Stu said. "Man, that's rough."

"What, you wanna purchase a nice casket on a layaway plan? You never even met the guy."

"So, what'd you do to him?" Stu said, taking the feet.

"Nothing. Guy threw a heart attack."

"Uh-huh. Good one, Clem."

"Swear to God. Guy suddenly looks like he's got gas pains, and boom. Dead."

They waddled toward the hole, their glossy green burden swinging between them. On Clem's count they slung it in. They stood at the edge, hands on hips, staring down. Stu looked like he was about to say something when a cellphone went off, its ring a digital copy of an old telephone's.

"You gonna get that?" Stu said, pointing into the pit.

"Shit," Clem said. "We can't leave that on him. Someone might hear it."

"How they going to hear it through four feet of dirt? Not that anyone's gonna come out to this fucking dioxin fiesta in the first place. Whole place reeks of acetone or some damn thing."

"We're not leaving it on him, Stu. Go get it."

Stu climbed into the pit, carefully straddling the body. He cut open the garbage bags with a pocket knife and rooted around until he found the phone. He handed it up to Clem and climbed out. Clem put it in his pocket and reached for his shovel.

"Don't seem right to just dump him like this," Stu said. "You think maybe we should say a few words?"

Clem made the sign of the cross and cleared his throat. "Here lies a dead guy," he said. He looked over at Stu, then back to the green package below them. "End of story."

ELEVEN

SABRINA SAT IN FRONT while Owen drove and Max took his siesta in the back bedroom. It was unlawful to be out of the seats while the vehicle was travelling down a highway at sixty miles an hour, but it was useless to try and talk Max out of it. The afternoon nap, according to Max, was just one of many things he and the great Winston Churchill had in common.

The desert rolled by on either side. They passed the turn-off to Laughlin, and the huge letter C that marked the town of Chloride. They sailed by Kingman, and then it was miles and miles of cactus.

"They look fake," Sabrina said. "They look just like the plastic ones, except they're all different sizes."

The temperature gauge said it was 104 Fahrenheit outside; the air conditioner was working overtime. Owen became acutely aware of the scent Sabrina was wearing, something incomparably fresh and clean that increased his desire to bury his face in her graceful neck.

"Those are the Hualapai Mountains," he said, just for something to say.

"So that's what the Hualapai Mountains look like."

"You're making fun of me, aren't you."

"Why, yes, Owen. I am."

He tried to find a music station that wasn't playing country, and finally gave up. Sabrina pulled out an iPod with an FM attachment, so for the next stretch they listened to Dido.

"I like her," Sabrina said. "She's a bitch, but vulnerable—like me, I guess."

"Don't say that." Owen pulled out to pass a spavined Buick that was belching black smoke. "You may be vulnerable, but—"

"Tell me something, Owen." She turned her whole body round to face him. "What's a grown boy like you doing travelling around the desert for the summer with his uncle?"

Owen smiled and pulled back into the slow lane. "Pretty weird, huh?"

"Tell me, though. Isn't he too old to be your uncle?"

"He's my great-uncle. But really he's more like my stepdad."

"What happened to your parents?"

"It's kind of like what you went through, only I was younger. I was ten." Owen told her the story of the car crash, and his brush with foster care.

"God," Sabrina said. "I don't think I would have recovered from something like that."

"It turned out Max was the only relative I had. When he heard about my situation, he applied for guardianship and I've been with him ever since."

"Pretty eccentric guy."

"Oh, you don't know the half of it."

"Well, if he loves my dad, he's got to be a crook. Made you part of the life, right?"

Owen looked at her, her green eyes bright, daring him to admit it. "I don't know what you're talking about."

"Yes, you do. You're forgetting how I grew up." She touched his knee, warm palm through denim, quickly gone. "It's okay. You don't have to pretend around me. You do these, uh, road trips every year?"

"This is the last one. I mean, I like to see the country and all—it's been a real education—but I'd like to spend at least one summer just hanging out."

"Listen, don't you have a girlfriend back in New York? She must hate it when you take off like this."

"No girlfriend. Not at the moment. What about you? You said Bill was not a boyfriend."

"Nope. Haven't had one of those in years, and I don't want one. Boys are just too . . . too everything. Personally, I find females a lot easier to take. Which is why I'm a total lesbian."

"Get outta here," Owen said. "You are not."

"How the hell would you know?" A sudden deep furrow between her eyebrows hinted at an as yet unexpressed temper.

"Because there's nothing about you that says lesbian. Everything about you says guys, guys, guys."

"Oh, really. Here you are driving across country in a trailer with an old man who's not your father, you want to be onstage, and you've got no girlfriend. Do you ever have just the tiniest suspicion that you might be gay?"

"No, actually, I don't."

"Uh-huh. And tell me how exactly it is you know you're not gay?"

"Very simple." Owen sat up straight and looked out at the highway. He cleared his throat, thinking how best to put this. Finally he said, "I know I'm not gay, Sabrina, and I'll tell you exactly why: if you were to disappear right now, this instant—if I was to never see you again for the rest of my life, never hear from you, never again have any contact with you whatsoever— no matter how many girls—women—I might meet and be friends with over the years, no matter how pretty they might be, how smart or how sexy, I will never, ever forget how you look in that red tank top right now."

Sabrina looked down and shook her head slowly from side to side, but Owen could see the dimple of a smile in her cheek.

"I'm not exaggerating, Sabrina. You and your red tank top are in my head for all eternity."

"And that's how you know you're not gay."

"That's how I know I'm not gay."

"Well," Sabrina said, "despite how I may or may not look to you, I personally find women a whole lot more attractive than men. Men are such lunks, so completely insensitive. All they want to do is drink beer and watch sports. And let me tell you, despite what the movies might have you believe, they are perfectly terrible in bed."

"And how'd old Preacher Bill take the lesbian news? Bible-thumpers aren't usually too forgiving when it comes to loving your gay neighbour."

"I never discussed my sexual preferences with Bill."

"Good choice. Not worth getting stoned to death."

"The reason I didn't tell him was because he was so obsessed with me, and obsession just gets worse the more obstacles you put in the way—or didn't you ever notice that?"

"I have to tell you the honest truth," he said.

"What's the honest truth, Owen?"

"I've always had a real soft spot for lesbians."

"Yes, sir," Sabrina said. "I bet you have."

Bill Bullard stood in the dining room of his compact little bungalow and read the note for the fourteenth time.

> Dear Bill,
>
> I'm sorry to leave you like this, especially with such a nasty bump on your head, but it's time for me to go. You've been kind, but you're just too nuts about me, too nuts in general, and too fond of hitting people.
>
> Please don't try to find me. Let's just remember the good times, okay?
>
> I wish you nothing but the best,
> Sabrina

Bill set the note down on the dining room table. He was a security man, for Pete's sake, he carried a gun, he was good at hitting people, he used to be a cop. In short, he wasn't supposed to cry. But he wanted to, he wanted to bawl like a baby. He rubbed a hand over his scalp and felt the gauze taped around his skull. In the mirror he didn't look as bad as he felt. The bandage sat at an almost jaunty angle, and it made his eyes look bigger and more sensitive. Noble even. The total effect was kind of war veteran, though he had never been in the armed forces.

Feeling dizzy, he went over to his blue leather couch and lay down, the TV remote digging into his back until he pulled it out and tossed it onto a matching blue leather armchair. His head throbbed and a wave of nausea travelled up to his throat; the room, blue and white as a china plate, spun around him until the white bits stretched and thinned into cirrus. Lying on his back provided no comfort. He turned, ever so slowly, onto his side and curled up with his hands pressed between his knees like a child.

That reminded him to pray. He hoped that Jesus would forgive his not getting onto his knees in his current state. He wanted to avoid the likely blasphemy of vomiting in mid-prayer.

"Oh, Jesus, who suffered for my sins and the sins of mankind and who bought with your blood our everlasting redemption and salvation, I beg you, please bring Sabrina back unto me. Please bring her back, and I will do anything, anything at all, you may see fit to demand of your lowliest, most miserable servant."

Servant.

He was so tired of being a servant. Fifteen years a cop, five of those a detective with the LVPD, and he was still a servant. He'd been working for Baxter Secure Solutions for four years now, making hardly more than half what he had earned as a detective. Between alimony and child support for kids he got to see twice a year, his financial future filled him with dread.

His plan had been to stay a cop for twenty years, then take his pension and open a private business—possibly as a PI, possibly in security—and hire a bunch of guys to do the actual dirty work. But the chief and the mayor had apparently had different plans for him. They didn't like his methods, even though his methods got results—great results, in fact.

There is an essential truth about working Robbery: you can't be a nice guy. Nice guyism is a definite no-no. You work Robbery, you're trucking with scum from daybreak to nightfall. Yes, there are victims to deal with, and yes, they are upset, but once you've extracted descriptions of the stolen items and ruled out insurance fraud, an investigator doesn't have a lot to do with the victims. In Homicide you have to hold hands, you have to walk on eggs, you have to be half social worker. Not in Robbery.

Bill Bullard modelled his detective work after the foreign policy of the presidents he loved, Reagan, Bush I and the much-misunderstood, much-maligned George Bush II. You are merciless with your enemies, generous to your allies, and if you have to befriend a bad guy to get a worse guy, you do it. And so he had developed a stable of very dependable, very helpful hard cases as his CIs. You didn't want to have dinner with them, you didn't necessarily want them in your home, but you did want them on your side when it came to catching bigger fish. That entailed ignoring a lot of crimes not directly relevant to your investigation. You don't nail the guy for what you have on him— you get him to give you information on other, badder asses, guys on whom you had nothing, nada, zip.

Thus it was that Bill had cultivated certain relationships that in the cold light of civilian life looked pretty questionable. In the course of trying to bring down Sammy Gibbons—an evil bastard who had been running a team of kids who robbed patrons of ATMs—he had relied on one Artie Doyle, known as Conan, who had a history of rape, robbery and aggravated assault. When it came out in court that he had let Conan get away with numerous frightening activities in order to bring down Gibbons, not only did the case against Gibbons go up in smoke, but Bill lost his job.

Five years later he still couldn't believe it. Conan was not that bad an actor, not compared to Gibbons, but this is the justice system we are stuck with—a system that sees fit to dispense with the services of its finest investigators.

Oh, the blackness of the pit into which he tumbled after that! Looking back, it was amazing to Bill that he survived it. Then his wife had left him—for weeks he had stayed in his house with the shades pulled, hardly getting out of bed, barely able to eat. No one came knocking on his door to see if he was all right, and several guys from work wouldn't even return his calls.

If daytime television had been any better, he might still be lying in bed to this day, but finally Oprah and Dr. Phil just drove him out of the house. He began to look for things to do, physical things, like painting his porch and repairing the picket fence that ran around the perimeter of his property.

But the fence was hardly worth painting, the way it kept tilting closer and closer to the ground. The gate was totally unusable and had to remain open at all times as an additional prop. So he set about repairing the thing—a big mistake, since he'd never worked on a fence before and was unprepared for certain difficulties. Just removing the old fence posts proved a formidable task, involving the digging of holes even bigger than the concrete base of the posts. Then you had to haul them out of there.

The result was he had to dig all new postholes, and that proved all but impossible, the desert soil was so rocky. One day he was toiling away at this in ninety-degree heat, blinded by sweat and rage, when a cheerful voice said from behind, "Looks like you've got kind of a tough job there."

Bill rubbed the sweat from his eyes and looked at the bleary image before him: a diminutive man in a short-sleeved shirt and necktie wearing the kind of glasses that had gone out of style sometime in the sixties.

"Ronnie Deist," he said, pointing to the east. "I live half a block up."

Bill introduced himself, leaning on his posthole digger.

"I could help you with that. I used to be a contractor and I still have the tools."

"Oh, yeah? And how much would that cost?"

"Nothing," Deist said. "I'm a neighbour. I'd be happy to help."

"Well, if you know how to dig a posthole and set a fence, I could sure use you."

First Deist told him where to rent a gas-powered posthole digger. Bill hadn't even realized such things existed. When he got back from the rental place, Deist had returned dressed in serious contractor's clothes and with a pickup full of tools. They spent the rest of that morning pulling out the old posts using the truck, and then Deist produced a picnic hamper packed with sandwiches and lemonade.

"Man, you come prepared, don't you?" Bill said.

"Oh, that's my wife. She's one of those people who always makes sure other people eat. I'd probably forget lunch myself, or grab a McDonald's or something. I'm not as smart as she is."

Bill found he simultaneously really liked Deist and didn't trust him. He was the most cheerfully self-denigrating person he had ever met. Also the most relentlessly happy. Deist whistled, he told dumb jokes, he commented on anything that passed by, always in a positive way. As they sat in the shade eating turkey sandwiches, he praised Bill's choice of house and location, admired Bill's strength in how he handled the posts. You couldn't get him to say a bad word about anybody—the Congress, the mayor, you name it, he had a kind word for them all.

The mayor had just been convicted of influence peddling, and all Deist said was, "I've done things I've been ashamed of. I'm sure the mayor has done lots of good things, and he'll find ways to do more."

By the end of the afternoon the fence was fixed.

"Are you sure I can't pay you something?" Bill said. "I've taken your whole day, and I now have a good-looking fence, thanks to you."

"You don't owe me a thing," Deist said. He mopped at his brow delicately, and wiped sweat from his glasses. "I enjoyed working with you."

"But why'd you do it?"

Deist shrugged. "It was quite selfish, actually. I knew it would be good for *me*."

"I gotta say, you strike me as about the happiest guy I ever met, short of a retard or two."

"I'll try to take that as a compliment."

"How do you do it? Are you on tranks or something?"

"No, no. It's Jesus who makes me happy. Some years ago I put my life in the care of the Lord, and nothing but good has flowed to me from that decision."

"You're kidding. You're born again?"

"I don't use that expression myself—it has political overtones I'd rather not be associated with. But I am a Christian, yes. I believe that Jesus Christ was God made man, and I should model my life in all ways possible after him."

"I don't recall any fence-fixing in the Bible."

"Jesus was kind. I try to be kind. But I didn't come here to convert you, I just couldn't stand to see a man wrestle with a fence post all alone on such a hot day." Deist grinned. He had a sizable gap between his front teeth. "And now I better skedaddle or my wife will have my hide."

Bill wiped his hand on his pants and put it out to shake. "Ronnie, I can't thank you enough."

"You're welcome. I enjoyed it."

"You're weird, you know that, right?"

Deist smiled, flashing that gap again. "My wife says the same thing." He climbed into his truck and backed out onto the street.

"Hey, Ronnie," Bill called out. "Which church you go to?"

And that was how he'd turned his life around. He attended the local Baptist church that weekend, had himself dunked a couple of weeks later, and he had never wavered in his faith since. It didn't take him long to realize that most born-again Christians were not as cheerful as Ronnie Deist. But they were solid people, they had a fallback position, they had a bedrock belief in God's wisdom that could not be shaken, and once Bill introduced that belief into his own life, that life began to improve.

He got the job with Baxter Secure Solutions, he started taking night courses in computer security and forensics, and the Bible became his constant solace. Now that he knew there was a purpose to every little bit of suffering he had to go through, it became easier to endure. Being fired, being alone, well, God wanted him that way, obviously. Being fired was what had led him to God in the first place, and being alone was what left room in his heart for God to take up residence there.

And then He had brought him Sabrina. All right, it was not a conventional romance. A wedding date had never looked in the least likely. And physical comforts? Well, God didn't want you to be plucking that particular fruit unless you were married, so clearly right now he wanted Bill Bullard celibate for reasons that might or might not become clear in time.

But poor Sabrina. That girl was so lost. She'd had such disadvantages. Raised by a criminal, for one—hard to imagine a bigger handicap than that. How could you develop a moral code when your old man was a professional thief?

They had met at work. Bill was covering the day shift at the Flamingo, and he'd caught her coming out of a twelfth-floor corner suite in a maid's outfit. It was only a matter of luck, really. He'd been up on the floor because a female guest was complaining that one of her many suitcases had been stolen. It had taken Bill all of about five minutes to determine the real story. She had complained the previous day about elevator noise in her tenth-floor room, so they'd moved her. Somehow they missed a suitcase that had been tucked in the back of her closet, and it had remained behind in the other room.

As Bill was coming out of her room, he saw this very attractive maid emerging from the suite at the end of the hall. Bill happened to know that the twelfth floor had already been cleaned, so he went to ask her a thing or two.

"Sorry," she'd said. "I'm new here."

He'd then asked for her hotel ID, which was clipped to her belt. It turned out to belong to someone else entirely. The only thing she had in common with the photo was dark hair. He cuffed her right there in the hall while he looked through her maid's cart.

"Well, if that don't beat all," he'd said, pulling two purses out of the cart. "You always wheel cash and valuables around in a cleaning trolley?"

"I have no idea how that stuff got in there," she said.

He took her down in the freight elevator to the security office, sending his junior to go work the lobby. The normal routine was to get a name and take a photograph, and then call the police to send a car. A security man was essentially just a witness. She had told him her name—phony as it turned out—and he had taken the picture. He had even had his hand on the phone, ready to dial.

Then she said, "Please don't call the cops." Normally, of course, he would have ignored such a request. He had arrested more than a few women in his time on the force, most of whom broke down in tears right away, and he had always found it easy to ignore. Some had hinted at the possibility of sexual favours in exchange for freedom, and he'd ignored that too. He booked them all. But that was before Jesus had come into his life.

Sabrina hadn't burst into tears. She had just explained, pretty accurately, how things would go if she was arraigned on a break-and-enter charge: the bail, the trial, the last-minute guilty plea and—since this was a first offence—the suspended sentence. "I just don't see it doing me or the owners of that property any good, do you?"

"And where in creation did you get the idea that I'm here to do you good, young lady?"

"I don't know. Something in your face, I guess. Something tells me there's more to you than your job."

He knew, despite the evident sincerity in those green eyes, that this girl was fast-talking him, but somehow it didn't matter. Las Vegas was full of beautiful women, and sex was readily available; it wasn't that. Something about Sabrina got to him in a way that was new, and for the first time he sensed what Ronnie Deist called "the touch of the Lord's guiding hand." Bill Bullard was being called off the bench to help with the Lord's game plan.

"If I were to let you go, there would be certain conditions," he had said, amazed at himself even as the words left his lips.

"Such as?"

"Well, you'd have to come to church with me for one."

"Are you serious?"

"And not just once. You'd have to come once a week for a couple of months."

"That's possible. I'm not saying I'll do it yet. What else?"

"You'd have to let me help you."

"What, you're a priest now? A social worker?"

"No, I'm just a man who sees a person in trouble. You tell me you got no money and your landlord's kicking you out end of the month. You'd have to let me help you find a job and a place to stay."

"Okay, fine," she said. "But if you think I'm going to sleep with you, you can dial the cops right now."

So Bill set about trying to bring Jesus into Sabrina's life. He put his all into behaving the way Ronnie Deist would have— cheerful, helpful, relentlessly correct—a gentleman from morning till night, protective of the weaker vessel. And oh, what a vessel: that smile, those eyes, that obviously divinely crafted shape. Sabrina was so pretty she made his knees wobble. But here she was in Las Vegas, where she'd had some idea of becoming a croupier. Her daddy's rap sheet hadn't helped her there. Then she'd been working as a waitress at Bistro Monty, and the manager had harassed her so much she'd had to quit.

First thing Bill did was contact Luigi Monticello, the

eponymous owner of Luigi's. When he was still on the force, Bill had gotten a crooked health inspector off Luigi's back, and the old spaghetti slinger had never forgotten it. Sabrina aced her tryout shift, and was soon working a couple of nights a week. Score one for the Lord.

On the apartment front, he had not been so lucky. He had gone over the papers and the Internet ads relentlessly, but the studio apartments they looked at were either uninhabitable or too expensive for her ever to save any money. After three weeks he'd suggested she move in with him. Strictly platonic, he'd promised, and he'd meant it. Lord knows he'd meant it.

Sabrina kept her part of the bargain by going to church with him every Sunday. Although she was always polite about it, it was obviously not "taking." He'd ask what she thought about the sermon and she'd just smile and shake her head. "Not for me," she'd say. "Sorry, Bill. Not for me."

When she finally had to move out of her apartment, she did agree to come and stay with him. "But let's get this straight," she had said. "The minute you put a hand on me, or come into my room, or make the least sexual suggestion, I am out of there, is that understood?"

"I have no problem with that," Bill said. "You see, Sabrina, my faith has taught me to be grateful for all I have, and you'd just be doing me a favour in letting me share some of that happiness. No cost to you whatsoever. Except the church. The church deal stays the same."

When she first moved in, she'd stayed in her room all the time. He had to coax her out of there like a stray, talk her into watching a little TV or sitting in the living room over a beer.

Now and again he would indulge in some Bible talk, trying to open her up to the idea that God is not just for Sundays. When the moment seemed apt, he would call up a telling story from the Old or New Testament. Sometimes she listened, nodding thoughtfully. Often she laughed.

"You're such a wacko, Bill," she'd say. "You know that, don't you? You're a religious wacko."

"If by that you mean the life and death of Jesus Christ informs my day from morning to night, then yes, I hope I am a religious wacko."

"See, only a wacko would say something like that."

Bill remembered the spark in her eye when she'd said that, the rueful way she shook her head, black hair swinging, and it pricked his heart. It was the good things that hurt the most—her smile, her laugh. His life was a gutted hulk without them, even if Jesus was still around.

"The Lord must want something of me," Bill told himself, sitting up on the couch. "He's sending me this pain for a reason. He wants me to learn something. He's telling me it's not over. There's more in this particular lesson plan for Bill Bullard."

From a cluttered desk drawer he pulled out a portable hard drive, plugged it into his computer, and booted up. Bill did not pride himself on a great many things, Lord knew he had his limitations, but he did have a certain gift of foresight. Sabrina was not always gently amused by his efforts to protect—and, all right, correct—her, and this led to arguments and shouting and even a swat or two. And one night, after things had reached a particularly unpleasant pitch and he was certain that Sabrina was planning to catch the next flight out, he had attached a FireWire to her PowerBook and sucked out a copy of her entire hard drive.

He opened it now on his own computer and warmed up by taking a scroll through her music files, recognizing almost none of the so-called artists listed there. Neil Young, Leonard Cohen, that was about it. What the hell was Arcade Fire? Was that a band? A movie? Bjork? Wolf Parade? How could you listen to people with names like that?

Her photos were more interesting, although ultimately disappointing. A more than passing familiarity with online porn had given Bill the notion that young women liked nothing better than to photograph each other masturbating. Sabrina had apparently resisted the temptation. Even when they were blurred and obviously drunk, her friends remained completely clothed. There were lots of pictures of someone called Aunt Rachel—in fact, she had her own folder. And she occurred a lot in another file called Dallas 2007.

Sabrina's email was more revealing. Between its Sent file and its address book, it contained everything a man on a mission could want.

At Wickenburg, the highway became 60/89, and Max took the wheel. His nap had left him grumpy and uncommunicative, and the three of them travelled in silence. Owen blasted aliens on his laptop for a while, and read some material he had downloaded about Tucson, but he had trouble concentrating—not because of Sabrina this time. He kept seeing Pookie in his mind's eye, bald head and goofy smile. Why would anyone want to hurt Pookie?

It was late when they arrived in Tucson, and they had trouble finding the trailer park. As soon as they were parked, they couldn't wait to escape the Rocket, so they unhitched the car and went into town.

"Ugh," Max kept saying as they passed miles of concrete buildings on eight-lane streets.

They had a late dinner at a Mexican joint called the Poca Cosa, but even a couple of margaritas failed to cheer Max up. He asked Sabrina what her plans were for the next day.

"I guess I'm not sure," she said.

"You can still stay with us if you don't have anywhere to go," Owen said. "I mean, if you want to come along to El Paso and see your dad . . ."

Sabrina smiled, shook her head. "That's okay. You two have been great, but I can look after myself."

Now it was Owen's turn to be depressed.

When they got back to the trailer, Max went straight to bed. Owen made popcorn, and Sabrina sat beside him on the couch to watch an old Clint Eastwood western. She fell asleep about halfway through, and Owen—he didn't exactly stare—but he observed her out of the corner of his eye. She was out like a little kid.

She woke immediately when he switched off the TV.

"Why'd you turn it off?"

"You weren't watching, and I've seen it too often."

She stretched, revealing a good deal of midriff. "What's Max so upset about? It's not because of me, is it?"

"Max is just moody."

"But he seems different from yesterday. Did something happen in Vegas?"

"We had some bad news. Family news. I don't want to talk about it."

"I thought all your relatives were in England."

"I really can't talk about it."

"Okay."

She reached out and touched his cheek, which made him wince.

"You have a nasty bruise," she said.

"Yeah. Preacher Bill has a wicked jab."

Sabrina shifted on the couch and planted a kiss, feather-light, on his cheek. "You've been really good to me."

He turned his face slightly, and this time she kissed him on the mouth. She gave it just a second, then sat back.

"It's too bad you're not a girl," she said. "I'd probably rip your pants right off."

"How about if I put on one of your dresses? Would that help?"

"I don't own any dresses. And I don't ever want to see you in one, either. Even though you are pretty cute."

"Yeah?"

"Now he's digging for compliments. That's it, I'm going to crash."

Owen lay on the couch staring at the blank television while she got ready for bed. He tried not to listen for the sound of her clothes coming off.

Max woke up in a better mood and was *pom-poming* and *tiddle-tiddle-tiddling* under his breath as he fussed around the Rocket's galley. He sprinkled raisins into the oatmeal, whipping the porridge around the pot as if he were baking a cake. Owen always sat with his back to this, because it gave him a terrible urge to yank the pot from Max's hand and bonk him over the head with it. Sabrina sat sleepy-eyed over her coffee, not a morning person, apparently.

"We have some time to play tourist today," Max said. "I trust our navigator has made plans?"

"There's a couple of options I'm considering."

He was looking at Sabrina across the table. Even with her eyes all puffy and her hair messed up, she looked great. *Especially* with her eyes all puffy and her hair messed up. Owen began to understand an advantage of marriage: getting to know a person backstage, so to speak.

Max set bowls of oatmeal before them. "Where are we going, then, my prince?"

"I have the perfect spot for our criminal history theme."

Owen drove them all to Tombstone, where they walked the wooden sidewalks among locals dressed up in period costumes. They saw a horse-drawn hearse once owned by Wyatt Earp, and in the window of the *Tombstone Epitaph* a real-estate ad informed them that "the mild year-round climate and low humidity make Tombstone an attractive place for retirement."

"Hey, Max. Maybe you could retire here."

"Please do not mention that word to me again. I have no wish to be buried in Boot Hill."

They watched an animatronic re-enactment of the shootout at the O.K. Corral, jerky robots playing Wyatt Earp and Doc Holliday.

"Appalling wigs," Max said. "I don't see why you go to the trouble and expense of building a robot and then ruin it by making the wig out of horsehair."

Afterwards they sat in the shade at an outdoor café and had sandwiches and lemonade. Beyond the storefronts, the Dragoon and Whetstone mountains loomed. A quiet descended on the three of them, and Owen knew that Max was worrying about Pookie and what it might mean for the rest of the trip.

When they got back to Tucson, Sabrina insisted on moving to a hotel. "Don't worry," she said, seeing their reaction, "I've managed to save a little bit, thanks to Bill, so I'll be okay." She went over to Max and thanked him for everything.

Max rose to his feet with much huffing and exclamation to receive a hug. "Sweet Lady," he said, "I hope we shall meet again. When I visit your sainted father in Texas, I hope to hear from him that you have fulfilled your filial duty."

"I'll think about it," Sabrina said, but her smile was faint.

Owen drove her to the Delta. He wrote out his cellphone number and handed it to her as the doorman took her suitcase.

"Um, listen," he said. "I don't know how you feel, but I'd really like to see you again."

"You mean in New York?" Sabrina looked up at the tower of the hotel as if consulting it. "Owen, I've pretty much decided to leave crime and criminals in the past."

"I told you," Owen said, "this is our last road trip. Max is going to retire, and I'm going to be at school full-time."

"Let me think about it, okay?"

"You have my number. Just think 'yes,' okay? Yes is good."

TWELVE

"WHAT STATE OR NATION is divided by the Great Dividing Range?" Roscoe held his beer up to the light, inspecting it like a chemist.

"Existence," Max said. "It divides the living and the dead."

Roscoe shook his head. They were sitting at a table in the Red Rose Tavern, the kind of bar that looks friendly at night but in the daytime looks tawdry and forlorn. It reeked of last night's cigarettes, the fashion for clean lungs having yet to reach Tucson. The only other patrons seemed to be the two blobs sitting at the bar, one in a stetson, the other in a John Deere cap.

"The United States," Owen said. "We'll be crossing the Great Divide in a couple of days."

Roscoe shook his head again. "Australia," he told them, "is home to the Great Dividing Range."

"Well, now that we've passed Geography," Max said, "perhaps we can get down to work."

"We're not waiting for Pookie?"

"Pookie won't be joining us on this outing," Max said.

Roscoe looked from Max to Owen, and back to Max.

"You may not want to join us either," Owen said.

Max gave him a sour look.

"You have to tell him," Owen said.

"Pookie seems to have gone astray," Max said. "We've not been able to raise him, and he's made no effort to contact us."

"That's alarming," Roscoe said. "That's not like Pookie. You think he's . . ."

"Crossed the Great Dividing Range? I've no idea."

"You think maybe he got pinched?" Roscoe said.

"That's another possibility," Max said.

"It's okay if you don't want to come with us tonight," Owen said. "It might be a little riskier than we thought."

Roscoe stared out the window at the parking lot. "You pay me half if I bail now?"

"Expenses. Not half."

"It's not my fault Pookie's . . . whatever."

"How do we know it's not your fault?"

"You're not calling me a rat, I hope."

"Roscoe, I have called you many things over the years—base Hungarian, cutpurse, and once I believe a rhesus macaque—never a rat. But perhaps inadvertently you mentioned our adventures to someone less discreet than yourself—possibly you were overheard."

"I'm not an idiot, Max."

"Well, I don't know what happened to Pookie. But I do know I'm not paying you for a job you don't do. As I say, expenses for getting here, and even your overnight, but the whole fee? Only if you play your part in the show. Look, help us pull this one off and we're off to bigger and better things in Dallas. Maybe we could cut you in for a one-time percentage on that one."

Roscoe raised an eyebrow. "What kind of percentage?"

"Five. Am I not the world's most reasonable man? Mind, this is strictly a one-time offer. And you have to do this show as well."

"I'm in." Roscoe shrugged. "I need the dough."

Bradford Blake had made so much money in hedge funds that even a self-confessed glutton like himself really couldn't use any more. Once you've got the fourth house, the racehorses, the sports team, what can you do? Buy a fifth house? Consequently, he now put his money into political causes, that is to say, the campaign funds of extreme right-wing Republicans. Name it—gun lobby, missile shield—if it upset liberals, Bradford Blake was all for it. Lately he had developed a taste for owning newspapers.

He was aided in this by his pretty wife, Cassandra, a conservative columnist ten years his junior, who had recently become a favourite on the talking-head circuit. She was a piquant presence, not afraid to heap scorn upon the poor and praise upon the lucky. Most liberals were reluctant to appear on camera with her. Somehow those sparkling blue eyes, those erotically swollen lips, rendered greed sexy and concepts such as world peace synonymous with erectile dysfunction.

Owen had gleaned most of this from an unflattering biography. The author had revelled in the details of the couple's extravagant parties, their sailing adventures, and most of all Cassandra Blake's insatiable lust for jewels.

The party tonight was to be a relatively subdued affair of eight people, nothing like the San Francisco show. There would be no point trying to sneak in as caterers. This time, speed would be the crucial factor. The plan had originally been for Max, Pookie and Roscoe to work with the guests in the dining room once everyone was seated. Owen would be upstairs emptying everything of value from Cassandra Blake's jewellery box into a pillowcase. With Pookie out, it was more risky but still doable.

Owen and Max waited for Roscoe in the parking lot of the shopping mall where they were supposed to meet, but Roscoe didn't show. Five minutes after the appointed hour, Max said, "Our valiant friend must have had second thoughts."

"The odds *are* different now that Pookie's missing."

"Pookie didn't know what our next show was going to be, so despite his having vanished in a puff of smoke, the odds remain exactly what they were: favourable. How many people know when Bradford and Cassandra Blake got married? Or that they always celebrate their anniversary in Tucson, where they met and where they still keep a house? We do a lot of research, young man, which is why we always come out on top."

"How do we know it wasn't the Subtractors who grabbed Pookie, and now they have Roscoe too? And Roscoe *does* know the plan for tonight."

"How could the so-called Subtractors—who don't exist in the first place—have got on to Roscoe?"

"Maybe he and Pookie had already decided on a hotel. If they got Pookie, Pookie could have told them where they were planning to stay."

"Rubbish," Max said, and started the car. "Absolute twaddle."

The Blake house was in the exclusive Foothills area, with the Santa Catalina Mountains rising up behind it. Unlike their Connecticut colonial, or their London townhouse, or their Fifth Avenue penthouse, the Blakes' Tucson abode was a long, low bungalow, mostly glass, with a central living area and two wings branching off to the east, giving it an unexpected, asymmetrical look.

Max himself was looking a little asymmetrical, as this time he had opted for an utterly hairless pate that reflected the street lights as they drove. He finished it off with a straight nose that made him look rather like a window mannequin. Owen was wearing a dark wig, medium long, and an artful goatee, almost perfectly square. With the darkened eyebrows he looked roguish, an up-and-coming film director you might see on the cover of *Details* magazine. *Hollywood's whiz kid talks about his life, his loves, and his meteoric rise from Juilliard to Hollywood's A-list . . .*

Max stopped the car just before the Blakes' driveway. He switched off the radio and the air conditioner and they were plunged into a deep hush. No houses were visible, not even the Blakes'. The evening light crept across the hills in a thousand shades of gold and red.

"Any questions before we make our entrance?" Max said.

"This is scary, Max. We need at least two guys in the room where they're eating, and we don't even have Roscoe. It's too easy for someone to make a break for it—and then we're in big trouble."

"We have the cellphone jammer, do we not?"

"It's not enough, Max."

"Here's what we do: you enter the far end of the house—couldn't be easier with this Swedish modern monstrosity—you liberate the goodies and come back out."

"Good. We skip the dining room altogether."

"We do no such thing."

"Max, we almost always get more from the bedrooms than from the guests."

"But Cassandra Blake is a jewellery horse. Her friends will try to outdo her."

"How do we cover kitchen staff and the dining room at the same time?"

"After you come out, we go in through the kitchen and bring them into the dining room with us."

"Max, last week this was a four-man job. This morning it was a three-man job. We're making a mistake here."

"Cowards die many times before their death, my son."

"It's not cowardice, it's common sense. You're not thinking clearly."

"Improv, boy. Improv. You're an elderly little sod, in your way. I am supple-brained and creative, while you, my infant, are becoming more hidebound by the minute."

"Max, I really don't like this."

"Fine. I'll do it myself. You wait here. Back in a trice." Max grabbed the door handle.

"You'll get yourself killed." Owen reached out and caught his arm. "And I can't stand the thought of you dying in that bald head."

———

Max cut the phone wire, a largely theoretical manoeuvre since the real threat would be from cellphones and the jammer would take care of those. He was careful not to cut the burglar alarm wire, which would have set the thing off. In any case, with the house full of guests, it was certain to be switched off.

Architectural Digest had told them which room was which. They used glazier's tools to remove a windowpane from the master bedroom, and Owen climbed in. Max stood guard in a clump of trees nearby, bald head gleaming in the moonlight.

Once inside, Owen went straight to the door and checked the corridor, which was so long it seemed to taper to a dot. There wasn't a sound from the dinner party; it was too far away and the house was too well built.

Chokers, necklaces, earrings and bracelets were strewn in magnificent disarray across a mahogany dresser. Owen checked his disguise in the mirror, dark wig and goatee nicely in place, which was good, given the tiny security camera above the door.

With a sweep of his arm he cleared the top of the dresser of three necklaces and several bracelets, all glittering with diamonds. Then he upended a jewellery box into his sack. In a top drawer, a row of TAGs and Breitlings and Rolexes sparkled on a roll of blue velvet. Into the sack with the rest.

He was out the window in less than five minutes. The sack went into the trunk of the car, then it was round to the back door and into the kitchen. It was important not to hesitate here. The Asian couple in the kitchen silently raised their hands at the sight of Max's revolver.

"Don't be alarmed." Max put a finger to his lips. "We have reason to believe there are burglars in this house. Into the dining room, please."

The couple went in through the swinging door, closely followed by Max and Owen. The guests had not yet sat down to dinner, so they had to continue through the dining room into the living room. Upon stepping onto this new stage, Max became instantly Australian.

"Good evening everybody, my name is Bruce Whittaker of the Australian National Wealth Reallocation Service. Now, pay attention." He pronounced it *attintion*. "The gun is loaded, and for your own safety I must ask you to deposit all valuables in my assistant's bag: rings, watches, jewellery of all sorts. Heroics of any kind will have repercussions of the most catastrophic order." *Ketastrophic*.

"Who the hell do you think you are," Bradford Blake said, rising from a leather chair. "You get the hell out of here."

"Sit, mate, sit." Max brandished his pistol, a new one Owen had never seen. "We don't want this little thing to go off. Now behave yourself and there'll be no worries."

"What do you want?" It was Cassandra Blake who spoke. She was seated on an elegant suede couch between two guests.

"The good life, my dear—comfortable shoes, a fine single malt and a hot tub—same as everyone." Then, to the group: "Cellphones into the sack, if you please."

They were robbing one of the most beautiful rooms Owen had ever been in. There was a fire roaring in a shoulder-high fireplace and a huge painting of a picnic scene that looked like something you'd see in a museum. He went from each person to the next, sack extended like a trick-or-treater's, acutely aware of how undignified a pursuit robbery is.

Aside from the two cooks and a maid in uniform, Owen counted seven people around the room. He was pretty sure he had seen eight place settings on the dining table.

"Aren't you a little old to be doing this?" Cassandra Blake said to Max.

"*Siventy*," he pointed out, "is the new fifty. Though I gotta say, doll-o, that necklace looks so fetching on you I've half a mind to leave without it."

"If you had any conscience, you would. My husband gave me this."

"Into the bag, if you please. Enjoyed your piece on gayism, Mrs. Blake. Canny coinage, 'gayism.' I imagine Mrs. Wood found it amusing too."

He nodded toward Victoria Wood, a fortyish blonde seated on the couch beside her film producer husband. More than one gossip column had hinted that Cassandra Blake and she had enjoyed a torrid lesbian affair the previous summer while their husbands were embarked on a hairy-chested sailing venture in the Pacific, far beyond the reach of tabloids.

"I don't understand," Bradford Blake said. "Why would Victoria find it amusing?"

"That looks an exy timepiece, sir," Max said. "Into the bag, if you please."

The maid stepped forward with a thin silver and jade bracelet.

"Not necessary, my dear," Max said.

"Why not?" she said. "I am with them."

"But not *of* them. Now, if you'll just be seated . . ."

Owen had collected five cellphones, half a dozen watches and bracelets, and the pearl necklace. He held up the sack.

"All righty, then, time for us to say cheerio. Please remain seated until the robbery has come to a complete and final stop. Do not attempt to call the police and do not attempt to follow— or you'll be hearing from my associate." He gestured with the gun. "Thank you for your co-operation."

They were halfway to the front door when a man sprang from a closet and tackled Owen, bringing him down on the hardwood floor.

"Son of a bitch," he was yelling. "You filthy son of a bitch."

His breath smelled of Scotch. He yanked the bag out of Owen's hand, and Owen reached for his pistol. One loud bang was usually enough to settle people down.

Before he could fire, there was a loud *crack-crack*.

Then the air was full of screams. The man staggered and fell backward into an armchair. Just above his belt, two dark stains were spreading across his shirt.

Owen stood frozen between the bleeding man and the door to escape.

"Move," Max said. "We haven't got all night."

Owen grabbed the sack and blundered out the door, Max following.

They ran to the car, Max wedging himself behind the wheel and starting it. Through long training he resisted the urge to floor it, and they cruised out of the tranquil neighbourhood in a slow agony.

Owen switched off the jammer and fumbled in the sack for one of the cellphones. He dialed 911 and asked for an ambulance to be sent to the Blakes' address.

"I need your name, sir."

"No, you don't." Owen dropped the phone back into the sack. "You shot the guy, Max. I don't believe it, you actually shot the guy."

"I don't know how it happened!"

"You loaded real bullets is how it happened. We never use real bullets. Or so you've always said. Are you going to tell me that all this time you've been using real bullets?"

"Of course not! I always use blanks! It was a new gun. Spider Weems was hard up for cash. Sold it to me for a hundred."

"Fully loaded."

"Yes, I must have forgot that bit."

"Max, that was a stop sign!"

Max swerved to avoid a smart car, which had a surprisingly loud horn, and headed for the expressway.

"You've probably turned us into murderers. We're both going to end up in the goddamn electric chair, and some poor innocent guy is going to end up dead. Jesus, Max, what if he has kids?"

"For God's sake, it was an accident!"

"Yeah, great. Remind me to try that one on the judge."

———

They left the car in the parking lot and entered the mall separately as a bald man and a goateed youth, emerging fifteen minutes later as innocent tourists. They left the stolen car in the lot and drove the Taurus back through town toward the trailer camp, Owen at the wheel.

"Bright side," Max said, "that shot probably saved us from a lengthy semester at Oxford."

"What about the guy's life, Max?"

"I value yours more. This is our fifth adventure together. I don't see why it should be a surprise that sometimes things can go wrong."

"Max, you didn't used to shoot people. We have to abort the rest of the trip and head home. And you have to retire for good."

"Never, lad. Banish Max and banish all the world."

"This is no time for Shakespeare! This is real life! Those were real bullets! We've caused real pain!"

"You've missed the turn."

Owen made a U-turn at the next intersection. They parked in the shadow of the Rocket and went inside.

"What did you think of the accent?" *Ek-cent.* "Bruce Whittaker, strite outta Queensland, at yer service."

Max embarked on a recitation of Portia's speech on mercy, translated into Australian. In other circumstances it might have been funny, but now it was unbearable. Owen turned on the kitchen light and peered into the sack. He was trying mightily to behave as if this had been a normal show, no disasters.

"We should sort out the cellphones first. We can dump them in a mailbox tomorrow. Look at this necklace I found upstairs. It was right in front of the mirror. She must have been trying it on just before the guests arrived."

"Let's just stash it for now, laddie."

Owen loosened a couple of screws and pulled back the dishwasher, and Max handed him the sack. He was tucking it into their hidden hutch when Max said, "Good God. What the hell are you doing here?"

Owen whipped around to see who he was talking to.

Sabrina was lying on the bottom bunk, just now raising herself on one elbow.

THIRTEEN

"You're back," she said, her voice fogged with sleep.

"The girl's gone deaf," Max said, moving closer to the bunk. "I asked what you were doing here."

"Bill turned up at the hotel. He was waiting in the lobby. Luckily, I saw him before he saw me."

"How did he know you were in Tucson," Owen said, "let alone which hotel?"

"Well, he does work in hotel security."

"She called him," Max said. "Didn't you? You called him and told him where you were."

"I didn't. I swear."

"If you didn't call him," Max said, "the only way he could find you would be to follow us—which he could not possibly do, because when we drove out of Las Vegas he was still in the hospital."

"All right, I did call him. I mean, I dialed him—he wasn't there. I just left a message saying I hoped he wasn't hurt too bad and that I was sorry for how things worked out. But I didn't speak to him or tell him where I was."

"If he has connections to the cops," Owen said, "or maybe the phone company, they can pinpoint the location of a cellphone to the nearest tower."

Max's brow furrowed into Shar-Pei–like folds. "I begin to suspect, young lady, that you haven't told us everything there is to know about Preacher Bill."

"I guess I should have mentioned . . ." Sabrina winced, and pinched the bridge of her nose. "I just—I didn't want to scare you away, that's all."

"What are you talking about?" Owen said. He was surreptitiously nudging the dishwasher back into place.

Max wheeled to face him. "Our damsel in distress here—our sweet, innocent, saintly young lady—failed to mention that her mentor, her *man,* also happens to be an officer of the law." Then, turning back to Sabrina: "Isn't that right?"

"You gotta be kidding," Owen said. "He's a cop?"

Sabrina nodded miserably. "Not *is* a cop. *Was* a cop. He quit years ago. I guess I should have told you."

"Why didn't you?" Owen said.

"Because the devil child knew that if we'd had the slightest idea she was consorting with a copper, we'd have nothing to do with her."

Owen sat down at the kitchen table. He looked at Max. "Still, I don't see how it's that big a deal. What difference does it make?"

Max went into lecture mode, hands on hips. "The difference, my son, is that he's connected to an organization that is very good at tracking people down. He has access to networks, faxes, radios. By now he's probably got her picture on every bloody cop computer in the country."

"You're right," Sabrina said. She grabbed her coat from the top bunk. "I'll go."

"How did you get in here, anyway?" Max said.

"Oh, come on, Max. My dad taught me a *few* things."

She brushed by Owen. He grabbed her arm. "Wait," he said. "You don't have to go anywhere."

"Yes, I do. Max just said I do."

"No, I didn't," Max said. "Though at this moment it is an extremely attractive thought."

"Max, even if somebody should recognize her, we're not going to get into any trouble. We're just on holiday and Sabrina's along for the ride."

"I don't like surprises," Max said. "This was not the way the Pontiff brought you up, I'm sure."

"Oh, please. My father is no bloody hero."

"John-Paul would never teach you to mislead friends who try to help you."

"Okay, Max. I'm sorry. I should have told you right away."

"Right," Owen said. "And what—we would have left her there in the parking lot with that Bible-thumping nutcase? Let him beat her half to death?"

"Never. I have a few faults, but cruelty to the fair sex is not among them. I would have done everything the same."

"So, fine. In other words we'd be exactly where we are at this moment."

"Not so. For one, I would have confiscated Her Highness's cellphone and mailed it to Ouagadougou before she could alert the entire bloody country as to her whereabouts. Hand it over, hell spawn."

She pulled out her cellphone, but instead of handing it over she began to dial.

"I'm calling a cab."

"You don't need a cab," Owen said. "You can stay with us. Max, you promised your friend you'd look out for her."

"I know. But that was before I realized she was being followed by an insane policeman."

"He's not insane," Sabrina said.

"Yes, he is," Max and Owen said together.

Bill Bullard entered the hotel room and switched on the light. Getting access had been no problem: Baxter Secure Solutions provided the security for half the hotels in the Southwest, and this one happened to be among them. If he wanted to park himself in their lobby keeping an eye on traffic for a few hours, hotel management had no problem with it.

Tracking down Sabrina's cellphone hadn't been too hard either. He had help from a friend at Nevada Nextel—well, not a friend, exactly. Bullard had once caught the guy with an under-age hooker, and had held it over him ever since.

The hardest part was getting time off work. Lance Baxter was not a congenial person, and about as far from a Christian as it was possible to be without being an outright Satanist. Bill could have just phoned in sick—he still had bandage on his head, even if it was now reduced to a small square of gauze—but sometimes he was too honest for his own good. He told Lance he needed time off for compassionate reasons, he had to help a friend who was in an emotional crisis. Really, he should have known better.

"Oh, God," Baxter had said.

Right off, this was a response guaranteed to upset Bill. "Lance, how many times have I begged you not to take the Lord's name in vain?"

Baxter couldn't have cared less about Bill's religious sensibilities. "This is about that girl," he said. "I knew it, the minute I saw you with her. She's too young for you, Bill. What the hell are you thinking?"

"I'm thinking of her welfare, Lance. I'll allow that sometimes I can be selfish, but this is different. My motives are entirely altruistic. Sabrina is a confused person in need of help."

"Helping a nubile young waitress?" Baxter said. "We all know what that means."

"No, you don't."

"You've got a daughter her age, for God's sake."

"There you go again."

"She's the same age as your daughter, Bill. Admit it."

"Peggy-Ann is eighteen. Sabrina is a young woman of twenty. Anyway, I don't see why you got to pitch a conniption about it. All you gotta do is switch a couple of shifts around."

Baxter spoke in a tone he had almost certainly picked up at a management training seminar. "Believe it or not, Bill, the rest of us at Baxter Secure Solutions get tired of covering for your spiritual retreats and your prayer breakfasts and your emotional crises." Baxter swept an arm at the bank of monitors on his office wall, as if all the cameras in his arsenal were sick of Bill's problems too. "Why should we always be making accommodations? I thought God was supposed to be looking after you."

"He is. He's looking after you and me and the whole wide world right now. Obviously that don't mean we up and quit our moral responsibilities."

Baxter shook his head. His cellphone rang and he picked it up, squinting at the tiny screen. He switched it off and put it back down. He no sooner did that than his land line, a bright red phone designed to imply security at a national level, also began to ring. He punched a button and it went silent.

"You've got a real jones for this girl and you can't even admit it. You're obsessed, Bill, I can see it a mile away."

"Think what you want," Bill said. "I know what's in my heart."

"Uh-huh."

Baxter took out his Mont Blanc and scribbled a note to himself. That was just like him, to make a note on a Post-it with a fountain pen.

"All right, Bill, but you owe me one. And I want you back Monday at the latest. You'll be doing graveyard."

"Lance, I'm fifty-five years old. Let the younger guys do graveyard."

"Are you so tight with the Lord you can't see when a mere human being is doing you a favour? Get the hell outta here."

Fifty-five and still taking orders; it was enough to make a grown man cry. Bill always tried to be humble, the way Jesus was, but Jesus was half divine and clearly had an advantage or two.

Now, Bill's first glance at the hotel room confirmed that Sabrina had not somehow snuck past him. Her jeans were strewn across the end of the bed, which was otherwise unrumpled. Her backpack was on the floor. Her suitcase was open on a fold-out stand, and it squeezed his heart to see how full it was.

Bye-bye, Bill, it said, I've lit out for good. She had taken almost all her clothes, not that she had a vast wardrobe. You'd think that someone so beautiful would have closets full of the latest fashions, but Sabrina owned almost nothing.

He knelt beside the bed and sniffed the jeans, burying his face in them and breathing deeply. "Don't go," he said. "I swear, I will buy you everything you need. I will be your provider and you will be my helpmeet."

The suitcase contained mostly T-shirts, though she hadn't packed the yellow one that said *Cancún*.

He found the dark skirt that he yelled at her for wearing because it showed too much of her legs. Those beautiful legs that sent waves of lust riding through his body. He didn't want other men lusting after her that way.

"I was yelling more in pain than in anger," he said to the hotel room now.

But he remembered how the expression on her face had changed. How the muscles in her cheeks had gone slack, her eyes dimming to a darkness that he recognized was fear. Fear, and something worse: contempt.

"Oh, Lord, why did you send me this beautiful creature, if not for me to take under my protection?"

She had used the shower. The bath mat was askew, and a towel was slung over the shower curtain rail. The air smelled of coconut shampoo. Girl things were set out neatly on the glass shelf above the sink: eyeliner, some kind of flesh-coloured stuff in a tube, lip balm. He opened the lip balm and touched it to his bottom lip, then the tip of his tongue. He picked up her hairbrush, put it back.

He went back to the other room and knelt again beside the bed, clasping his hands together until the knuckles whitened.

"Oh, Lord, help me bring Sabrina back, for she done truly lost her way. And woe betide those who led her astray, who made straight the way unto eternal fire."

He clutched a T-shirt in both hands and brought it to his face. A sob escaped his throat, but he checked the urge to weep. Mostly because he had a pretty good idea where Sabrina was headed next.

Max woke up. Cold metal was pressing against the base of his skull, as if he had fallen asleep with his head resting on a pipe.

He could see the lights from the trailer park, white orbs in the window, which was open. He could smell the faint smells of oil and gas from someone's badly tuned motor. A dog barked in the distance and, farther off, yobbos guffawed.

He reached behind his head and felt the pipe, palpated the little ridge at the end pressing up against his skull. The sight. He sat up, back pressed against the head of the bed.

Wyatt Earp was sitting on the bed beside him, knee-high boots resting on top of the covers. Doc Holliday was perched sideways at the foot, drinking from a silver flask. They were the animatronic creatures Max had seen the day before.

"New wigs," Max said. "Is that what you've come for?"

"We don't need no steenking wigs," Wyatt Earp said. His mouth moved in the most unsettling, jerky motion, out of sync with his words.

"You scared yet, fatso?" Doc Holliday sneered at him from the foot of the bed. "You should be."

"The wigs," Max said. "I'll just get up and fetch them for you."

Wyatt Earp put an arm around his shoulder. It felt just like you'd expect a robot's arm to feel, squeezing him so that he could not even squirm. The barrel of the gun pressed against his temple.

"You first," Doc Holliday said, making a pistol of his fingers. "Then the boy."

"Oh, no. Not the boy," Max pleaded. "Not the boy."

The bang went off in his ears like a cathedral bell. He felt the bullet crash into the bone behind his ear. He would only have a second or two to save Owen. It took all his strength to raise his right hand, bending at the elbow. He grabbed the barrel of the revolver. It was scorching hot, the metal searing his hand. He couldn't hold on. He pressed his pillow to the back of his skull to staunch the wound and passed out.

Sometime later, he peeled the pillow from his head and opened one eye. The pink fringe of morning glowed in the Rocket's window, and the room was gunslinger-free.

FOURTEEN

MAX WAS NOT A MAN TO CLING TO A MOOD, Sabrina had to give him that, and breakfast always seemed to make him positively sprightly. Her storied father had been a spiky bundle of negativity in the morning. Set your juice glass down too hard on the kitchen table and he'd reach across and give you a swipe on the ear. All you usually saw of him were his hands gripping the newspaper, which he snapped and rattled as if it were responsible for the outrages it reported. His moods made mornings a time of trepidation for Sabrina and her mother, and she realized now, sitting in the sunny nook of the Rocket, that they coloured her perception of breakfast to this day.

Max was humming and whistling in the galley, fixing coffee and poached eggs. He commented, cajoled and exclaimed over his cooking in several different accents. Just in the course of cracking eggs he went through Scottish, Irish, Indian and a Southern black bluesman accent that made Sabrina laugh in spite of herself.

"You're a one-man United Nations," she said. "Doesn't it get crowded in there?"

"Desperately, my dear, desperately," he said, setting a plate in front of her. "Eat 'em while they're hot."

"These are great," she said, sprinkling salt and pepper on two perfect eggs. "I never actually ate poached eggs before. It must be an English thing."

"One of the many amenities we gave to the world, along with Shakespeare, Sir Larry and the Beatles."

"Don't forget slavery," Owen put in.

"Slavery existed long before the British Empire, boy."

"Not in this country."

"Please. No politics at breakfast."

Owen switched on the television at low volume, flipping channels until he found a local news show, *Breakfast Television with Rick and Rona*. It was one of those set-ups where two manic hosts make jokes at each other between reading the news and interviewing people involved in unusual pursuits.

The male half of the show went solemn at the next item. "A dinner party ended in bloodshed last night as two armed men robbed and terrorized guests at the home of Bradford and Cassandra Blake. Tork Williams is live at the scene."

A shot of the Blake residence showed crime scene tape and forensic officers coming and going. The reporter breathlessly recounted how the two men had interrupted the dinner and robbed the guests of cash and jewellery that "could be" worth up to half a million dollars.

"Local businessman Reeve Chandler was shot as he tried to stop the men. He was taken to County General, where he's in critical condition with gunshot wounds to the chest and abdomen."

Sabrina didn't like morning television, but Owen seemed riveted. Even Max had gone still to look at the screen.

"A security camera got a shot of the two men as they made their getaway out the front door. One of them is an older man—described as an Australian with a shaved head. The other is late teens/early twenties with dark hair and long sideburns."

The screen showed low-definition, jerky shots of the two making for the door, looking back over their shoulders. Their panic was obvious, the bald man with the gun still in his hand stopping at the door to turn around and brandish it again at the people they had robbed.

Max sat down and shook pepper all over his eggs, then let fly with a mighty sneeze. "Navigator," he said to Owen, between blowing his nose and wiping his eyes, "what's our heading?"

———

They set out east on US 80, straight into the morning sun. Sabrina sat behind Max and Owen, listening to Feist on her iPod. Her T-shirt and jeans were feeling a little lived-in, but there had been no question of going back to the hotel to retrieve her luggage, not with Bill parked in the lobby.

They passed a sign announcing Bisbee.

"How now, good Bisbee, what news?" Max said. "Owen, instruct us in the lore of Bisbee. How came it hither and wherefore."

Owen pulled out a Blue Guide and flipped through it. "Used to be a big silver mining place," he said. "Copper, too. Home of the famous Queen Mine and the Lavender Open Pit. In July 1917, a thousand striking miners were rounded up and hauled out of the state and dumped in the New Mexico desert."

"Respect for the working man," Max said, "is what made this country great."

The Rocket creaked and rattled along at a stately pace, Max tapping out rhythms on the steering wheel to music only he could hear. Owen turned a couple of times to look back at Sabrina and give her a small smile. He was cute, she had to admit. His uncle was peculiar, but Owen seemed much more solid than most guys his age, despite an upbringing that had to have been at least as unconventional as her own.

They passed Douglas, and continued through the Pedrogosa Mountains. Not that they looked much different than all the other mountains in Arizona—scrubby, with rounded tops, more like big hills than what she thought of as mountains. The light turned purple in the long shadows they cast, and there was something unsettling about them.

"The Chiricahua Apaches used to hide out in those hills," Owen told them. "Outlaws, too."

"Outlaws like who?" Sabrina said.

She wanted to hear Owen talk more. She liked his voice, and

the way he was interested in different places and things. But he just shrugged and said, "Billy the Kid."

To pass the time, Sabrina tried to read some of *Much Ado About Nothing* in the Collected Shakespeare she found beside the TV. It didn't seem nearly as funny as the movie, and she put it aside. She flipped through a case of CDs: there were obscure comedy items, a French instruction CD, Celtic folk tunes, Leonard Cohen, a complete John le Carré audiobook, a lot of Celine Dion, as well as Green Day and Broken Social Scene. There was also a set of three CDs called *Bob Hedge's Dialect Practice Sessions.*

Here and there US 80 offered a few miles of ragged asphalt, some abandoned buildings and more tumbleweed than anyone needed to see. They listened to country music on the radio and didn't talk much. Sabrina had never been on any road trips that took longer than a day. It was strange how you settled back into a reflective state. The washed-out glare of the sun, the procession of hills and cactus, the odd herd of goats, took on a gauzy unreality, totally disconnected from the air-conditioned interior of the Rocket.

"We have reached the City of God," Max said during one of the better stretches. "Somehow I didn't expect to find it in New Mexico, U.S.A."

He was referring to Lordsburg, which he slowed to cruise through. The place looked flat and insubstantial. Everything about it said "mining town of the 1880s" or thereabouts. The sun hammered down on the empty streets. The only thing moving was a ratty-looking yellow dog that trotted along with a self-important gait as if late for a meeting.

"Looks like no one's left in Lordsburg," Owen said. "Including the Lord."

"I hope that dog's all right," Sabrina said.

"That dog *is* the Lord," Max said. "It's the tail gives him away."

There was a brief flurry of excitement when Max saw a sign for Shakespeare.

"The Swan of Stratford lives! And who would have suspected it would be in the desert?"

"Relax, Max. It's just a ghost town."

"All the better. Hamlet, Banquo, Pompei? Will adored ghosts! An obvious must-see."

Owen waved the guidebook at him. "It's got nothing to do with Shakespeare. It was a silver mining place that went out of business. It's privately owned, and it's only open for tours on Tuesdays and Thursdays."

But Max would not be dissuaded. So they drove along miles of dusty highway until they came to the gate that contained the same information Owen had already reported.

"Bugger," Max said.

Beyond the gate they could see the main street, the low store-fronts and what looked like an old hotel.

"Billy the Kid worked in that hotel," Owen said. "But he didn't enjoy washing dishes, so he turned to a life of crime."

"A common but tragic flaw," Max said. "Antipathy to manual labour."

Not long after that, they were back on the interstate. "Did you know," Max said, "that the town of Deming has twenty-seven gas stations, twenty-one restaurants and thirteen motels?"

Sabrina looked up. "How would you know a thing like that?"

"The State of New Mexico tells me so." He pointed at a sign that contained exactly the information he had just imparted. Apparently, the State of New Mexico, or at least the part of it along the I-10, wanted to remind visitors of the treats that awaited them in each of its towns and cities. Signs popped up every few miles, keeping them completely, not to say relentlessly, informed.

"I refuse to stop anywhere with fewer than forty-three restaurants," Max said. "A man has to have choice."

Owen opened the CD player, pulled out the disc, and reached back for the case of *Bob Hedge's Dialect Practice*

Sessions. Sabrina got a look at the disc he was holding; it was labelled *Australian.*

Later that afternoon they passed the Continental Divide.

Owen flipped open his cell and dialed Roscoe again, but there was no answer.

"Oh, now, it's too bad the base Hungarian isn't here to see this," Max said. "Him with his Great Dividing Range."

"That's the Continental Divide?" Sabrina said. It was little more than a flat ridge of rock baking in the sun.

She had been pretty quiet since Lordsburg. Owen tried to steer the conversation around to Max's sales prospects in El Paso—the local theatre company, the drama department of the university, a couple of wig shops—but Max was oblivious. He recited some Lewis Carroll verses and told a funny story involving Peter Ustinov and a bottle of vintage port. Mile after mile of scrubland rolled by. The road was empty, wiser tourists realizing the desert is best travelled at night.

They passed through miles of Martian landscape, vistas, dust and weeds that eventually turned into pepper fields, and then they came to El Paso. They settled the Rocket in a campground that was near a crumbling old mission with a solitary priest smoking a cigarette by the front door. They all wanted to stretch their legs, but it was still too hot to enjoy a walk, so they ended up taking the Taurus to a shopping mall. It was like being inside a gigantic refrigerator, and they walked around the Gap and Banana Republic and American Eagle Outfitters until they felt crisp as cucumbers. They had dinner at a coffee shop that provided a car wash while they ate, and afterwards they went to see the new Tom Cruise movie. Owen had a funny sensation that the three of them must look like a family out together, as if they were normal.

Max went straight to bed when they got back to the Rocket, but not before another attempt to persuade Sabrina to visit her father.

"He's your friend, Max," she said without looking at him, "not mine. You go visit him if you want to."

"Unnatural child."

"He never really cared about my mother, never really cared about me. Why should I care about him?"

"When I wrote and told him I was planning a trip out this way, his only request was to ask me to check in on you. We wouldn't be together if he hadn't."

"Listen, Max, this man you admire so much treated my mother like shit right up until the day she killed herself by swallowing every pill in the house. So forgive me if my feelings about him are not exactly tender, okay?"

Max put his hands up in uncharacteristic surrender, backed into his bedroom, and closed the door with a sensitive click.

Owen switched on the TV and flipped through newscasts, trying to find one from Tucson. Sabrina fiddled with her iPod. They sat in silence together, grazing their separate media.

After a while Sabrina said, "Are you trying to find out if that guy's okay?"

"What guy?"

"The guy Max shot last night."

Owen started to protest, but she held up a slim hand and shook her head. "You're forgetting I grew up with a criminal too. I know the signs—the excitement, the adrenalin, the nerves. You have the hairpieces, Max is master of foreign accents, and I see from your CD collection that you've been practising Australian. I have to say, Owen, I didn't peg you for a violent person."

He flicked off the television. In the sudden quiet a distant siren threaded its way through the night. Someone in one of the other trailers was playing a banjo. All his life Max had taught him to never reveal what it was they did for a living, no matter who asked. "Discretion," he had told him a hundred times, a plump finger to his lips. "The world depends upon it, boy."

Owen had long lived in the expectation of one day facing an accuser. It just never occurred to him that it would be anyone he liked so much. Sabrina was right beside him on the couch, and he had to restrain himself from putting his arms around her. He found he wanted her to know everything about him.

"I'm not a violent person," he finally said. "Neither is Max."

"A man is in the hospital, Owen."

"He attacked us. We didn't hurt anybody, and then just as we're leaving he comes leaping out of nowhere." It sounded so lame, he felt his face begin to burn.

"Lucky for you," Sabrina said, "it looks like he's going to survive. They're searching for the bald Australian who shot him. And you say Max is not violent?"

"He isn't. He's just . . . losing it. We never carry anything but blanks. This time, unfortunately, he forgot to replace the real bullets that came with his new gun. And he's having these weird nightmares. He won't admit he's screwing up, and I can't get him to quit."

"Can't you take him to see a doctor, have some tests? Maybe a specialist?"

"Max hates doctors. They always tell him to lose weight. And he would never see a shrink, are you kidding?"

A television went on in the trailer next door. The *Tonight Show* theme blared for a moment before it was turned down.

"Don't let on to Max that you know about Tucson," Owen said. "I don't know what he'd do. Anyway, obviously it's kind of dangerous hanging out with us at the moment."

"Why? You'd tell the cops I was in on your jobs?"

"They might assume you are—aiding and abetting and all that. Actually, we've got worse things to worry about right now."

Sabrina raised her eyebrows, and Owen found it impossible to keep anything back. He told her about the Subtractors, and about Pookie and Roscoe.

"I heard of the Subtractors," Sabrina said. "My dad used to live in terror of those guys. I always assumed it was an exaggeration, a legend of some kind."

"Well, maybe it is. All I know is our friends are missing, so where are they?"

Later, when he was in bed, Owen wondered if he had said too much. Not that he was worried about Sabrina telling anyone. But a more gallant sort of person would have remained silent.

He felt his bunk rise up a little and go back down. Then up again, and back down. He leaned over the side.

Sabrina was looking up at him. "You want to come down here and visit for a while?" She nudged his bunk again with her feet.

"Uh, yes," Owen said, "but . . ."

"So why don't you?"

"You told me you were a lesbian."

"I did? Then I guess you must be my kind of girl."

Owen climbed down and she lifted up the covers to let him in. It took some manoeuvring to get comfortable in the narrow bed.

"I probably shouldn't tell you," Owen said after the first tentative kiss, "but I'm actually not all that experienced at this."

"Really," Sabrina said. "And you think I am?"

"Well, you are a couple of years older. I assumed, you know . . ."

"That I'd been around the block? A few miles on the old speedometer?"

Owen laughed. "Not like that."

She crooked a hand around the back of his neck. "I'm not a nympho, if that's what you're worried about. You're the fourth, to be exact."

Owen thought about that for a moment. "I guess you want to know how many for me too, huh?"

She shook her head and closed her eyes. "I have a strict Don't Ask policy."

"It's twenty-seven," Owen said. "Or maybe twenty-eight."

She sat up as if she'd been hoisted by a pulley. "Jesus, Owen, are you serious? What's the male word for slut? You're only eighteen, and you've slept with twenty-eight people? That's disgusting."

"Sorry," Owen said. "I didn't expect you to believe me—I'm just getting you back for telling me you were a lesbian."

"So it wasn't twenty-eight?"

"No. If I tell you how many, will you lie back down?"

"How many?"

"It's only been two."

"Really?"

She lay back down and he held her close—there wasn't much choice in the narrow bunk. They twined themselves together, and he felt the heat of her skin down to his toes, the heat of her breath on his neck. He was now aroused as hell, but also feeling tender in an unfamiliar way, and in no hurry; he wanted this to last. He kissed her cheek, and it felt like the softest, warmest thing he had ever touched.

"Two," he said. "Pretty pathetic, huh?"

"You think I'd be more impressed with ten? That a high number would make you more manly?"

"Seems like it's supposed to."

"Being more manly is not something you have to worry about, Owen."

She kissed him, reaching under the covers, and soon he wasn't worrying about anything at all.

Afterwards, when they had lain in silence for a while, Owen sighed and said, "That was amazing. Astounding. That was really, really—I don't have words for it. I feel—I don't know whether to shout or cry."

"I know what you mean. Well, maybe I don't," Sabrina said, her voice in that silky region between a whisper and full speech. "Why don't you tell me?

"You mean aside from the fact that you're the most beautiful person I've ever met?"

"Oh, come on. I bet you say that to both the girls."

Owen laughed. "It just feels so good that you actually know who I am. I mean, you know the truth about me—about me and Max—what we are, what we do. And you still—well, I mean you seem to, at least—like me. Nobody's ever really known me before. No girls. No guys. Nobody except Max."

Sabrina touched his lips with a finger. He took hold of her hand and they lay side by side for a long time, talking quietly, sharing their memories of growing up in households where the money came from crime.

"The thing is," Sabrina said, "living with a criminal—or being one—is like living on the *Titanic*. You just know it isn't going to end well."

FIFTEEN

STU QUAIG WAS STARING INTO THE MIRROR on the open closet door, checking out his hair for the forty-seventh time, it seemed like, pinching and prodding it into artful little peaks. Clem had to admit the colour looked good, some kind of mustard yellow highlights he'd had added to relieve the monotony of brown.

"Did I tell you how much I hate my haircut?"

Clem picked up the May issue of *Handyman* and thumbed through it. "Why, no, Stu, you didn't. Please go ahead."

"I hate my haircut."

"There, you feel better now?"

"I told her a quarter inch, no more." Stu held up thumb and forefinger to show him what a quarter inch looked like. "And she says sure. Starts off fine, cutting the back, the top, I don't see anything wrong. Then she gets to the front, I'm seeing two-inch hunks of hair falling into my lap."

"You should of stopped her."

"It was too goddamn late to stop her. What am I going to tell her, put it back? Reattach it? Hey, Ming, you think you could graft that back to my head so I don't go out of here totally fucking bald?"

"I hope your dissatisfaction was reflected in the tip," Clem said, flipping pages.

"Tips are how they make their living. I'm not gonna cut off her income over it."

"I'd have given her nothing. Asians don't feel pain like we do."

"She holds up a mirror to the back of my head, where there used to be hair, and says, 'What do you think?' and I say, 'I think you cut it too short.' And she says, oh, she had to do this and that to make it sit right. I expect to come out looking like Jude Law, instead I'm sitting here with a head full of nubs."

"So why go to Sassoon?" Clem said. "You spend like eighty bucks or something and you're coming back in tears."

"Because they're the best, that's why. They have a *training* program. It takes time to become a Sassoon stylist."

Clem tossed his magazine onto the floor. "I been going to the same barber for twenty years. Mikos. Eight bucks, I get a great haircut and Mikos is happy with a two-buck tip."

"Yeah, but your hair looks like shit."

"It suits me."

"Let me tell you," Stu said as he shut the closet door. "A total makeover would not be wasted on you, Clem. You could stand a little improvement in the presentation-of-self department."

"At least I don't got a head full of *nubs.*"

There was a sound of rattling chain from the bathroom. "You ever try Hairlines?"

"The dog is speaking again," Clem said. "Shut up in there, Rover!"

"Hairlines. Small chain out of New York. You get the best of both worlds. Trained stylist, but they don't charge you Sassoon prices. I've been going there for years."

Stu stepped back into the bathroom for a second, looking down at Roscoe. "You got good hair," he said. "What do they charge?"

"Twenty plus tax and tip. And the girls are major cute."

"Twenty bucks, huh? Maybe I'll check 'em out. Place nice?"

"Sure. You know, lots of black. Lots of mirrors. Music's too loud for my taste, but I got sensitive hearing."

Stu left the bathroom and Roscoe climbed out of the tub. He put the toilet seat down again and sat. It seemed like a year he'd been chained to the bathroom sink in this motel. According to the soap, it was a Motel 6. He had to sleep in the bathtub, and every time one of these bastards took a dump, he had to be in the damn bathroom inhaling it. At least the one called Stu had the decency to pull the shower curtain shut.

He looked at his bare feet, the two gauze bandages where his baby toes used to be.

"Hey," Roscoe called out, "he claimed to have shot forty-four men with his Colt Thunderer before he himself was shot in the back following a barroom altercation in 1895."

"Who the fuck knows?" the one called Clem said. "Theodore fucking Roosevelt."

"Was it Billy the Kid?" Stu said.

"John Wesley Hardin. Known as the Fastest Gun in the West. There were several songs about him, none of them true, however. Bob Dylan, you have to wonder if he did any research whatsoever."

"You really get a bang out of this trivia shit, don't you?" Clem said.

"It passes the time."

There was a long pause after that. Just the sound of the television as someone flipped channels, and magazine pages turning.

"So, you got any more questions for us?" Clem said.

"Yeah, how about you unlock this chain and let me out of here."

"No," they said.

The theatre department at the University of El Paso was planning a production of *Lady Windermere's Fan,* and Max took the opportunity to provide them with several high-quality wigs. It was not a huge sale, but it was excellent cover, and the university itself was quite entertaining, having been built for some reason in the manner of a Tibetan lamasery.

After that, he drove over to the hospice affiliated with Thomason General, where John-Paul Bertrand, alias the Pontiff, alias Sabrina's father, was dying on the third floor. Sabrina and

Owen were sightseeing. Even at his age Max found it difficult to believe someone so young and pretty could be so heartless.

The Pontiff lay in bed in a wash of sunlight, a shrivelled, shrunken thing. His previous address had been the Huntsville state prison, and usually inmates put on weight from the lack of activity combined with a steady diet of television and candy bars. Either that or they inflate themselves into rippling muscle-men by relentlessly pumping iron. But the shape under the sheets was scarcely more substantial than a child's.

His face was turned away from the window, the mouth slightly open. A comb-over was plastered to his skull, and a hundred hairpieces appeared in Max's mind as improvements. One bony hand was splayed on his chest, no watch, no jewellery. The stalky neck, the bony hand, the hollowed cheeks—the Pontiff was Coventry after the Blitz.

Max sat down beside the bed, the small chair creaking under his weight.

The eyes fluttered open. Bombed-out eyes.

"Magnus Maxwell at your service."

"How long you been here?"

"Mere moments, squire. Moments."

"Sorry. All I do is sleep all the time. Well, doze. I never actually sleep. Sleep . . ." He let the word dangle, as if it were the name of an old friend fallen in battle.

"I brought you something." Max propped the stuffed angel he had found in the hospital gift shop on the nightstand.

"To see me on my way. Thanks, Carl. That's kind."

"Max, old son. There are a million Maxwells in the universe, and no doubt one of them is Carl. I, however, am Magnus—known to all and sundry as Max. You asked me to look in on Sabrina, remember? I'm happy to tell you she is very bonny. Socking away the gold, planning to go back to school."

"Sabrina." The Pontiff coughed weakly, but even that small strain made his eyes water. "She'll be glad to see the last of me."

"Not a bit of it. She was so happy to hear they let you out," Max said. "Finally saw the error of their ways."

"Department of Corrections is not equipped for . . ." The bony hand gestured at the curtains, the television, the pale blue walls.

Max touched the IV unit. "Stoli?"

"No." John-Paul looked at the saline drip and grimaced. "We've had a parting of the ways, vodka and me."

Where was the Pontiff? Where was the sly thief? The party animal? The robust friend yelling jokes and insults, slapping you on the back? Who was this *thing,* this *carcass* that had taken his place?

Max pulled out a bottle of Stolichnaya from his sample case, and two glasses. "It's time the two of you made up," he said, proffering a shot.

The Pontiff made no move to take it. "Only good thing about all this," he said, in the dry remnant of his old voice, "you lose your taste for alcohol. Stuff never did me any good."

"Rubbish," Max said. "I've seen you hold forth in bistro and tavern, in song and rhyme and just about any form that would suit one of the world's natural born master thieves." He leaned forward confidentially. "You remember the party after the Chemical Bank job? You rented the house in Seaview? What a time we had then, hey?"

"Stupid."

"It was worth it just to see Bobo Valentine dressed up as Wonder Woman."

"It was all stupid."

"Ach, man, don't tell me you have regrets! Regrets aren't for the likes of us."

"What's your name again? Sorry, between the chemo and the radiation . . ."

"You remember me—Magnus Maxwell. Old Max. The one and only."

"Let me tell you, Max, you and me, we're a dime a dozen. Not even a dime. A thief is nothing but a parasite."

"But I only prey on parasites, your grace. That makes me a metasite, a net contributor to the economy."

"Call it anything you want, pal. A thief's a thief." The Pontiff was taken by a series of feeble coughs. With the bruise-coloured circles under his eyes, the sunken cheeks and papery skin, he was a wisp of life, as if there would soon be nothing left of him but the tiny rasp of a voice, and when that was gone, nothing at all.

He took a drink of water—a slow process, even with Max's assistance with glass and straw—then he continued.

"I took things that didn't belong to me—out of greed and selfishness and laziness. Couldn't be bothered to get a real job, do something positive in this world. I got more respect for the guy mops this floor. I got more respect for the guy fixes the toilet. Those people are adding something, and they don't do it for big bucks and they don't do it out of some cockamamie philosophy and they don't think the entire world should pay them to do nothing."

"You were a tower of strength," Max said, "a leader of men."

"An asshole leading assholes. It's not like I was running a research team. My advice to you is get out while the getting's good."

Max decided to change tactics. "Sabrina's hoping to visit soon."

The Pontiff closed his eyes and shook his head. "Girl hates me."

"Not possible, my liege. Nothing ill can dwell in such a temple. I told her I'd be visiting you and she said, 'Tell him I'll be there, soon as I can.' Absolute monster of a boss, Luigi. Wouldn't give her even two days off."

"Sa–bri–na." The Pontiff's thin rasp separated the three syllables as if they were unrelated, as if they didn't add up to a word, let alone a person.

"The very girl," Max said. "I remember you requisitioning a bicycle for her first Communion."

"Uh-huh. You see any family here?"

"Well, hmm, time and distance do sometimes beggar the sweetest intents."

"No, my friend, no one's coming. My family got sick of me a long time ago. All those years, I never cared what it meant to Paula, my line of work. She never knew if she'd be seeing me from one day to the next, one year to the next. Finally got sick of my lies and evasions. I don't blame her. It just wore her down, and she offed herself. Sabrina's never gonna forgive me for that. Why should she? So spare me your bullshit, old man."

Max tried again. "Listen, Ponti. Why don't you come on a road trip with me and my boy? We're travelling cross-country in a luxurious vehicle."

"I don't want to die in a vehicle."

"Your holiness, allow me the honour—"

"Your holiness. What is that?"

"Don't you remember? You were known as the Pontiff, being named John-Paul—and also owing to a certain infallibility."

"Obviously. Which is why I spent seventeen years in jail."

It was amazing to Max that such a frail creature as the Pontiff had become could contain such quantities of negativity. Of course, the dreary little room with its plastic glasses and straws, its faint smell of urine, its lurid TV clamped to the ceiling, was not conducive to good cheer.

"Come for a ride with me," Max said. "Get some fresh air! Make a world of difference."

"Tell you the truth, pal, I don't even remember you."

Max bowed his head. "I grieve to hear it."

"I don't have a clue who you are."

"Max Maxwell, né Magnus."

"I know who you *say* you are, but I just don't know who you *are*. You think you're a character, right? Think you're colourful. But you're just another blowhard got lots of personality and no fucking character. There's no *person* inside that belly of yours. And one day the belly shrivels along with everything else and you end up a fucking zero. Less than a zero—a minus sign, a decimal point, empty fucking space. Get used to it, my friend." The bony hand gestured again: the empty chair, the nightstand devoid of gifts and cards. "This is the way a thief dies."

Max was uncharacteristically quiet as they drove through at least a hundred miles of the desert that is west Texas. The plains and cactus looked as if all moisture had been sucked out of them thousands of years ago. A pale yellow light cast the world in a sickly, overexposed glow.

But Owen was feeling great. He had to look back at Sabrina every five minutes or so just to make sure she was real. He could not believe he had slept with so beautiful a creature. And she for her part had developed a new smile, where just one corner of her mouth lifted, a smile of complicity. He wished Max hadn't con-fiscated her cellphone. Even though she was sitting about two feet away, he would have sent her a text message saying, "Stay Forever," followed by a million exclamation points.

Max was driving with fierce concentration. He spoke without taking his eyes from the road, as if addressing the hot asphalt and the desiccated landscape it traversed. "Young lady," he began, "you have made no inquiry concerning your father."

"No," Sabrina said from the back seat, "and I'm not going to, either."

"I shall tell you how he's doing anyway."

"Knock yourself out."

"Your father, I regret to say, is clearly mortal," Max said. "Growing more mortal by the hour. The body is suffering, no question. But the spirit of the man! He's driving the staff crazy with all the visitors. People bringing gifts, telling stories about the old days, wishing him well. Wanting to touch the hem, so to speak. I was moved, I don't mind telling you."

Owen feigned deep interest in a Blue Guide.

"And not a word of complaint about his illness," Max went on. "Well, you could see it in the sweat on his brow, of course, and his eyes watering from the pain. Blamed it on allergies, the old master." Sunlight glinted on the tears that now wet Max's own cheeks.

"We saw this tiny Napoleon museum," Sabrina said brightly.

"The man is on his deathbed. Can you not relent?"

No answer. They drove awhile in silence. Then Max said, "Why on earth is there a Napoleon museum in El Paso?"

"No one knows," Owen said, "but they had a pair of his boots and a bunch of books that he owned. And we saw the cemetery where John Wesley Hardin was buried."

"John Wesley? The religious founder?"

"The gunfighter," Owen said. "One of the meanest ever. He shot one guy just for snoring."

"No one could hold that against him," Max said. "And what delights do you have in store for us today?"

"I'll tell you when we get there."

The Guadalupe Mountains brought some relief to the monotony of the drive as they continued east through fields of prickly pear, cholla and agave. They stopped for lunch at a state park, where they saw mysterious pictographs. Whenever they stepped out of the Rocket, the ferocity of the sun seemed to suck the breath out of their lungs.

When the sign came up for the Carlsbad Caverns, Max was all for it until he saw the vast squat oval of the natural entrance. "No, no," he said. "Impossible."

"Come on, Max, they're supposed to be spectacular. They'll be all lit up inside."

"I refuse to go underground until such time as mortality may require. You two go ahead. I shall meet you here in the Rocket exactly two hours hence."

So Owen and Sabrina got to explore the caves in the company of sixty or seventy tourists. After the brutal sun of the parking lot, the cool of the caves was pure balm. Owen lent Sabrina one of his sweatshirts. The sleeves hung down past her wrists, giving her a waiflike look that didn't suit her at all.

They walked through strange cathedrals and chapels of limestone. The immensity of the earth lay above them, but the soaring ceilings relieved any gloom. A couple of times he took her hand to help her up a slope, thrilled by the heat of her small fingers against his palm. He would have held her hand for the entire rest of the day, but Sabrina detached herself each time.

Stone glittered and gleamed in shapes of waterfalls and organ pipes. Clusters of stalactites tiny as straws pressed up against columns bigger than anything that had supported the Parthenon. They saw dazzling mineral deposits, carpets of gypsum dust, and the shimmer and bustle of microscopic cave life.

When they came out into the sun again, Sabrina said, "Thank you for taking me there, Owen. It's something I'll never forget."

She pulled off the sweatshirt and handed it back to him. A photographer operating a small stand near the exit asked if they'd like a picture for two bucks, and Owen said sure. He took one of Sabrina and one of them together, and Owen bought both. ·

"I look silly," Sabrina said, handing back the photo.

Owen shook his head. "You are so wrong." As they crossed the parking lot, he said, "You know, I think being around you makes me dumb."

"Dumb as in quiet or dumb as in dumb?"

"Both. I'm having trouble speaking. Am I just, like, the nerdiest guy you ever met? I can't handle this."

"Can't handle what?"

"You. Being around you. You make me too happy. I keep feeling like there's something urgent I have to tell you, but then I can't speak."

"Sounds like a nightmare."

Owen shook his head. "Definitely not. Whatever the opposite of a nightmare is, that's what I'm having."

The Rocket was dark, the bedroom door closed.

"I better wake him up," Owen said. "He tends to get confused if he naps too long." He rapped on the bedroom door. "Max? Max, you really missed something. The caverns were awesome. Max?" Owen knocked louder before opening the door. The bed was empty. "Shit. He's gone somewhere."

"It's awfully hot," Sabrina said. "Maybe he decided to wait inside the shop."

Owen pulled out his cell and dialed Max's number. There was a dull humming sound. Sabrina checked the far side of the bed and found Max's vibrating phone, holding it up for Owen to see.

Coming in for the landing, that's the tricky part—or at least that's how Max thinks of it. He is aloft somewhere (where *exactly* is another blank spot on his instrumentation), and he is flying blind, drifting blind really, because he has no sense of direction. He is a balloon, not a powered craft.

He might call himself a UDO if that term were available to him at the moment, an unidentified drifting object, because he is certainly drifting, having no clue as to his exact location, and definitely unidentified, having for some reason no mental access to certain personal records—for example, his name.

The (he assumed temporary) misplacement of his identity was not nearly so alarming as the monolithic unfamiliarity of his surroundings. It was not for lack of signs, landmarks, hints and indications. There was that greyish breast of a mountain in the distance, surrounded by less impressive folds of agricultural cellulite. It was the sort of geographical formation you looked at and said to yourself, Ah yes, there's _____, I must be near _____ (home, Mum's place, the office).

And there was a black and white sign, a shield-shaped piece

of tin fixed to a metal post that said *East 180*. It was full of meaning, Max knew. It was like looking at a bottle full of a rosy translucent liquid, condensation dripping down its elegantly curved sides. It was meant to be drunk, begging to be drunk, but what it might be, or be called, or taste like, he had no idea. How could he? He had never seen this sign before. But he had the feeling that it contained important information, information that *someone* would understand.

Family, said the picnic bench on which he was perched. Definitely a sense of family at this currently empty table. But unmoored Max had no idea at this moment if he could expect a family to claim him or even if he had a family. *Vehicles,* said the line of cars, trailers, SUVs parked just to his left between the picnic tables and the washrooms. Yes, he retained the fact that those were washrooms, his underwear still a little damp from his having recently peed in one of them. But as to vehicles, well, he had walked up and down that row of angled chariots several times now and not one of them looked familiar. His anxiety was further stoked by the undeniable observation that the vehicles were constantly pulling away, only to be replaced by other, no less unfamiliar, vehicles. The tool of logic was still apparently available to him, and he employed it now, caliper-like, on this observation: he must be connected either to one of the vehicles that had already departed or to one that had not yet arrived.

His mind perched on this pillar of reason for a few moments, but the perch was not nearly as secure as he wished, because the logic widget had a certain implacability about it and was now presenting to his awareness two other possibilities: 1) that he had no connection to any vehicle that had ever been anywhere near this place, wherever it was; and 2) that no such vehicle was ever going to arrive.

An unfamiliar thrumming set up in his chest, which he supposed was fear, and he was hoping it would go away. *O, let me not be mad*—where did that come from? He could see the letters, black Gothic script snaking across the pale fog of his mind.

Family, the bench said again. Did he have one, whoever he was? Had he lost track of them while he was in the washroom relieving, none too nicely, his bladder? Here came a family now. Father: khaki shorts past the knee, colourful shirttail out, and enormous running shoes; Mother: honey blonde, ponytail, mid-size breasts under T-shirt emblazoned with obscure image; Child: girl, elevenish, body straight as an arrow, with the skinny legs disproportionately long, sipping from an enormous drink.

Max sat a little more erect on his perch. He tried for an expression that was alert, approachable, a face ready to be recognized. This could be them. This could be the family he belonged to. I would have to be the grandfather, he reasoned. He further arranged his face into bland benevolence, the way a deaf person hedges his expression into a smile that could be taken either as agreement with the statement he has just failed to hear or simple recognition, possibly even the anticipation of a disagreement.

The little girl handed off the large drink to Mommy and looked toward him. Max smiled at her, saying nothing; he was a last Christmas present under the tree, waiting to be opened. She should be yelling something like, *Hey, Grampa, aren't you getting into the car? We'll leave you behi-ind!* Then he would hop off this uncomfortable table and join them in their private conveyance.

Time formed a cocoon of sorts around him, seemingly disconnected from other people's hours. Within this cocoon, an image visited him, fleeting and gossamer, tantalizing: a woman, roundish in proportion, friendly of face, holding a shirt as if caught in the action of ironing. She asked him a question. It was English, but he didn't recognize the words. She finished with an interrogative lilt on a single syllable. His name. His mind reached out for it, a feather hammocking its way down to the earth. He snatched at it. Gone.

Wisps of identity threaded the air before him, ungraspable. Self-knowledge dancing on the tip of his mind. *Come, let me clutch thee.* Had someone said that to him? A frisky nun, perhaps? Was he perhaps a priest of some sort? No prayers came to mind; very little of anything was coming to mind.

Certain intelligences were reaching him from the periphery of his being. Sweat was beading on his brow, rolling down his ribs. It was hot sitting on this bench in the open sun. No one else was doing this, he noticed. The only tables that were occupied were in the shade.

But best not to move. Someone would come to claim him. Yes, _____ would come. And she would be . . . female. His wife. The lack of a ring told him that he was likely not wived, but surely _____ would come. A son-in-law? That would imply relationships that seemed as remote to his ken as yet-to-be-discovered moons.

Ah. Another family group approaching. Twelveish boy, fourteen-ish girl, short round dolphin-faced momma, and a choleric man muttering red-faced into a communications device. Arrange brows, lips. Bring cheek muscles to bear. I might be yours. I can be safely approached and even transported out of this hot, lonely sun.

Owen and Sabrina left the Rocket and headed back across the scorching parking lot. The gift shop was packed with tourists examining Carlsbad books, DVDs and geological samples. No sign of Max. They checked the washrooms, the video exhibit. Nothing.

They approached a gallery attendant seated on a stool just inside the door, an Asian girl in a uniform that was too big for her.

"Have you seen a big English guy wandering around on his own?" Owen asked her. He gave her a detailed description, right down to the shorts and the argyle socks.

"No, I'm sorry," the girl said with a jarring Texas accent. "Y'all might ask in the shop, though. Maybe he might coulda gone there?"

"Thanks."

A cashier in the shop remembered seeing Max, but it had been at least an hour ago.

"Here's what we do," Owen said to Sabrina, trying to keep calm, although his heartbeat was shifting from allegro into presto. "You go that way through the galleries and I'll go the other way, and I'll meet you back here in ten minutes. There's no way we can miss him if he's in there."

"Ten minutes. Okay."

Owen walked to the end of the gallery tour and went in through the exit. The attendant was chatting on a cellphone and didn't notice him. Sabrina passed him on her way through in the other direction.

"Well, he's not in the washrooms, he's not in the gallery, he's not in the shop," Owen said when they met up again outside the shop.

"Maybe he changed his mind and decided to tour the caverns."

"Max never changes his mind. If caverns are bad, they're bad forever."

"Well, where else could he be?"

They checked the Rocket once more, but Max was still not back. They went to the main pavilion and reported their problem. A couple of minutes later Max was paged over the PA and asked to report to the information desk.

"Sometimes he gets a little, uh, bewildered," Owen said to the woman at the desk.

"You mean he might not know who he is?" She had hair that was way too blonde for her age.

"It's possible. It hasn't happened before, but it's possible. If I give you a description of him, could it be given to all the rangers?"

"We can give it to them by radio, hon. But it won't reach into the caves, just to the entrance and exit."

Owen left his cell number with her in case Max should turn up.

When they were back outside, Sabrina said maybe they should call the police.

Owen laughed. "Are you kidding? He'd never forgive me. It's possible he wandered off along the highway. I'm just gonna have to look for him."

They detached the Taurus and left the Rocket in the lot. Owen made a left at the entrance and continued in their original direction. Air shimmered and seemed to liquefy above the asphalt.

"It's so hot," Sabrina said. "I hope he's not walking along the shoulder."

"You keep an eye on the right side, I'll keep an eye on the left."

They drove a few miles, taking it slowly, annoying the cars behind them. Owen stopped at a service centre with a McDonald's, but no one remembered seeing Max there. A little farther and they came to a rest stop, just washrooms and a few picnic tables in the shade.

"There he is," Sabrina said.

Max was seated at a picnic table, contemplating an apple in his hand as if it were a grenade. Owen called to him the instant he stepped out of the car, but Max didn't even look.

"Max?" he said again as they got closer.

This time Max looked up, but the expression on his face was vague, uncertain, unMaxlike.

"Max, are you all right?"

Max looked from Owen to Sabrina, his brow a landscape of perplexity.

"It's me, Owen."

"Yes, yes. Well, of course I know that." There was no conviction in his voice. "And the wife, obviously."

"Max, what are you doing here? Why did you take off?"

"Bit tired, to tell you the truth. Needed to sit down."

"You wandered away from the caverns, Max. We were scared to death. We didn't know what happened to you. How did you get here?"

"I don't know. We're related, you and I?"

"Max, I'm your nephew. Your adopted son. I'm Owen."

"Owen, yes. And your lovely wife."

"We're not married, Max—Sabrina is a friend. Let's get back to the Rocket."

"Rocket? No. You frighten me."

"Not a real rocket, Max. The Winnebago. Come on, you better lie down for a while."

Eventually they talked Max into the car and drove back to the caverns. Max gave no sign of recognizing the Rocket, but he was happy to lie down in the bedroom and close his eyes. He was asleep within seconds.

Owen was afraid to make any more stops after that. They drove for hours, not saying much. The highway unfurled across the Llano Estacado, an endless mesa dotted with tiny, unexpected lakes. Finally there was something green other than cacti—fields of cotton and alfalfa that stretched to the horizon. It was dark when the first oil pumps began to appear, and then they were in the land of stampedes and rodeos. Sabrina read out directions well in advance of the crucial turnoffs as they rolled along the vast expressways of Dallas–Fort Worth. With a minimum amount of confusion they found a suitable campground not too far out of town and parked the Rocket for the night.

Max was still fast asleep.

SIXTEEN

SABRINA LEFT EARLY IN THE MORNING to go and visit her aunt Rachel—her mother's sister—who had lived in Dallas her whole life. Max was still in bed, and she thought it would be best if Owen could be alone with him for a while.

Spending time with Aunt Rachel was like shooting rapids—exhilarating, but not something you wanted to do every day. Sabrina had hardly been in her aunt's kitchen half an hour before Rachel was lining up the day's activities like a squad commander plotting a covert operation.

"Honey, a girl cain't be without her wardrobe. That's like a magician without his wand, an angel without his wings. We are gonna take you right downtown, and we are gonna get your hair cut, and we are gonna buy you some clothes. We can't have you slouching across the country looking like Little Orphan Annie. Oh, honey, I am so glad to hear you left that religious zealot. There's only one thing worse than an atheist and that's a born-again bonehead. Could you not have got your luggage forwarded to you somehow?"

"The hotel says it's gone. Actually, what they said was, 'Your husband took it when he checked out.'"

"The man's a robber and a thief. Not to mention violent, possessive and downright mean."

"Good Christian, though."

"If that man's a Christian, I'm a Tibetan nun. Where's he get off stealing your clothes?"

"He's not all bad, Rache. He took me in at a really bad point in my life."

"Don't you go mistaking plain old ordinary lust for Christian charity. Personally, I've had it with Christians—Muslims, too—and the Jews can go take a flying—Honey, look at your nails. Those hands look like you've been tunnelling out of San Quentin. I can see we are gonna have to make a day of this. Now tell me again who it is you're travelling with?"

"A guy named Owen Maxwell and his uncle."

"How old is Owen?"

"Eighteen. Just two years younger than me."

"I know how old you are, honey. You're sweet on him, aren't you?"

"Not really. Maybe a little."

"More than a little, princess. I know the signs. How'd you meet this handsome young dog?"

"He saw Bill hitting me and screaming his head off in a parking lot and he intervened. Naturally, Bill beat him senseless."

"And I have no doubt he was quoting chapter and verse the whole time," Rachel said. "Honey, we are just gonna have to indulge in a little post-traumatic stress shopping."

Rachel took her to Neiman Marcus, Saks Fifth Avenue and so many boutiques that Sabrina lost count. Even though she was nearly thirty years older than Sabrina, Rachel seemed to know what the younger generation liked and where to get it. Sabrina bought a pair of Buffalo jeans on sale, a sleeveless blouse, and a green hoodie that managed to be light and cozy at the same time.

"Honey, that colour is made for you. Suddenly you got eyes like a movie star."

As an extra surprise, Rachel picked out a simple pendant, silver with a drop of turquoise.

"Rachel, I can't. It'll take me ages to pay you back."

"Who said anything about paying me back? Pretty little thing like you, it's a pleasure to dress you up."

"But these things aren't cheap."

"Don't you worry about it. Pierre left me very well provided for."

Rachel's husband, a Dallas tax attorney with the un-Texan name of Pierre, had died of lymphoma more than ten years ago. These days she was seeing a younger man named Ken, and she seemed inclined to keep him, though she showed no inclination to marry again.

"You want to know the secret of a lasting relationship?" Rachel said, setting her shopping bag on the sidewalk so she could flag a cab.

"I imagine there's more than one," Sabrina said.

"No, there's actually just the one: fellatio. Constant, expert fellatio." Rachel stepped out into the path of an oncoming cab, forcing him to halt. "Give him the kind of experience money can't buy and that man will be by your side forever."

"God, Rachel. I thought you were going to say 'ruthless honesty,' or 'a compatible sense of humour.' And you come up with blow jobs."

"Everybody's got their theories. Mine happens to be backed up by a lot of hard evidence, pardon the pun." She held open the door of the cab for Sabrina. "What say we head home and have ourselves some lemonade on the veranda?"

When they brought their lemonade out onto the back porch, Bill Bullard was on the bottom step, cap in hand.

"Jesus Christ," Rachel said.

"I'm going to ignore that," Bill said. "But you can be certain the Lord won't."

"Mister, you go straight back where you came from. You are not welcome here."

"Ma'am, with all respect, I did not come here to see you. I come to see Sabrina."

"Well, Sabrina doesn't want to see you."

"I reckon the young lady's old enough to speak for herself."
Bill shifted his weight, cocking a hip and leaning one hand on
the newel post at the bottom of the porch steps, the other on
his hip. The posture pushed his belt even lower beneath his
abdominal overhang.

"How did you find me?" Sabrina asked.

"Finding people is one of the things I'm good at."

"But I never told you about Rachel."

"Not in so many words, maybe. Everybody has an address book."

"You went through my laptop? That's a pretty sneaky thing to
do, wouldn't you say?"

"I believe it's my duty to protect you. Sometimes protection
demands extraordinary measures."

"You son of a bitch," Rachel said. "You are lower than a snake's
belly in a wagon rut. What kind of man goes through a woman's
personal belongings?"

"A man who is concerned for her welfare. Sabrina, may I talk
with you in private?"

"There's nothing to talk about, Bill. I don't want to be around
you anymore. You're too possessive, you're too violent, and you're
too religious."

"I have my faults and my weaknesses, Lord knows I do. But
there is no such thing on this earth as too religious."

"Tell that to the people who died in the World Trade Center,"
Rachel said. "Tell it to all the so-called witches been burned at
the stake. Why don't you just turn around and get your ass off
my property?"

"I'd like to talk to Sabrina first."

"She just told you she don't need to talk to you."

"It's okay," Sabrina said.

"Honey, you don't have to talk to this creep."

"Really, Rachel. I'll be all right."

Rachel looked from Bill to Sabrina, and back to Bill. "I will
be watching you right here from this veranda," she said. "And

if you try to haul this young lady off or harm her in any way, I will have the police on your ass so fast it'll make your head spin. And trust me, Dallas cops aren't gonna give a shit you were a cop in some lame-ass sink trap like Las Vegas. They'll just assume you're stupid and corrupt, like every other Bible-thumpin' dickhead."

"I'll keep that in mind, ma'am. Thank you for clarifying."

Rachel sat down on a wicker chair, making the ice in her lemonade clink.

Sabrina went down the steps and crossed the lawn to a white wooden swing hanging in the shade of an enormous tree. There was a rumble of distant thunder and a heavy dampness in the air. Bill stood before her, cap in hand, looking as penitent as it was possible for a man of his body mass index to look.

"Sabrina," he said, "I behaved like a jackass, and I am truly sorry. I hope you can find it in your heart to forgive me."

"I have no trouble forgiving you, Bill—for what you did to me. But you beat the guy who was kind enough to intervene, and forgiving you for that isn't up to me."

"Okay, I am sorry for that too. I know my temper can occasionally get the better of me. It's an affliction the Lord has donated to me as a test. I hope to do better on that test in future. I've prayed on it."

"You're always praying, Bill. If you go around beating people, it doesn't make it better that you pray about it. Nobody cares if you pray or not, but they do care if you smack them around."

Sabrina sipped from her lemonade and pressed one foot into the grass, pushing the swing around in a tiny circle. From the direction of the veranda came the clink of ice cubes.

Bill twisted his cap. "I've been thinking maybe I could enrol in one of those anger management courses? Much as I hate the idea of therapy and all that group candy-ass wallowing. Makes my skin crawl, to tell you the truth. But I'd be willing to undertake it, if you'd come back with me."

"I can't go back with you, Bill."

"But you said you forgive me."

"I do. I just don't want to live with you."

"Aw, Sabrina, don't you know by now I love you like to die? I'm nearbout crazy with it. I'll do better, I promise. I'll make a solemn vow, and you know I would not swear falsely."

"How did you know I'd be here, anyway?"

"I didn't. But I was pretty sure you'd be in touch with your aunt, even though I can't help but notice that that lady is a piece of work. I was hoping to prevail upon her better nature to get a message to you, that's all. It was just one of the Lord's tender mercies that he saw fit to bring you to me just as I arrived."

"Luck, in other words."

"You say luck, I say the Lord. Who do you think's in charge of luck?"

The last of Sabrina's lemonade clattered up the straw. "Bill, thank you for taking me in when I was down. I'm grateful for it— really I am—but I'm moving back to New York and that's that."

"Have some mercy, now. You are crushing my spirit. Truly."

"I'm sorry, Bill."

"Won't you at least think on it?"

"There's nothing to think about. I don't suppose you'd be able to send my stuff to me when I have a place of my own?"

"Matter of fact, I brought your suitcase with me. Backpack too. I'm not a brute, Sabrina. I knew there was a good chance you wouldn't appreciate my offer to take you back. Figured I'd leave 'em with your aunt if it come to that."

"You have them here?"

"They're in the car."

To Sabrina's horror, Bill knelt on the grass as the first raindrops began to fall and clasped his hands in front of his chest. This brought a furious rattle of ice cubes from the veranda.

"Sabrina, looky here now. I'm on my knees. Do you know what that costs a man of my prideful nature? This is me, William P.

Bullard, begging you. Abasing myself before you. Heaven sake, girl, what more can you require of a man?"

"Well," Sabrina said, "I'd rather just have my luggage."

"He gave it to you?" Owen said. "He didn't hit you again, did he?"

"No, he didn't hit me. He tried to get me to go back to Vegas with him. I actually felt sorry for him."

He touched her shoulder. "Don't be sad. I'm really glad you didn't go back with him."

"Back with whom?" Max said as he came into the Rocket, spotted with rain and carrying a bag of groceries. He had the most remarkable powers of recovery Sabrina had ever witnessed. He didn't seem even the slightest bit troubled by his demented episode of the day before.

"Bill showed up at my aunt's," Sabrina said.

Max set the groceries down on the table and mopped at his brow. "My dear, please tell me that isn't true. Have you been phoning him again?"

"He snooped through my address books. He figured I'd show up at Rachel's and he just happened to be there when we got back from shopping."

"And now I suppose he's followed you back to our very doorstep and we can look forward to having a Bible-spouting former constable on our tail for the rest of our natural lives."

"He didn't follow me. I made him promise not to."

"Oh, good. It's a truth universally acknowledged that no law enforcement officer, former or otherwise, would ever break a promise."

"Max," Owen put in, "she said he didn't follow her. Did you see any strange cars outside?"

"I did not. But my mind misgives some consequence," Max said, pointing upward, "yet hanging in the stars."

"It's not as if he's still a cop. He just wants Sabrina back. He doesn't know anything about us, why should he?"

"My lad, I know not. But I do know the former Officer Bullard has popped up, gopherlike, in two separate locations, and I am not yet so feeble-minded as to put it down to coincidence. The young lady is fetching—not to mention the daughter of my long-time friend—but forgive me if I find it unnerving to be associated with an actual police magnet. My dear," he added to Sabrina, "I mean that in the most affectionate way."

SEVENTEEN

THEY'D BEEN FOLLOWING THE OLD MAN AND THE KID since Vegas, and now the girl too. They got Tucson from Pookie—his hotel booking in the datebook section of his PalmPilot. Roscoe had given them Dallas, and Zig had insisted on lugging the sap all the way to Dallas in case he might know any more. There were only half a dozen RV parks in the Dallas–Fort Worth area, and of these only two had facilities big enough for vehicles the size of Max Maxwell's Winnebago. Which was how they'd tracked them to the Texas-T trailer park. Clem and Stu had split the bird-dog duties, meaning Clem had to waste his entire day following this girl around, and he could not for the life of him figure out why.

Clem seriously believed that if he stayed in the car another minute he was going to go out of his screaming mind. Parked in the McDonald's lot, staring at the Texas-T sign—pretty soon they'd have to haul him off to a psychiatric hospital, to spend the rest of his days drooling before a TV set playing *America's Funniest Home Videos* or some other lame-ass show he'd never watched except by accident in a bar maybe.

He'd been here for two hours now, rain tapping on the car roof and dribbling down the windshield. He couldn't listen to the radio any longer without running the battery down. He snatched up his cellphone and called Zig.

"How much longer you expect me to do this?"

"Do what?" Zig said. "What are you doing?"

"I'm parked outside the goddamn trailer park waiting for something to happen. I'm telling you, the girl's got nothing to do with these guys' business. She's a friend or relative or something. Spent the day shopping, for Chrissake."

"Who with?"

"Some dame. Friend, I think. Older. Absolutely nothing of interest happened."

"They see anybody else?"

"No one. Well, there was one guy come out of the old lady's place when they got back from shopping. Could be the broad's husband, I don't know. Anyway, girl took a taxi back here an hour ago and I'm—Hang on, there's a cab coming out of the park now. Yeah, it's her."

"Stay on her."

"Zig, I'm getting sick of pissing in a bottle here. Why the fuck am I watching this girl?"

"Because we don't know if she's part of this crew or what."

"Well, let Stu do it."

"Stu's watching Max and the kid downtown, and I'm watching Jeopardy Joe here. Don't you lose her, Clem, or I'll light up your ass, I swear I will."

Clem threw the phone down and pulled out into the traffic, wipers flapping. The cab was two cars ahead. He snatched up the phone again and switched it off. What was Zig doing all this time? Probably screwing one of his underage druggies too stoned to know any better.

"Fuck you," he said, and threw the phone in the glove compartment.

"There's no way we can do it," Owen said. "Not without Pookie and Roscoe. You checked out the new wing."

Max steered the Taurus through the Dallas traffic, which seemed so used to sunshine that it was utterly stymied by rain.

"It's a hospital, my boy. Hardly a fortress. My plan is not only feasible, it is elegant. A good round plan. The lobby will be filled with doctors and lawyers and do-gooders all drinking to excess. They're opening a wing—they're not expecting to get robbed. All those speeches, they'll be stultified."

"Max, just yesterday you didn't know your own goddamn name."

"That is a low blow, lad. I refuse to dignify it with a reply."

"Max, you've got four mezzanines looking down on the lobby where everyone's going to be. You've got four huge exits. And there's going to be newspaper photographers, TV cameras, who knows what else?"

"I fear no cameras. A disguise is a disguise whether on camera or in the flesh. As to mezzanines—"

"Max, please. You're scaring me. What's the point of doing reconnaissance if you're going to ignore everything you find out? Besides which, since when do we rob hospitals?"

"We wouldn't be robbing the hospital, we'd be robbing the rabid right-wing lunatics who attend such things. Need I remind you that it's to be called the Thomas P. Craine Center for Reconstructive Surgery? Do you know who Thomas P. Craine is?"

"Just because he's a rich Republican doesn't mean he isn't doing something good. Hey, watch out!"

Max had suddenly pulled over in front of an FTD shop, eliciting even more horns from behind.

"Flowers to Tucson," he said. "That fellow who was injured."

"The one you shot, you mean."

"There's no need to call a spade a bloody shovel. It was a workplace accident. You mock my finest instincts."

The florist was a Korean man dressed in a soccer jersey and a fisherman's cap. An old newspaper clipping was taped to the cash register: "From DMZ to DFW: Korean Poet Kim Wa Yeung's Long Journey from Word Power to Flower Power." The transaction took forever owing to Max's insistence on discussing Shakespeare with the florist. When they were finished, Owen bought a dozen miniature daffodils.

"Why this sudden urge for daffodils?" Max inquired, back in the car.

"They're for Sabrina," Owen said.

"Careful, laddie. She hasn't had your upbringing. The Pontiff, bless him, was not what you'd call a family man. Business with him was not seasonal—no, no, he was a full-time thief—and I fear his daughter has paid the price. But to return to the subject at hand: I don't want to rule out a ripe prospect at the first sign of adversity."

"Max, have you totally forgotten yesterday? It's okay—it's not your fault you're getting old and your synapses maybe don't fire the way they used to—but you didn't even know your own name. You're not in any shape for a big show. It's not even an option. You might as well hang a sign on your back that says 'Arrest Me.'"

Max wouldn't listen. He was feeling fine, never better. Yesterday had been a fleeting episode. One was only human. Mountain molehill. They went back and forth on the subject all the way to the campground. They were still arguing when they opened the Rocket's door.

"Max, remember what you used to tell me? 'One has to have the courage *not* to pull a job.'"

"Tush, boy. You mistake the howl of fear for the song of reason. Hang on . . ."

"What's wrong?"

"The dishwasher's been moved."

"You moved it when you came back from visiting the Pontiff."

"Just so. And I set it back exactly as always."

Max got down on his knees and slid the dishwasher away from its fittings. Usually you had to unscrew two braces in the floor before you could do that, but they were loose. His head disappeared into the gap as he reached around behind the machine.

"It's gone."

"You're kidding."

"All of it."

"You're kidding me."

"See for yourself."

Owen dropped the flowers on the table. He got down on the floor and felt behind the dishwasher. There was nothing at all in the hutch.

The two of them stood in the galley, speechless.

After a minute Owen noticed the rack across from the bunks. "Sabrina's suitcase is gone. So's her backpack. They were up there next to mine."

"She robbed us," Max said. "The filthy little scrubber robbed us."

"Jesus, Max. It's far more likely the Subtractors got her. Or *someone* got her. Whoever got Pookie. Whoever got Roscoe. Now they've got Sabrina. Why would you assume she ripped us off?"

Max held up a piece of paper. Owen grabbed it from him and read the following:

> *Owen, Max,*
> *Opportunity knocks and I hope as fellow thieves you will*
> *understand. Thanks*
> *for everything!*

"The filthy, cozening slut."

"Don't call her that, Max."

"Obviously she noticed the dishwasher the other night. The false witch was feigning sleep when you stashed the stuff, and now she has stripped us bare. And you bought her flowers," Max said, laying a damp, heavy paw on Owen's shoulder. "How positively heartwarming."

EIGHTEEN

THEY WERE ON THEIR FOURTH HOTEL NOW, the Monte Carlo, keeping to the more luxurious ones since it was likely Sabrina was "feeling pretty flush," as Max put it. But none of the desk clerks recognized her from the photo they held up, the one of her at Carlsbad.

They sat down in the Monte Carlo's plush lobby for a breather.

"Max, we're acting like a couple of amateur detectives here. Doesn't that bother you?"

"The woman has done me bold and saucy wrongs," Max said, mopping his brow. "She must be found."

"Think about it," Owen said. "If you were Sabrina, would you rob us and then head for a hotel? I wouldn't. I would head straight to the nearest airport or train station—and where does that leave us? Are we going to head out to the airport and ask every ticket clerk if they've seen her?"

"The vixen was bound for New York, was she not? That narrows it down."

"Max, we're not going to find her in Dallas. We *might* find her in New York if she really does head back to school there."

"Maybe she rented a car. We should check rental outlets."

"There must be hundreds of them in this city. Anyway, why rent when you could buy? She could go right out and buy herself a Mustang—she said that was her fantasy."

The moment he said it, Owen wished he hadn't. Max snapped his fingers and said, "Fire up the laptop, kid. We'll need a list of Ford dealerships."

"I don't have the laptop on me. Let's go outside and get some air."

He took Max by the elbow and led him to a bench still damp from the earlier rain. Beside them, a bronze statue of an oilman ignored the pigeon balancing on his bronze hard hat. Owen had a sudden deep yearning for the streets of Manhattan, for the squirrels of Stuyvesant Town, for his life to come at Juilliard.

"I can't accept it," Max said. "I've been robbed by a mere slip of a girl. It must be a bad dream. Wake me, boy, wake me. Queen Mab is riding my cerebellum."

"We're just going to have to live with it."

"It's too humiliating."

"The stuff she took? Two weeks ago we didn't own any of it. There's no point getting upset about losing it now."

"There's every point."

"Let's just head home. It's time to call it a day."

"Desist, surrender monkey." Max stood up with much groaning, pressing his hands into the small of his back. "I have another plan."

"Great, Max. I can't wait."

Max stood on tiptoe, a surprisingly delicate manoeuvre for one so middle heavy, and addressed himself to the bronze figure.

"I, Magnus Max Maxwell, am determined to get very drunk."

Max's "plan" dragged them through several drinking establishments. Owen was sticking to Coke, but after his third it was beginning to taste horribly sweet and he was having to pee every ten minutes.

Their current stop was Jimmy's Roustabout Tavern; Owen hoped it would be the last. It was full of oil-drilling paraphernalia and murals of famous gushers. It was not a spot that appealed to people who were actually in the petroleum business, but it was clearly a hit with the criminal element. This may have had something to do with the proprietor, Jimmy Coughlin, who looked only slightly younger than Max and had tattoos of dragons flaming up his forearms.

"Jimmy, old son," Max said over his tower of stout. "You remember John-Paul Bertrand, our sainted Pontiff?"

"Sure, I knew JP before he got sent up to Huntsville."

"It's his daughter has my attention just now."

"Robbing the cradle, aren't you? Even I have some standards."

"Jimmy, I assure you, although she has attacked me in my heart's core, my purpose is nothing romantic. In brief—"

"Max." Owen squeezed his elbow hard and spoke right into his ear. "Max, cool it."

Max didn't even notice. "In brief, she has absconded with goods and chattels not her own."

"She ripped you off? Really? The Pontiff's kid?"

"A kid no longer. Her comely form doth cloak the heart of a jackal."

"And you think she's in Dallas?"

"Yes." Max slapped the bar. "The slyboots must be found. Justice must be done."

"Max," Owen said between his teeth, "for God's sake shut up."

"Ooops. Pardon," Max said to Jimmy. "The poor lad is pixilated by her. She's not only run off with my treasure, she has run off with his heart. Tell me something, James, what has happened to that thing we all held so precious?"

"What thing would that be?"

"Honour, old son. Honour among thieves. What has become of it?"

"That's actually pretty funny, Max. You're the only person my entire career I heard mention it."

"No, it's true, I tell you. We must all aim to meet the standards set by our beloved Pontiff. I do hope he's feeling better. He was looking a bit peaky the other day."

"Oh, he's definitely feeling better," Jimmy said.

"Excellent news! He's out of hospital?"

"He's out of hospital," Jimmy said.

"His health," Max said, raising his glass. "Very fine news indeed."

"Max," Owen said, "he means he's dead."

"Heard it on the news this morning," Jimmy said, wiping a glass.

"Dead? Who's dead?"

"The Pontiff, for God's sake," Owen said.

"Oh, no," Max said, slumping on his bar stool. "Oh, lamentable day."

"Poor Sabrina."

"Poor Sabrina!" Max roared at him, spraying stout. "She wouldn't even visit the man! Her own father lying on his deathbed, and she wouldn't even visit."

"At least he had friends there," Owen said. "I guess, if you're gonna die, you want to have your friends around."

"Just so, lad. Just so." Max raised his glass again, nearly sliding off his seat. "To a happy end in the comfort of loved ones. Can't ask for more than that."

It was not unusual, particularly in pubs, bars and taverns, for people to assume that Max was drunk. He was, after all, loud, voluble and occasionally obnoxious. But the truth was, Max rarely drank to the point of intoxication. Too much ale interfered with his performance: he would start to forget his Shakespeare, he would have to interrupt his own histrionics with frequent trips to the men's room, and, worst of all, he would lose control of his mouth, releasing compromising information in quarters that were, to say the least, insecure.

Tonight there was no question: Max was in his cups. As soon as a thug or ne'er-do-well would enter, he would sail toward him, listing badly. None of them knew who he was talking about. They were too young to remember the Pontiff, and Max's woman troubles didn't interest them. One or two of them looked like they might reply to his questions with violence. Owen couldn't get him to shut up, and he couldn't get him to go back to the Rocket.

Max was muttering morosely into his pint of stout when a man sat down beside him. Owen noticed he had a cool haircut and a lightweight pinstripe suit that made him look like a hip lawyer, if there could be such a thing. He ordered a margarita and stared up at the Sports Channel behind the bar, where a baseball player was being interviewed while unrelated captions unreeled beneath his image.

The man swivelled around, bored. He didn't pay Owen any mind, but when he saw Max he squinted a little.

"Max?"

Max gave him a bleary look.

"Max, is that you? Stu Quaig, Max. We worked together one time."

"Stu?" Recognition seemed to pull him from a heavy fog. "As I live and breathe, the very man. How now, good Stu?"

"I'm fine, Max. How you been?"

"Couldn't be better. My nephew, Owen. Owen, this is Stu. Freelancer I was foolish enough to hire."

They caught up on mutual friends. Whatever became of Bobo Valentine? Is Sylvester still in stir? Shame about the Pontiff.

"Max, I think we better head home now," Owen said for the tenth time.

"Nonsense, boy. Just got here." He batted Owen away like a troublesome fly and turned back to his old acquaintance. "Good man Stu, speaking of our hallowed Pontiff, peace be upon him, were you aware he had a daughter?"

"Never met the man in person," Stu said. "Don't know anything about him."

"He had a babe," Max said. "One Sabrina. And that babe has

now grown up. I promised Ponti I'd look in on her now and again while he was away at Oxford."

"That's a good thing to do for a friend," Stu said.

"Good, it turns out, is not always wise. Because this baby witch, this Sabrina, this devil child in Guess jeans has made off with my score, my security, my nest egg, my rainy day fund, my little something to fall back on. The girl has rooked me. And from this moment on," Max said, raising a hand in oath, "I, Magnus Max Maxwell, do consecrate my life—or whatever frayed, splayed and gossamer threads may remain thereof—to finding the little horror."

"What are you going to do when you find her?"

"I shall do such things as will be the terror of the earth."

"You're not going to do anything to her," Owen said. "Max, please. It's time to go home. Don't listen to him," he said to Stu. "He makes shit up. He'll say anything when he's had too much to drink. Come on, Max, let's go."

"Yeah, I figured," Stu said.

"I shall be extremely sarcastic," Max said. "I shall be a verbal Subtractor. I shall attack her with cutting remarks until, writhing in guilt and shame, she hands over my swag."

Stu leaned forward and said in the quietest voice, "Let me get this right. Some girl stole your score?"

"Thou sayest true."

"The entire thing?"

"Kit and caboodle."

"Max, have you ever thought about retiring?"

"*Et tu,* Stu? I can't bear it. Sweet Jesu, such a handsome score it was, too."

"Max," Owen said, taking him by the shoulders and shaking him, "can we please get the hell out of here?"

NINETEEN

WORKING FOR ZIG WAS AN UNPREDICTABLE BUSINESS. When it paid, it paid well—fine restaurants, fancy clothes, buy yourself a cool stereo—but there were times when you'd be better off hoisting garbage cans with the sanitation department. Clem had been sitting in the car for the entire day—turning the wipers off and on, and his lumbar region going at his spine with a couple of shivs—and why? So he could keep an eye on this stupid girl. She was cute, all right—she had the kind of body Clem had never got close to without handing over hard cash. But the truth, at least as Clem put it to himself, was that this girl probably knew nothing about nothing.

In fact, when she got out of the cab, a suitcase and backpack got out with her, and she lugged them into the Ford dealership. This was not someone with a deep connection to the guys they were closing in on. But he had to sit there and wait while she examined all the Mustangs, and follow her when she took one out for a test drive. She didn't take long to make up her mind, but then he'd had to sit there with his back screaming at him while she dealt with the paperwork.

It didn't make sense. One minute she's living in a trailer with a couple of thieves, the next she seems to have moved out and she's buying a car. How does that work? Part of him wanted to pose this question to Zig, but Zig was in a pissy mood and Clem didn't feel like putting up with it. While he was chewing this over, something interesting finally happened. The girl's still inside finalizing her car when a beefy guy in a forest green Chevy Blazer pulls up right behind Clem and kills the motor but doesn't get out of the car. He sits there staring across the street at the dealership as if he's going to eat it.

It was the same guy he'd seen coming out of that broad's driveway, same Chevy Blazer. So why is he sitting here watching her go car-shopping? Maybe he's related to her in some way, a rich uncle. But if that's the case, why is he just sitting there watching? Or maybe he's got a jones on for the girl and he doesn't want the wife to know. But if that's the case, how did he know to find her at this dealership? He hadn't been following her; Clem would have seen him.

Clem didn't like having him right behind, so he got out of the car as if he'd just arrived and bought himself some time on the meter, put the ticket on the dash, and went for a little walk. Nevada plates on the Blazer, he noticed, and kept walking. Had he followed her here all the way from Vegas?

Clem went into a convenience store and checked out the magazines, keeping an eye on the guy and the dealership. He bought the latest *Woodworking* to read in the car.

When he came out, the guy was gone. Ten minutes later the girl came out. She put her backpack into the trunk, and Clem had to admit, watching her bend over, that she was one hot babe.

"I am so fucking sick," he said under his breath, "of beautiful women."

The salesman was looking happy as hell, trundling her suitcase. He hoisted it into the trunk, they shook hands, and she zipped right out of the lot.

Clem followed her out to Highway 80, and was wondering just how far he was supposed to stay on her tail when she pulled into the first motel that came up, a Red Roof Inn. Man, parts of Texas were about as ugly as a place could get. The glass towers of Dallas glinted in the background, but right here there wasn't anything in sight that wasn't concrete or cinder block, including this Podunk hotel.

Clem parked at a gas station across the street, pretending to be having pressure trouble with his tires, keeping an eye on the motel for half an hour, forty-five minutes. He thought of calling Zig to ask how long he expected him to watch this girl, when who should turn up again but the beefy guy in his forest green Blazer.

He swung into the parking lot and drove dead slow past the room with the fire-engine red Mustang out front. He stopped just for a moment, then swung back out on the highway the way he had come. This put Clem in a tough spot: should he stick with the girl or follow the guy? If the guy was a cop, Zig would want to know about that.

"Time to make a decision, Clem," he said to himself. It wasn't as if he was just a lackey. A man had the right to use his own judgment once in a while, even at the risk of sending Zig into a rage. The girl looked to be settling down for the night, and Mr. Beef could mean real trouble.

"Hell with this bitch," he said. He tore out of the gas station lot and caught up to the green Blazer, careful to keep a car or two in between. He stayed on the guy all the way into Dallas, right downtown to the Hyatt Regency Hotel.

When Stu got to the Motel 6, Zig was waiting for him. Roscoe was handcuffed once again to the bathroom sink. Well, they could let the guy go now; they wouldn't be needing him anymore.

"Where you been?" Zig said. "I'm starving. Sitting here listening to the *Jeopardy* meister in there." He slipped his shoes on and started tying the laces.

"Wait'll you hear," Stu said. "I got some real interesting news."

"Fine. Let's go eat. There's an A&W down the road. I got a sudden yearning for a root beer."

"Great idea," Stu said. "A little root beer sounds good about now." Thinking, *Root beer?*

A voice called from the bathroom: "Hey, bring me something back too, okay? No onions."

"She ripped off the whole thing?" Zig said, wiping mustard off his mouth. They were sitting at a table in the A&W. Place was pretty deserted this time of night. "This girl totally wiped him out?"

"Totally."

"Man, that guy should retire."

"Exactly what I said," Stu said.

"You sure he wasn't playing you?"

"No way."

"Because if Max figured out you were following him, he coulda invented this whole scenario just to put us off the scent. He's old, but he's no idiot."

Stu took a slug of root beer. It was a lot sweeter than he remembered it. "No way, boss. He was completely hammered, crying in his beer. Had the kid with him, and the kid was smart enough to try and shut him up, but he wouldn't listen. Poor bastard's got no clue where the girl is."

"Yeah, but we do," Zig said, and pulled out his cellphone. "Lemme call Clem."

Before he could dial, the phone rang in his hand.

"We're at the A&W just down from the motel," Zig said into the phone. "Where the fuck are you?" He shook his head, listening. "Tell me you haven't lost the girl."

Stu watched the corners of Zig's mouth turn white.

"Well, that's just great, Clem. Nice one . . . I don't give a shit. Come to the fucking A&W." Zig put the phone back in his pocket. "I don't believe it. Asshole lost the girl."

"We'll find her again," Stu said. "Let's see what he has to say."

Clem came in a few minutes later and ordered a burger from the counter. He brought it over to the table, in a surprisingly good mood considering the shit he was in with Zig. Zig hadn't said a word since the phone call, replying to Stu's attempts to cheer him up with grunts and sneers.

"There's something weird going on with this chick," Clem said as he sat down with a burger and a Coke the size of a bucket.

"Exactly," Zig said. "So why the fuck aren't you on her tail like I told you?"

"I hadda make a choice," Clem said, taking a huge bite out of his burger. His words came out garbled and smelling of dill. "There's some guy following her. Big guy in a green Chevy Blazer."

"Really?" Zig said. "Green, huh. That's fascinating."

"No, listen. She leaves the trailer park in a cab, no one following her except me. I tail her to some dame's place in a fancy neighbourhood: wraparound porch, driveway a mile long—you know those kinds of places? Anyways, I tail them while they shop in practically every store in Dallas. I tail them back to the fucking mansion. Couple of minutes later, this guy rolls into the driveway in the green Chev. I didn't think anything of it at the time—figured he's married to the older dame, big deal.

"Okay. Cab arrives and picks up the girl. I follow her to the trailer park, then to a Ford dealership. By now I'm thinking no way she's connected to Max and the kid, 'cause she's got her suitcases with her and she's buying a car. Then this guy pulls up behind me and he's watching her. There's no other customers in the dealership. Same big guy, same green Blazer—Nevada plates, too, I notice."

"So what?" Zig said. "What do we care where he's from?"

"Lemme finish." Clem took a chomp out of his burger, sucked some Coke from his straw, and chewed his way through the story. "Guy drives away, right? I wouldn't have thought anything of it, except for what happened later. Chick buys a bright red Mustang. I follow her. She drives outta town, not far, and checks in at the Red Roof out on 80. Ugliest part of Dallas you ever saw."

"Yeah, yeah. Just tell the fucking story."

"So I'm parked in the gas station across the highway, I'm wondering how long I'm gonna be sitting there, when the guy shows up again. Third time."

"The guy in the Blazer?" Stu said.

"Same guy." Clem nodded, wiping his mouth. "So, way I figure it, I got two choices: stick with the girl, or follow this guy and find out who the fuck he is."

"What do I care who he is?" Zig said.

"He could be a cop," Stu pointed out. "Or he could be working with Max, maybe. Somebody we missed."

"I don't think so," Clem said. "I followed him to the Hyatt Regency. Room 3114. I don't think any cop is gonna be staying at the Hyatt Regency while he's on the job."

"And the girl's still at the Red Roof?"

"Okay." Here Clem swallowed a huge bolus of burger and washed it down. "There we got a problem. I went straight back from the Hyatt, but when I get to the Red Roof the Mustang's gone."

"That doesn't mean she checked out," Stu said.

"I went into the office, asked around. I made it look like I just had the hots for the chick. Not hard to believe. Guy behind the counter gives me a smirk and says, 'You're too late, pal. She checked out.'"

"You lost her," Zig said, very quiet.

"Well, yeah, but who the fuck expects her to check into a motel and check out an hour later? I mean, what is that about?"

"Maybe she saw the Blazer guy," Stu said. "Recognized his car and got spooked."

"Whatever," Clem said. "Anyways, why's it such a problem? It's Max and the kid we care about, right?"

"As it turns out," Zig said, "we care about the girl. Deeply. Why don't we finish this conversation in the car, I'm a little sick of these A&W colours."

The three of them headed out to Zig's car, Clem still clutching his gigantic Coke, and Stu with a burger wrapped in foil.

"Christ," Zig said. "I can't believe you bought a burger for Mister Wizard."

"Guy hasn't eaten all day. Don't see why he should starve."

"Hate to see food go to waste, though," Zig said. "We ain't gonna be needing him anymore."

Clem got in the back seat. "So why are we interested in the girl all of a sudden?"

"Because she's got the score," Zig said, still very quiet. "She ripped off the old man."

Clem let the straw drop out of his mouth. Coke descended slowly down the tube.

"You're shitting me."

Zig eased his automatic out of his jacket. "Why, no, Clem, I'm not."

"Maybe it's not so bad, boss," Stu put in, eyeing the gun. "This Blazer guy seems to know exactly where the chick is all the time. He's right on her. We should have a talk with him."

"Did I ask your opinion?"

"No, just let's think this through."

"I already have."

Zig turned, and the noise in the confined space of the car was deafening. The bullet went through Clem's Coke, exploding it, and into his chest. He slumped to one side, and Zig put another one into his head.

"Jesus Christ," Stu said. "The fuck you doing, boss?"

"You want some too? Is that it?" Zig pressed the automatic into his rib cage.

"No, I'm just a little fucking nonplussed is all."

"I knew I should've never worked with a loser like that. The fucker." Zig put his gun away.

"Great, boss. Now what do we do with him?"

"Them, not him. You're gonna take the *Jeopardy* genius over to that goddamn construction site we saw under the expressway and have him dig a grave. And make sure it's big enough for two. They'll lay that expressway over them and no one'll ever know they're down there in Hoffatown."

Owen got Max back to the Rocket and left him crashed out on the bed. He lay on his own bunk, trying to read *The Magus,* but he couldn't stop thinking about Sabrina. He wasn't angry so much as bewildered. Bewildered? That did not seem the right word for the pain that was hovering inside his chest just now.

Max woke up a short time later, groaning theatrically and massaging his temples. He continued his lamentations over a pot of tea in the dining alcove. Owen was about to turn the light out when Max pounded a meaty fist on the table. "Of course!" he bellowed. "The very man."

"Max," Owen said, "it's time to go to sleep."

Max slapped the table smartly with both hands. "All those hotels we talked to, all those desk clerks, not one of them remarked, 'Isn't that funny? Someone else was asking after this girl just two hours ago.' Not one of them said that."

"Why would they?"

"Out of surprise, if nothing else. And when I asked each one, flat out, if anyone else had been asking after her, not one of them said yes. Not one of them even blinked or looked the slightest bit nervous about the question."

"And you find this astonishing because . . ."

"Because of Bill. Preacher Bill, aside from being an intellectually challenged Jesus freak, is obsessed with that thieving, ungrateful siren. Pathologically obsessed, according both to she who must not be named and to sober observation. He followed her to Tucson. He followed her to Dallas. He showed up at her aunt's. So my question is, why isn't Bill looking for her now?"

"He probably is."

"Then why isn't he asking around about her? Why isn't Bill, born stalker and monomaniac, lurking in hotel lobbies? Why isn't he howling outside our door? I'll tell you why—because he already knows where she is."

"I don't know, Max. He doesn't seem all that smart to me."

"I warrant you, sir"—Max flapped his hands against the table in a series of tiny slaps—"Billy Bob Bonehead knows exactly where the tigress hides."

The one named Stu hadn't driven very far when he pulled over into a parking lot. From what Roscoe had seen so far, Stu was the comparatively sane one of the three, but he was agitated now—sweating heavily, cursing every other car, and driving off the shoulder and back on, over the white line and back, though the car didn't smell of alcohol. And now they were sitting in the parking lot of an insurance company, closed at this hour. There were no other cars in the lot. It was raining again, and Roscoe wondered if this would be the last time he would hear that sound, fat drops exploding on metal.

"Okay," Stu said, "I'm gonna let you eat your burger now."

"My hands are cuffed behind my back, Stu. Why don't you take the cuffs off for a second—or at least put 'em in front?"

"No way. I'll feed it to you."

He unwrapped the foil from the burger, and the smell of fried meat billowed through the car. He held the burger in front of Roscoe's face, and Roscoe took a big bite. These guys hadn't been too regular about feeding him, so it was definitely the finest burger of his life. This was a good sign, wasn't it? They wouldn't buy him a burger if they were planning to kill him, right?

"You want some root beer? I got you a root beer."

"Root beer. Sure. What's going on, Stu?"

Stu didn't answer. He held out the paper cup and straw, and Roscoe took a long sip. The ice had melted, making the root beer watery, but it tasted as good to him as champagne. For the next few minutes Roscoe couldn't do anything but eat and drink.

"Man," he said when it was done, "I give that burger a ten out of ten. Thank you."

"Sit back now."

Stu started the car again and pulled out into the traffic.

"Where we going, Stu?"

"I told you. The train station. Ship you home."

"You're going the wrong way. I've been to Dallas before. I know where the train station is."

"We're going to the suburban one. Less crowded."

"Uh-huh. Stu, are you aware there is root beer all over your back seat? Blood, too. Looks like someone had a hell of an accident back here."

"That's right. Someone had a hell of an accident."

They passed turnoffs for Plano and Rockwall. Roscoe hitched forward a little on the seat.

"Where's Clem, Stu?"

"Who knows? Took the day off."

"Took the day off, huh? He know people in Dallas?"

"Search me. I don't know Clem that well."

"No? You seemed to get along pretty good. I figured you two for—well, not old buddies exactly—but long-time colleagues, so to speak."

"We've known each other awhile."

"So would this be Clem's blood on the back seat here?"

"Stop talking."

They drove another ten minutes, then Stu exited onto a boulevard that ran under an expressway. It was down to one lane owing to construction. He veered around a ROAD CLOSED sign and pulled off onto an undeveloped area that was just scrub grass and sandy soil. He switched off the car, and there was only the clatter and hiss of the expressway overhead.

Stu got out and took a shovel out of the trunk. He opened the back door. "Okay, Jeopardy. Now we dig."

"You expect me to dig my own grave?"

"Don't panic. It's not for you."

"Why am I here, if it's not for me? What happened to the train station?"

"It's not for you, I said. It's for Clem."

"Uh-huh. Zig killed him?"

"Just get out and start digging."

"Start digging or you'll what? Frankly, Stu, I don't see a lot of downside if I just sit right here in this car. What're you gonna do, shoot me?"

Stu looked off in the distance and sighed. "I knew you were gonna say something like that." He folded his arms and looked up at the sky—or where the sky would have been if they weren't underneath an expressway. The overhead traffic sounded like a waterfall.

"Anyway, how am I supposed to dig with my hands cuffed behind my back?"

"I'll cuff 'em in front."

"And then I come at you with the shovel. Bash you over the head."

"And I shoot you. Okay, fine. You're right. That doesn't work either." Stu leaned on the shovel, thinking. "I could shoot you in the balls."

"You think that's going to improve my digging? Anyway, I don't think you're like that. It was Zig and Clem took my toes. No, no. You want a grave dug, pal, you're gonna dig it yourself. I'll just sit right here and watch."

"Fuck," Stu said. He flung his jacket into the car and started digging. Even though the expressway afforded some protection, a stiff wind had come up and was blowing rain all over him, though not enough to soften the ground. He soon started cursing.

"So what'd he kill him for?"

"Who you talking about?"

"Why'd Zig kill Clem?"

"You said that. I never said he did."

"You said the grave was for Clem. Why'd he kill him?"

"Because Clem did something he shouldn't have. Zig doesn't like people who don't listen."

"So what'd Clem do that he shouldn't have?"

"What do you care?"

"I don't—but you should. You're the one gotta work with the guy. What'd Clem do that got him the death sentence?"

"He was supposed to keep an eye on a certain party, and he didn't do it." Stu's words came out between jabs of his shovel. "And now we don't know where that party happens to be. I recognize it may seem like an overreaction."

"Oh, no, Stu. Anybody'd do the same."

"I admit Zig can be unreasonable."

"Well, here's a question for you—not trivial, for once. Here's a guy shoots someone he works with for making a mistake. And here's you. You saw him do it. What possible reason could Zig have for letting you live?"

"He respects me. He didn't respect Clem."

"Uh-huh. It seems pretty clear you don't need me anymore. Which means you know where Max's score is, or you know who knows. Are you betting your personal well-being on the notion that Zig can't wait to share that money with you?"

"I know what you're trying to do. You're trying to sweet-talk me."

"Yes, I am. But that doesn't make what I say any less true."

"So you think I should let you go. On the possibility that Zig's gonna kill me."

"More than a possibility, Stu. Stop digging, for God's sake. You and I have been around the block. We know how people work.

Right away I figured you three guys out. You tell me if I'm wrong. There's you: tough guy, get-ahead guy, but not a berserker, not a thug. Right?"

"Pretty much."

"Then there's Clem. Not the smartest guy in the world. A follower. Kinda scared. He'll do stuff he knows is wrong, real wrong, if it keeps him in good with the boss. Might even kill, if push comes to shove. Right?"

"Yeah, I'd say that pretty much covers Clem."

"And Zig. Zig is a fucking psycho. Zig does not care how far he has to go to get what he wants. Knew it the minute you guys grabbed me. There's no connecting with that guy. He's missing whatever it is makes one human being recognize another. That's why he formed the Subtractors. That's why he works this way."

"Subtractors?" Stu laughed and started digging again. "That's a good one. You thought we were the goddamn Subtractors?"

"I can't imagine what gave me that idea."

"We're not the Subtractors. The Subtractors are just a legend, man. The Subtractors are just a scary story."

"Tell that to my fucking feet, Stu."

"Naw, Zig just liked the legend, that's all. Everybody's heard about this mythical gang—why not live off their reputation? Act like you're this invincible force of darkness, who's to know?"

"So if you're not the Subtractors, what's the deal with Zig's nipples? Being chained up in a bathroom, I got to see more than I wanted."

"Word is, he was in D block at Sing Sing. He was in a beef, owed a lot of dough, and he was gonna get hit. So he did it to himself to get transferred."

"Like I say—a guy who'll do anything. So, if you think he's going to let you live after all this, you're out of your mind."

Stu's shovel clanked against rock. "Fuck."

"You beginning to see my way of thinking?"

"No, no. I'm just hitting bedrock here." Stu's face was glistening with sweat. He was about two feet down. "What's in it for me if I let you go? What am I supposed to do for work? Guy's gotta make a living."

"I don't know. I could put a word in with Max. If he knows you saved my ass, he might do something for you."

"I worked with Max one time. He was good for a laugh, but he's past it, man. Way past it." Stu had to rest on his shovel again, his face was dripping. "You think he might cut me in?"

"He doesn't even cut me and Pookie in. But you'll get some work. Max is a good guy to have on your side. Knows everybody."

"Fuck it." Stu threw down the shovel. "Okay, you convinced me. How about you help me dump Clem and then we hit the road together?"

"Deal."

"Get outta the car and I'll take off the cuffs."

Roscoe got out of the car. His feet stung where the toes were missing, and every muscle in his body ached from being chained in the bathroom for days.

"I hope I don't regret this." Stu was fumbling in his pocket for keys. He found the right one, dropped it.

"Hurry up, man. I think I saw a car pull in over there."

"Over where? I don't see anything."

"Under the cloverleaf. I could be wrong."

Stu found the key and undid first the leg bracelets, then the handcuffs.

A pair of headlights rolled up to them and went out.

"Fuck, it's Zig," Stu said. "Let's beat it."

They got into the car, but before they could move, the headlights came on again and Zig swerved in front. Stu threw it into reverse, spitting dirt as they jerked backward. A bullet slammed into metal.

Their own headlights were on now, and they could see Zig standing in the glare like a scarecrow, gun hand pointing.

Stu spun the wheel so that the passenger side was between him and Zig.

"Fuck, man," Roscoe said, ducking down.

"It's the only way back to the—"

The glass above Roscoe's shoulder shattered and Stu slumped sideways, a black hole in his temple. Zig was coming toward them, a black shadow in the cones of light.

Roscoe climbed over Stu and pulled up the seat release, pushing the driver's seat all the way back. That left just enough room to sit on top of Stu and still reach the controls, even if his head was pressed up against the roof. He put it in drive and floored it.

Another shot hit the rear door.

As the car clattered onto the access lane, he could just see Zig climbing back into his car.

"You all right?" he said over and over again to Stu, but he already knew the answer.

TWENTY

"Oh, Jesus, son of the Father, light of my life, please, if I am worthy, send Sabrina back to me. Help me to win her back, for I know I can do everything through Him that gives me strength."

Bill Bullard was on his knees before a round glass table in the corner of his Hyatt Regency living room. This time it was the honeymoon suite. Bill took one of the miniature Jack Daniel's he had set out on the table, cracked it open, and drained it in one go.

"Heavenly Father, through whom and in whom all things begin and end, I thank you for helping me to find the woman of my life. And now I pray that you help me, a sinner—oh, I know I am not worthy—to help her."

He checked the laptop that was open beside the minis. He clicked Update and the onscreen map shifted slightly, showing a squat red arrow on US 80 about one hundred miles east. She must have checked out of that Red Roof pretty early.

"Now, Lord, I ask you to grant unto Sabrina the perception to see into my soul and recognize that my life is consecrated to her, second only to You, almighty Lord. Let her see that she is enthroned in my heart in a place inviolable."

He opened another JD and drained it.

"Lord of the Covenant, if that is asking too much, or if you feel I must be further tested, I beseech that you vouchsafe unto me the strength, the wisdom and the tenderness to win her heart. I hope and pray with your help to win her back, not just for me but for You, that I may set her feet once more upon the path of righteousness."

There was no more Jack Daniel's. He opened a Rémy this time, sucked a little out of it, and made a face.

"Oh, and please don't let me hit her anymore. Grant me the strength to keep my temper. I mean, except in the most egregious cases."

There was a knock on his door. He got up and opened it to a man in a blue suit, white shirt, red tie, holding up an ID card.

"William Bullard?" Zig said. He'd conned the name out of the front desk, using the room number. "My name's Zigler. I'm a state-licensed investigator. Would you mind if I ask you a few questions?"

Bill looked closer at the license. Nevada. It appeared to be genuine, but you could buy anything fake these days.

"Questions about what?"

"May I come in? I won't take up much of your time. My car's out front begging for a ticket."

Bill let him in and shut the door. He sat down in a chair near the balcony and motioned for Zig to do the same. Zig looked around, taking his time the way a real PI might. The suite was impressive— couch and chairs, huge desk, flat-screen TV, and that was just the living room. This Bullard character must have some dough.

Before Zig could ask his first question, the guy pointed a finger at him. "You musta had to be a cop before you became a PI. Where were you on the job? Vegas?"

"Santa Barbara."

"Yeah? Who'd you work with?"

"Mr. Bullard, are you on intimate terms with the staff of the Santa Barbara police service?"

"No."

"Then maybe you could just let me ask my questions."

Bullard sat back with a smile. "Fire away."

"I'll get right to the point. I'm working for a client who needs to get something of his returned. Something precious that was taken from him."

"Blackmail, you mean."

"I'm not at liberty to say." Zig cleared his throat. His only contact with private investigators was through the movies. He didn't have a clue how they might act or what they might say in real life.

"In the course of our investigation, my associates and I keep running into you and your green Chevy Blazer, and frankly we're wondering what your interest in this case might be."

"Case? I'm not involved in any case. I just happen to be looking for something myself. Some*one*. You used the word precious. Well, this person is very precious to me."

Zig smiled. "I can understand that, Mr. Bullard. She's very beautiful."

"Yes, she is."

"Judging by the way you're keeping tabs on her, you probably know she's been staying with one Max Maxwell and an individual who may or may not be his nephew, called Owen."

"I'm aware of that," Bullard said. "I didn't know their names. That who you're interested in?"

"Very." Zig sat forward and spoke in a low voice. "May I tell you something in confidence?" He was happy with that *may*. Never used the word himself, but a private investigator would for sure.

Bullard shrugged. "Knock yourself out."

"These men are professional thieves."

"Uh-huh. Why you telling me?"

"I'm trying to be helpful to you. Because I'm hoping you'll be helpful to me. I need to interview the young lady in question. I believe she has information crucial to my case." *Crucial*. Another good word.

"I doubt very much that Sabrina knows anything about their business. She only met these yahoos a couple of days ago."

"You know she's been staying with them? And where?"

"A trailer park," Bullard said.

Zig laughed. "I have to say, Mr. Bullard, you're outclassing us on every level. You must be on the job yourself. How did you know about the trailer park?"

"You oughta try praying now and again, Mr. Zigler. You'd learn a lot of things."

"No, really, I have a professional interest here."

"I just pray for insight. You should try it."

"Do you have any reason to think she might be coming back to you? Have you talked to her?"

Bullard shook his head. "She doesn't answer her cellphone. She'll come back, though. I've prayed on it, and I believe with the Lord's help I can persuade her."

"I see. You prayed on it."

Bullard just shook his head again, slowly this time, as if in pity, as if there were secrets too deep for the likes of Zig to fathom. His cellphone rang and he peered at the tiny screen before answering.

Zig stood up and mouthed the word "washroom." Bullard pointed.

"Who'm I talking to?" Bill said, stepping out onto the balcony to take the call. It was sunny now, but humid from yesterday's rain. The screen on his cell said *Sabrina*.

"You can call me Owen."

"You're using Sabrina's phone. Put her on."

"She isn't here. She left the phone behind."

"Don't bullshit me, boy. Sabrina wouldn't do that."

"Okay, you're right. I took it from her. I didn't want her calling you."

Bill looked over toward the washroom. He did not trust this so-called PI, not by a long shot.

"Are you who I think you are, boy?" he said into the phone.

"We met the other night in Vegas. You beat me up in a parking lot."

"You're the kid tried to interfere?"

"It was nothing personal. I just wanted you to stop hitting her."

"You got spunk, kid, I'll say that for you. Short on common sense, though. Tell me something, boy."

"What's that?"

"What did I get clocked with that night, a baseball bat? I woke up with one hell of a headache."

"Parking meter."

"Parking meter. There ain't no parking meters left in Las Vegas."

"They were taking them out, I guess. There was a whole bunch stacked up at the edge of the lot."

"That a fact. Well, I give you credit for resourcefulness." Bill glanced through the reflected Dallas skyline toward the washroom door. "I got company right now, why don't you state your business?"

"I have something for you from Sabrina."

"What would that be?"

"I don't know. I didn't open it. Kind of a fat envelope."

"Sabrina's got my number. Address, too. Why would she give you something to give me, that being the case?"

"Look, I'm doing you a favour. I didn't have to call."

"Why'd she give it to you, boy? Answer the question."

"I don't know. I don't know why she does anything she does. She's a confusing person."

"That's a understatement right there, is what that is." Bill raised a boot toward a pigeon that was sidling along the balcony railing. It flapped away. "But it still don't answer why she give it to you."

"Obviously, she doesn't want to see you in person."

"Obviously. Is that your word?"

"Anyway, she didn't give it to me, exactly. She took off in the middle of the night and she left two envelopes on the table— one for me, one for you."

"And what was in yours, boy?"

"A kind of apology, I guess you could say. For taking off without saying goodbye. But yours is fatter. Could be money in it, I don't know. Maybe photographs. Says Urgent on it. You want me to open it?"

"No, I do not."

"Okay, fine. Just give me an address, I'll drop it in a mailbox. Wish I'd never met either of you."

Bill chuckled. "Burned your ass good, did she?"

"Fuck you."

"Okay, kid, where you at right now, you in Dallas?"

"Yeah, but I'm leaving in about forty-five minutes."

"Fine. Bring it to me over at the Hyatt Regency. Room 3114. Keep in mind, if you try any funny stuff, you will pay the price."

The shower had one of those expensive rainforest heads, and there was a basket full of soaps and shampoos. Big soaps. There was a bidet, and a sparkling marble floor. Yes, it looked like Mr. Bullard earned himself a good dollar.

When he came back out, Bullard was still on his cell out on the balcony.

Zig took a gander at the other room. King-size bed with a big fluffy duvet, another flat-panel TV, must have been fifty inches, and hotel robe and slippers. The Gideon Bible was open on the bedside table. Did anyone actually read those things?

An eight-by-ten picture lay on the bed, a hot-looking girl in tank top and jeans. Zig recognized her from Clem's description— green eyes, dark hair, kind of a fuck-you expression on her face. He could see why this guy was obsessed with her. Body like that, yes sir, Zig could definitely work up an interest quite aside from the financial. He was equipped for all kinds of eventualities.

No female stuff anywhere in the room. No way she was staying here. So, if Bill knew where the hell this Sabrina was, where the hell was she?

Zig went back to the other room. He examined the round table where a white laptop was open, the screen dark. Zig glanced over at the balcony and casually pressed a key. The screen lit up with a map. He bent to look closer.

"What the hell you think you're doing?" Bullard said.

Zig grinned. "I see the Lord has opened his own website here, Mr. Bullard. 'Find My Girlfriend dot com,' is that what it's called? Let's see, what's this do?"

He hit Update. The map shifted and the red arrow took a step east on 80.

"Get away from there," Bill said. "I'm not joking now."

"Okay, okay, I'm cool." Zig backed away from the laptop, hands raised in the air. "Nice to see you and the Lord communicating by cyberspace."

"The Lord communicates through whatever media He pleases. Now tell me—you ain't no private investigator, so why you so all-fired interested in where Sabrina is at?"

"I told you, I need to ask her some questions. Beyond that, I'm not at liberty to say."

"Bullshit."

"Tell me something, Bullard. You're a religious man. You imagine you're a good influence on that girl?"

"I know I am. Sabrina suffered a godless upbringing. I'm doing my best to rectify that."

"I see. You think you're straightening her out?"

"Yessir. I have opened her heart on several issues. But there is none so blind as he who will not see, and she is still resistant in many ways."

"You advise her on the Ten Commandments? 'Thou shalt not steal' and so on?"

"I prefer to focus on the positive. The benefits of prayer and good works."

"Because it seems like she doesn't get the part about not stealing."

"What're you talking about, peckerwood?"

"It seems your little sweetheart ripped off Mr. Maxwell and his nephew. Relieved him of every last cent."

Bullard took a step forward, a manoeuvre that seemed to double his size. "You're lying to me."

"I swear." Zig raised a hand. "Hand me that bible and I'll swear all over it that she ripped them off. My associates saw them crying in their beer about it, and they don't have a clue where she is."

"And you want to get your hands on what she took, that it?"

"I didn't say that."

Bill drew his thirty-eight, ugly little black thing poking out of his fist. "You ain't going near Sabrina. I won't abide it."

"Okay, okay. Take it easy, Mr. Bullard."

"I will see you dead before I let you go near that girl."

"The way I hear it, it isn't me you have to worry about, it's that Maxwell kid. Last we saw, she couldn't keep her hands off him."

This was pure invention, and Zig realized immediately that he had overplayed. Bullard swayed as if he had been struck. He fired blind, catching Zig in his left arm.

Zig spun and fell. He rolled over and at the same time pulled out his own automatic. He fired up at Bullard and a spot appeared on his cheekbone about the size of a red dime.

TWENTY-ONE

SABRINA WAS ZOOMING ALONG A SCENIC ROUTE east across the southern United States. The CD player was going full blast with the Coldplay live album she had picked up at the Dallas HMV, the wind was whipping her hair into a full Medusa, and she was singing her lungs out. She'd checked out of the Red Roof about ten minutes after she'd spotted Bill's Blazer and spent a restless night at the Terrell Day's Inn, wondering how the hell he'd tracked her down.

She was pretty sure she'd lost him now; the rearview showed nothing but the Home Depot semi she'd just zipped by. And what could beat this? Swipe the swag and blast off, hit the highway running and no one telling you what to do. So here she was, in a microscopic denim skirt, a white tank, and a nifty pair of Calvin Klein sunglasses, having fun, thank you very much.

Or trying to. There were a couple of things she was trying hard not to think about. Her father, for one. As soon as she had got behind the wheel of this racy little car, she had had a change of heart. El Paso was 600 miles back the way they had come, and no one would be expecting her to go there, so she had phoned the hospice to make sure he would be able to receive a visitor. We've been trying to reach you, they told her. Your father died yesterday.

Which was why she was now taking the scenic route in the other direction. In a way, this little escapade was an homage to the old bastard. During the few times he was home and paying attention to her, Sabrina's father had taught her that theft could be a reasonable way to make a living, provided you boosted only those things that offered a good rate of return. It made no sense to risk jail time for paltry sums. If, on the other hand, you were looking at, say, buying a car, financing your education, or even just upgrading to a more comfortable lifestyle, well, that might be a risk worth taking.

She had hardened her heart to him over the years; her mother's suicide had done that. But she was discovering that death cancelled all debts, and already she was wishing she had not been so cold to him. It wasn't anger she was going to carry from now on, it was regret.

Even before she had learned of his death, her attitude had begun to change. It was being in the Rocket with Max that had done that. Seeing the frailty of old age, the foolishness. How could you stay angry at that?

Which brought her to the other thing she didn't want to think about. Owen.

Max and Owen entered suite 3114 and placed their sombreros on the table. You couldn't beat a Club Med sombrero for thwarting security cameras. Still, their entry had been delayed owing to the fact that Bill had not answered their knock and they were forced to seek out a chambermaid and stage an elaborate distraction. This involved Owen's pitching forward, throwing a series of baroque spasms across the hotel corridor, and foaming at the mouth. In the course of the chambermaid's panicked efforts to help, Max had relieved her of her pass-key. Then they had retrieved the sombreros from the stairwell where they had stashed them and come back.

"Hotel security," Max said, looking around. "Perhaps I missed my calling."

"What if he just stepped out for a few minutes?" Owen said. "If he comes back, he's going to go crazy, and I really can't face fighting that guy again."

Max put on a pair of gloves and opened the door. "Anybody home?" he called.

"Somebody is," Owen said, pointing.

A pair of feet stuck out from behind an armchair near the balcony. Owen crossed the room to take a closer look. "Jesus. It's Bill. He's been shot."

Max bent down and felt the man's neck. "Still warm," he said. "But definitely dead, poor sod."

"Come on, Max, let's go. We do not want to be explaining what we're doing in a hotel room with a dead guy."

"Eschew panic, lad. Panic is the mother of error. It would seem whoever aerated old Bill did not escape without a scratch." Max pointed to the smear of blood on the table, and another on the far wall.

"There's blood all the way over here," Max said, following the trail into the bathroom. "Lav's full too. He must've come in here for a towel to wrap himself up with. Shirt's on the floor, shot in the arm. He must've appropriated one of Preacher Bill's shirts after he patched himself up."

"Max, please. I'm feeling sick."

"In a minute, lad, in a minute. Cogitation is required. If I'm right that Bill here knew where the thieving Sabrina hides, there should be some indication in this room."

"Well, he's in security. He used to be a cop. He may have all kinds of ways of tracking people."

"True, lad. True."

Owen looked again at the bloodstained table. "There was a computer plugged in here—an Apple. You can tell by the cord."

"No doubt our wounded killer made off with it. A junkie looking for a quick sale? Unlikely. Perhaps someone who wanted information off the computer? Are there any other electronic devices about the place? A security man is likely to own many."

Owen took a quick look in the bedroom and came back. "Nothing but Gideon's Bible. Max, what are you doing?"

Max pulled his hand out of Bill's pocket, carefully holding a wallet by its edges. "I have established that the motive was not robbery. Several hundred dollars here."

"Max, I don't want to make money off murder."

"A noble sentiment, my boy. Then again, we didn't commit the murder. We discovered him pre-murdered."

"Max, put it back."

"Why? I can't see him needing it—the afterlife is almost certainly a cashless society. In any case, this is far too nice a point of ethics to determine just now. I'll just hang on to this, and weigh the matter at such a time and place as may seem conducive to fine distinctions."

He put the wallet, slimmer now, back into Bill's pocket and reached into another. This time he extracted a tiny phone. "Examine this, would you, boy? Electronics confound me."

Owen took it from him, a cherry red iPhone. "Top of the line," Owen said. "Wireless Internet, digital video, MP3 player, the works."

"Could one use it for actual communication?"

"What are you looking for, Max?"

"Well, let's discover who called him recently, shall we?"

Owen thumbed a few buttons until he found the right combination. "Sabrina! Oh, wait, that's me. I used her phone because it had Bill's number on speed-dial. Let's see what he's got on here . . ." Owen played with the buttons and squinted at the tiny screen. "Actually not much. Someone named Maria. That could be anyone—mistress, cleaning lady, hooker, who knows? Then he's got Office one, Office two, Office three. Then Sabrina—same number we have. And then he's got something called Star Trak."

"*Star Trek?*"

"Star Trak. T-R-A-K."

"What is a Star Trak when it's at home?"

Owen hit the button. The little screen lit up with the Star Trak logo.

"I've got their home page. It's probably going to want a password . . . No, wait, he's got it set to remember his password for
twenty-four hours." He clicked another button. "It's like MapQuest
or something. For finding directions. No, wait, it's a GPS outfit.
Max, you were right! He's been tracking her on GPS. He must
have put a unit in her suitcase."

"How absolutely diabolical," Max said with admiration.

"It's pointing to US 80. See, he probably had this screen open
on his computer and now the other guy's got it."

"Not a moment to lose, then. Exeunt all, in sombreros."

TWENTY-TWO

OWEN AND MAX had left the Rocket in the trailer park and were now barrelling along US 80 in the Taurus, the iPhone clutched in Owen's fist. The GPS readout didn't tell them Sabrina's speed, but she wasn't wasting any time.

She seemed to be choosing her route at random, sometimes sticking to the scenic highway, other times bounding onto the interstate. They tracked her across Louisiana, through two hundred miles of woody hills and Biblical injunctions. *Caution: Jesus has you on his radar,* one warned. *Are you ready for the Rapture?* inquired another. And Max's favourite: *How about a little (make that eternal) swim in a lake of fire?* The towns alternated between industrial wastelands and hamlets so microscopic they weren't on any maps.

They passed the boarded-up storefronts of Shreveport, and Max howled when they had to forgo the Riverboat Casino, which was not in fact a riverboat but a four-storey structure built to look like one.

"Are we closing in on her, boy? How are we doing?"

Owen checked the iPhone again. The tiny map showed Sabrina maybe sixty miles ahead.

"We're definitely closing the gap."

They stopped for gas in Gibsland (population 1,224), which, Owen informed Max, was the town where Bonnie and Clyde had met their grisly end. He even found a stack of postcards of their bullet-riddled bodies next to a news rack displaying the latest issues of *Edged Weapons* and *Varmint Masters.*

"Thank you for sharing," Max said when Owen handed him one of the postcards.

"Criminal history's our theme this year, Max. I don't see why that should change."

Bonnie and Clyde were nothing like the movie, Owen added when they were back in the car. "They killed a lot of people and didn't think twice about it."

"Is that meant to make me feel better?"

"It's just a fact, Max."

"Fact me no facts, boy. You're dealing with a big-picture man."

They drove past the shotgun shacks of Monroe, and not long after that they were in Mississippi. *Only positive Mississippi spoken here,* the road signs warned them.

"Only positive criminal history spoken here," Owen said. "So I guess you'd have to say Bugsy Siegel was a pioneering hotelier and Bonnie and Clyde were excellent drivers."

"You have a sarcastic side, lad. It somewhat mars your otherwise sterling character."

They stopped to pick up coffees at a roadside diner. Across the highway, a fly-blown storefront offered evangelical services. *Serving God 24/7,* the sign informed them. *You welcome, Jews.*

Owen fiddled with the iPhone, poking at the tiny buttons until the screen changed again. "She's about forty miles east of Vicksburg. Not so far now."

Not long after, they too left Vicksburg and Jackson behind.

"She's at Hickory now," Owen said. "Heading for Chunky."

"There's a town called Chunky? Why would they call it Chunky?"

"It's where they make peanut butter."

"I sense a falsehood."

A forest sprang up out of nowhere. Thick, dark woods lined either side of the highway. Roadside shrines began to appear. One was constructed entirely out of pop bottles, another out of seashells. All were decorated with Biblical verses and attended by furtive men who modelled their wardrobe on the Unabomber's.

They paused for meal at Mr. Waffle, which amounted to a three-course dessert, sweet enough to make Owen feel ill.

"American cuisine," Max pronounced, "cannot be faulted."

Owen wasn't listening. "She's stopped. Hasn't moved for the last little while."

Max's cellphone, which was next to his coffee cup, began to vibrate and skitter across the table.

"Get that for me, boy, would you? I'm digesting." In fact, he was thoughtfully probing his teeth with a toothpick.

Owen picked up the phone. "Hello?"

A familiar voice said, "How many possible phone numbers are there in any given area code?"

"Roscoe?"

"Seven million, nine hundred and twenty thousand."

"Roscoe, where are you? What happened to you?"

Max stopped picking his teeth and reached for the phone, but Owen dodged him.

"All you need to know, kid, is that if the Subtractors didn't exist before, they do now. At least, one of them does, and he's looking for some girl who stole your stash, or so he says. Guy named Zig."

"Zig is a Subtractor?"

"Bastard owes me two toes. He's killed at least two people and probably Pookie too. I would have called sooner, but they took my cellphone and I couldn't remember Max's number. I've tried about six million of those seven million combinations."

Max grabbed for the phone again and this time Owen let him take it. He signalled for the check and put some money on the table. After what seemed like an eternity, Max hung up.

Owen was already at the door of the restaurant, holding it open. "Max, for God's sake, hurry. It's Zig—and he's probably right on her tail."

"I am hurrying, boy. Consult your astrolabe. Where is the witch?"

———

As far as Zig was concerned, you could take Mississippi and shove it down the wood chipper. He was definitely not liking what he was seeing. For one thing, the accent was way too Southern for his taste. People sounded like the kind of yahoos just itching to whip a slave. If a catfish could talk, it would sound like a Mississippian.

The girl had got quite a head start. First he'd wasted time trying to find Jeopardy Joe, and then he'd had to deal with the guy in the hotel. Zig caressed his upper left arm where Bill had shot him. It was a through-and-through, but it hurt like hell.

And then there was the heat. Absolutely disgusting weather in this state. Las Vegas, Arizona, California too, it could be climbing to ninety degrees and you'd be dry as a bone. Here, even though it was only about eighty-five, Zig's shirt was drenched in sweat.

He smacked the wheel of the Explorer and cursed it. This was his back-up vehicle. He'd had the thing custom-boosted by the best car thief he knew, got it repainted a tasteful sky blue, and now the first summer he's driving it the a/c quits on him. Last service station he'd stopped at said it wasn't a matter of the fluid, the whole unit had to be replaced, and it just made him sick. You tried to maintain a certain standard of living while at the same time buying—well, all right, stealing—American, and you end up with a piece of crap. May as well have settled for some Korean rustbucket.

Having a taste for quality, Zig knew, was a double-edged deal. He'd once shared a cell with a guy doing hard time who had studied the Eastern philosophies to help him through it. One day Zig had expressed a longing for a pitcher of margaritas and an afternoon of teenage pussy, and his cellmate—Ozzie Starr was his name—told him, "Zig, there is no greater calamity than exorbitant desire."

"Says who?"

"Says Confucius."

"Uh-huh, and look where it got the Japanese. Sleeping in drawers, and subways so packed you need a key to take the lid off."

"Confucius was Chinese."

"Even worse. Look at the pollution, the child labour. How about a little exorbitant desire for clean air? How about a little exorbitant desire for democracy?"

Ozzie was sitting on the edge of his bunk, peeling the foil off a chocolate bar he'd squirrelled away somewhere. Zig couldn't help noticing the Eastern philosophies did not apparently advocate sharing your Mars bar with your cellmate.

"Confucius wasn't talking about political systems, bro, he was talking about personal happiness. If you're going to be happy, you can't be yearning for things you got no possibility of attaining."

"What's so exorbitant about beer and pussy?"

"Look around you, bud." Ozzie had waved his Mars bar at the steel bars, the peeling grey paint, the stainless steel toilet. "You see any teenage pussy in here?"

"So, according to you, if I get a hard-on for Luther T. down wing, that's gonna make me happier."

"Absolutely. Because that is a desire that has every chance of coming true."

"So Confucius say, Happiness is a huge black dick up your ass."

"No, Zig. Happiness is a huge black dick up your ass if that's what you *want* and that's what's *available*."

Fucking Orientals. Zig wanted the good things in life, and no Buddhist, Communist, Falun Gong claptrap was going to talk him out of it. Early on in life he'd developed a taste for good whisky, two-hundred-dollar hookers, and suits that made people sit up and take notice. He liked luxury cars and sunny climates, and by his early twenties he'd understood very well that the world does not hand such things to high school dropouts—unless they happen to play mood-altering guitar or have a tricky way with a basketball.

Right now, for example, instead of seeing a lot of useless Mississippi trees, and stupid little Mississippi towns populated by more spades than he'd seen in his entire time at Sing Sing, he could have really used a couple of weeks on a beach in the Bahamas, maybe take in some deep-sea fishing out of Bimini. He would park his ass on the back of a boat, stick a Cuban cigar in his mouth, and tan himself dark as a saddle. The fish were entirely beside the point. Unfortunately, his perennial cash flow problem demanded that he chase down some little slut he didn't even know because she happened to have her hands on a set of emeralds that—according to the news reports—could practically fucking *talk.*

Another Podunk town shot by. The laptop beeped and he eyed the screen. It was flashing an icon of a battery and a lightning bolt.

"Fuck you," Zig said. "Don't you do that to me. Not now."

He hit the Okay button and the map came back. He was definitely closing in on the bitch, and he hit the gas a little harder. She was a looker, he had to admit. He had the photograph he'd swiped from Bill's room on the seat beside the computer. Green eyes you could swim in, and a smile that was, well, let's just say you can keep Saint Pete. When you die, this is what greets you at the Pearly Gates—silky wings and a smile like this girl's. So, the order of business would be: scare the living shit out of her till she hands over the emeralds, have a little fun with her, then, sadly, switch off the light before you leave.

That switch was getting increasingly easy to throw, Zig noticed. There'd been Melvin; he'd had a pang or two about Melvin, mostly because it hadn't been necessary—he'd been too impatient. The Pookie guy had been an accident; you couldn't be held responsible for other people's health problems. But he was a little surprised at himself for doing Clem—that hadn't actually been part of any plan. In fact, that had made him feel pretty bad for a couple of hours. Stu? Well, the truth was he didn't know Stu all that well, so he didn't care that much. He'd been twiddling the radio dial for news all day. There was nothing about any bodies found in Dallas, other than Bill Bullard.

That was another no-brainer: guy shoots you, you have to kill him. According to the radio, the cops were looking for a man in a blue suit and a red tie, both of which he'd dumped a couple of hundred miles ago.

An Allied moving van in front of him forced him to slow down. Zig took the opportunity to hit the Update button on the laptop.

The little red arrow was pulsing near Lost Gap, less than ten miles ahead.

"Fuck you, Allied," he said, and swung out across the solid line, flooring it. A Mazda coming the other way honked incredulously, then hit the brakes and swerved onto the gravel shoulder, fishtailing in a cloud of dust.

Zig got back into his lane and tried to keep things at a good clip without screaming to be stopped by a trooper. Last thing he wanted was a conversation with some redneck in a Smokey outfit and aviator sunglasses. He had to get this babe's shapely butt in his sights in the next few minutes or he'd lose her for good.

TWENTY-THREE

SABRINA SWITCHED THE MUSIC OFF and then there was just the wind in her ears and the thrum of the Mustang's engine. The sun was burning bright and she was getting a little concerned about skin cancer. But how can you think about skin cancer when you're having so much fun?

This *was* fun, right?

She would have been having fun if it weren't for this little ache floating around under her rib cage. She kept hearing Owen's voice, that throaty whisper when he'd said, "God, you are so beautiful."

It wasn't the first time a man had said that to her, but there was an intensity about Owen that made her just know he really meant it, that he was truly thrilled to be with her. A quarrel developed between Sabrina the Romantic and Sabrina the Free.

Sabrina the Romantic: Owen saved me from a beating and I shouldn't have swiped his stuff.

Sabrina the Free: Oh, please. He's a guy. He just wanted to get into your pants. And you shouldn't have let him.

Sabrina R.: Owen knows stuff. He likes lots of things. He's curious and funny. I liked being around him.

Sabrina F.: He's a born thief and liar, and if the circumstances had been reversed he would've done exactly the same thing to you.

Sabrina R.: He seemed like he always wanted to give me things, not take them. Besides, we have a lot in common. How many guys am I going to meet who know what it's like to grow up in a criminal family?

Sabrina F.: Since when is that a recommendation? How many guys in Facebook put Professional Thief in their list of good qualities? You want to be free, you stay away from romantic entanglements, especially with junior criminals.

Sabrina R.: Yeah, but he made me feel so good.

Sabrina F.: Oh, please. Now we're going to be led around by the crotch?

Sabrina R.: Not just that way, in every way. He made me cheerful—not a word you hear a lot. That afternoon at Carlsbad was one of the best times I've ever had in my life.

Sabrina F.: Girl, don't be a fool. You got yourself a Mustang and the open road and a lot of money. The world is your oyster.

Sabrina R.: Then how come I feel so bad?

Sabrina F.: Take a look at yourself in that rear-view, honey. What could be better than the wind in your hair and a tank full of gas?

As a matter of fact, Sabrina did not have a tank full of gas. The needle was showing about an eighth of a tank.

A sign on the road said, *Been taken for granted? Imagine how God feels.* And then the red and white disc of a Texaco station appeared at the top of the next hill.

"I knew you'd have to stop sooner or later, sweetheart." The arrow was stuck on a service centre just east of Lost Gap. Zig held the accelerator steady at ten over the limit.

He passed a pickup truck that had an asphalt roller in the back. Then there was a yellow school bus. He rounded a curve that combined a Chevy dealership and a Dairy Queen, and then the Texaco sign came up on the right.

A couple of cars were jockeying around the pumps, but there were only a few vehicles in the Wendy's parking lot: pickups, minivans, SUVs, some dusty-looking Mazdas and Toyotas. Then he saw it: a brand new candy-apple Mustang with the top down, parked by the fence in the shade, a girl car if there ever was one.

———

Sabrina finished the last of her Coke and emptied her tray into the bin.

In the washroom she spent quite a while attacking her hair with a brush, without much effect. Her thighs were bright pink below the denim skirt, and the pale stripes of skin under her tank straps were vivid. Definitely time to put the top up, she thought as she stepped back out into the sunshine.

The Mustang looked cool out in the lot. Some guy had parked his gigantic SUV next to it, which made the Mustang look like a toy. He had the back door open, rummaging, and came out unfolding a map.

Sabrina got into the Mustang and put up the canopy. It worked like a charm, little motor whirring away. She was about to back out when the engine quit. She tried the ignition again— nothing. She waited a second, tried again. Still nothing.

"Damn." She reached into the glovebox for the owner's manual.

The SUV guy came into her line of sight and pointed at the hood of her car, eyebrows raised.

Sabrina rolled down the window. "I don't know what I did wrong," she said. "I just got the car yesterday and I haven't figured everything out yet."

"Try it again," he said.

She tried it again, but the engine stayed utterly inert.

"You just got this?" he said.

Sabrina nodded. "Yesterday. Better not be anything major."

"Naw, I bet I know what's wrong. My daughter has a Mustang."

"What's the problem?"

"Fuel injection is my guess. Brand new car, sometimes takes a few miles to settle in. Injection timing goes off and the engine just shuts down."

"You're kidding. Is this going to be a regular problem?"

"Shouldn't be. You want to just pop the hood and I'll take a look?"

"Um, I don't know where the release is."

"Just under your seat, to the left."

She pulled it and the guy raised the hood. Silence for a couple of minutes, and then she felt the whole front of the car dip down and up a couple of times, as if he was really yanking on something.

"Try it now!"

She hit the ignition and the thing turned over first time.

He put the hood down carefully and came round to the passenger side.

"That's fantastic," Sabrina said. "Was it what you thought?"

"Exact same thing as my daughter's. Fuel injection."

"Awesome. I don't know how I can thank you."

He opened the passenger-side door and got in.

"I do."

Owen clicked on Update.

"She's moving again," he said. "We can't be too far behind, but she's left the service station."

"Marvellous," Max said. "How are we supposed to know which car is hers?"

"We should be able to come right up on it. Maybe she got a Mustang like she was fantasizing about."

They drove in silence for a while, Max keeping it steady.

"We're just going to take our stuff back," Owen said. "Okay, Max? I don't want you going all King Lear on her."

"I only want what's mine, lad. I'm not a vindictive man."

Owen knew this was true, but he couldn't help adding, "I mean it, Max."

"It would behoove you to worry more about Zig."

"I'm trying not to think about that."

"Shit," Owen said. "I think we've passed her."

"We haven't passed anything but families with dogs and dune buggies for the past fifty miles."

"Pull over, Max. She turned off somewhere."

"There haven't been any turnoffs."

"Max, will you please for God's sake pull over?"

There's nothing like having a gun pointed at you to make you realize how much you want to live. Sabrina really didn't want to find out what it felt like to have little bits of lead whizzing around inside her. She thought of herself as a reasonably good talker, a diplomatic person amenable to compromise, and persuasive when she had to be. The question was, what kind of entity was this on the other end of that gun?

"Why'd you pick me?" she asked him.

"You know why."

"You want the car."

"If I wanted the car, the car would be gone."

"You want sex."

He used the gun barrel to push a strand of hair back from her face.

"It's not my primary motivation."

"So what do you want with me?"

"I got a whole inventory of reasons. They're growing by the minute. You certainly have a nice chest."

"Watch your mouth."

The man laughed. Not a pretty sound.

"You have a gun," Sabrina said. "It's not necessary to be an asshole as well."

He'd already made her turn off the highway onto a smaller road that twisted back the way they had come. Sabrina was keeping a close watch on the passing landscape, trying to memorize it. They were surrounded by trees now, and the forest was getting thicker and thicker—not at all what she had expected in Mississippi. She kept hoping they would reach some kind of open space. Where the hell were cotton fields when you needed them?

"Were you looking for me specifically?" she said. "Or did I just happen to be unlucky?"

"Luck's got nothing to do with it."

"So you were looking for me specifically."

"Affirmative."

"If that's true, how would you find me? Nobody knows where I am."

"Bill gave me directions."

"Bill wouldn't do that. Bill would come himself."

"If he could."

"What's that supposed to mean?"

"It means what it means."

"Is this a kidnapping? You imagine someone's going to pay a ransom? Believe me, I am not a person anyone's going to pay good money for."

"That's just low self-esteem talking. You might want to work on that."

They came to a dusty crossroads.

"Take this left," he said.

"Which will take us where?"

"Don't worry about it. Where's your sense of adventure?"

"Suppose I decide not to."

"Do that, and a bullet will enter your body. Somewhere painful."

Sabrina made the turn. It was a narrow dirt road, heavily rutted. An ancient real estate sign, shotgun scarred, came up on the right, advertising cottages for sale.

"You're thinking of buying a Forest View cottage?"

"Maybe I'll buy all of them," he said. "Open myself a money-making enterprise."

By the look of them, the Forest View cottages had been boarded up fifty years ago, having no doubt hit hard times after the interstate went through. There wasn't much other than trees to draw tourists or anyone else out here—no hills, no lake—and the road was a wreck that threatened to rip the floor out of Sabrina's brand new car.

They went a little farther and then the guy said, "Stop here."

A single sagging cottage on one side of the road. Other than that, no houses, no farms, just the road winding off through the trees.

"Switch off and open the trunk."

Sabrina switched off and pulled the trunk release.

"Show me the stuff." He clicked the safety off his automatic. "Now."

She got out and lifted the trunk lid. "It's in the suitcase."

He gestured with the gun. "Show me."

She bent into the trunk and undid the clasps of her suitcase. The canvas satchel she had lifted from Max and Owen was inside. She held it open for him to see.

"I like it. All right, put it back."

She closed the satchel and set it back in the case. As she was closing the trunk lid, she felt a sharp pain in her right hip and spun around.

"What the hell—"

The man held up a hypodermic and smiled. "Medication time."

"What the hell is that?"

"Short-acting sedative."

"You bastard."

Sabrina started back toward the front of the car. Her right leg was going soft.

He got in the seat beside her. "May cause drowsiness. Do not exceed recommended dose. Do not operate heavy machinery."

"Fuck you."

She hit the ignition, but her eyelids were starting to weigh several pounds each.

"You'll thank me later. Everybody likes a good nap."

"I'll kill you," she said, and made a swipe at him, but her hand fell heavily against his arm. Everything felt like it was wrapped in cotton.

"I won't do anything you haven't done before. I just didn't want things to get confrontational."

She felt herself being lifted and carried, and then the ground below her, a stick or something digging into her back.

When she woke up, she was face down. She had no idea how long she had been out. It could have been five minutes, it could have been an hour. Pine needles stuck to her face. Her body felt thick and heavy, as if her veins were full of syrup.

"That wasn't so bad, was it?"

"What did you do?" she tried to ask, but she could hear it didn't come out right. She started to move, lifting herself up on one elbow. Then there was another pinprick.

"No," she managed to say, and then she was out again.

Next time she woke up, she was looking at bits of sky, a canopy of trees.

She didn't feel as wasted this time. Maybe the shot had gone astray—or maybe she'd been out longer. She ran a hand over her face and sat up. The forest floor swayed beneath her like a hammock.

"Yoo-hoo," he said. "Hello there, sleepyhead."

She tried to stand but couldn't quite make it. He grabbed her wrist and pulled her back down.

"You have an interesting body, I have to say. Nice slow curves. Soft and hard in all the right places. Smells good. Tastes good. I took the scenic route, so to speak."

"What did you do, you creep?" She pulled her skirt back into shape.

"Well, let's just say you're not gonna enjoy riding a bike for a while."

Sabrina struggled to get to her knees.

"No, no, sweetheart, you just relax. We got all day here."

He reached behind and pulled up a small vinyl case, unzipped it, and pulled out another syringe. Sabrina rolled away from him and got to her knees, unsteady.

"Slow down there, sister. Time for your booster."

Somewhere beyond the trees a car pulled up.

"Keep your mouth shut," Zig said. "Or you're dead."

TWENTY-FOUR

CAR DOORS SLAMMED. Voices. One of them unmistakably Max's.

"Not a sound," Zig said, and gestured with the gun.

A twig snapped.

Sabrina made a run for it, forcing her legs to work. I'm going to get a bullet in the back, she thought. I'm going to die on this godforsaken road in this godforsaken state, and—

There was a gunshot and a tree spat bark at her face. She fell into some bushes. She could see Owen, and then Max, behind the trees on the other side of the road. How did everyone in the entire world know where to find her?

She crawled through the bushes, twigs and rock biting into her knees and shins. Zig jumped on her from behind and hauled her up by her hair, but not before she closed her fist around a sharp stone.

He gripped her arm like he would snap her wrist, forcing her to the edge of the trees. He yelled across the road.

"Come any closer, Max, the girl gets it."

Max's face appeared from behind a tree. Also a revolver.

"Zig? Is that you? I am extremely disappointed in you, Zig. A former classmate turning on me in my twilight years."

"You're a thief, Max. You should understand by now how thieves think."

"Nonsense, sir. You insult the profession."

"The profession doesn't care."

Sabrina brought the stone up hard and caught him in the side of the head. Zig staggered to one side, and she ran for her car.

Her legs were still sluggish and she nearly fell, but she made it. The keys were on the floor.

"Sabrina, wait!"

Owen's panicked face glimmered among the trees. She hit the gas.

"That girl has an impressive instinct for survival," Max said quietly.

"I think she's hurt," Owen said.

"Her welfare is not first among my concerns at the moment."

"Hey, Max," Zig called. His head appeared around the corner of the cottage. "What do you say we call it a draw?"

"There are two of us and only one of you. We have a vehicle and you do not. How is that a draw?"

"I'm more ruthless than you," Zig said.

"No doubt the late William Bullard would agree with you. Not to mention a brace of my colleagues. Clarify one point for me, Zigler. If you and your henchmen are the Subtractors, why are you minus two nipples?"

"That's a long story, Max."

"I have the time."

"I don't feel like going into it right now. I'd rather reiterate an earlier point: I am your basic ruthless criminal. I'm not all bad, but it would be fair to call me . . . uninhibited. Whereas you, on the other hand, are kind of a pussycat. I mean, you pride yourself on it, right? Max Maxwell, the gentleman thief."

"Appearances deceive," Max said. "The devil may take a pleasing shape."

"Max," Owen said quietly, "I'm gonna run to the car."

"Don't. He'll shoot you dead in your tracks."

"Well, you shoot at him first. Keep him busy."

"Don't be ridiculous. These are real guns, real bullets."

"On three. One . . ."

"Don't."

"Two . . ."

"Owen, for God's sake."

"Three."

Owen took off and Max reached around the tree, firing a series of shots across the road. Unfortunately, it didn't stop Zig from firing at the same time, and Owen had to dive right back.

"Okay," Zig called out, "now I have a question for you."

"Fire away," Max said. "So to speak."

"How are you going to get to that car without me putting a bullet through your head?"

"Can I rely on your good nature? On your reputation as a gentleman?"

"You could try."

Owen touched Max's shoulder. "How many bullets do you have left?"

"In a word? One."

"Shit. What about blanks?"

"There's a box in the trunk of the car."

Zig appeared around the corner of the cottage again. "Look, Max, I'm willing to call a truce here. Why don't you throw out your gun and we'll call it a day?"

"No deal," Owen called out. "You throw out yours first."

"No, thanks," Zig said. "But I'll tell you what I will do. I'll put it away."

There was a pause, then Zig stepped out into the open, hands in the air.

"Okay, look," Zig said. "I know you're not gonna shoot me in cold blood, and I'm not gonna shoot you either. I got my hands up. Gun's in my pocket. Just come out of there and we'll work this out."

Owen looked at Max.

"We can't trust him, lad. He'll kill us soon as look at us."

"You've got one bullet left. Are you willing to shoot him right now?"

Max shook his head.

"Maybe if we just toss him the keys to the car? Then he could drive away and there's nothing we can do about it."

Zig was coming toward them on the road. His hands were still in the air, but lower now.

There was the sound of a car coming, spitting gravel. Zig turned toward the noise.

The Mustang, coming fast. Zig reached for his gun, thought better of it, and started to run. The Mustang swerved and scooped him up off the ground, flipping him in a somersault up and over the length of the car. Sabrina pulled to a gravelly stop, did a three-pointer, and vanished once again up the road.

Zig lay still beside the road in a cloud of dust.

As Max crossed toward him, gun ready, Zig struggled to one knee.

Owen saw Zig reach, gun coming up. "Max! Watch out!"

Max fired, and Zig dropped the gun, slowly toppling to one side.

Max knelt beside him. Zig pawed uselessly at the dirt.

"Best take it easy, old son," Max said.

Zig stared at the blood soaking through his shirt. "Shit. Look at that."

"Sorry," Max said.

"It's not your fault."

"True enough, I suppose. Wages of ruthlessness. All that."

"Fuck, Max. I suppose I'm going to die now."

"It does look that way."

"Let's get out of here," Owen said. "We can phone an ambulance when we're back on the highway."

"Fuck that," Zig said.

"Is there anyone you want me to call?" Max said.

Zig was turning paler than any man Owen had ever seen.

"Let me think." He closed his eyes.

"Zig?"

He opened his eyes again. "I can't think of anyone." He squinted up at Owen, then at Max. "You know something?" he said. "This really sucks."

TWENTY-FIVE

AFTER THAT, THERE WAS NO QUESTION of continuing their trip, not even for Max. Aside from having just watched a man die, they had already missed the scheduled dates for two of their jobs, and the third, in Savannah, Georgia, was far too complicated for two actors. So they drove back to Dallas, climbed inside the Rocket, and limped home to New York.

In the weeks that followed, Max rattled around their two-bedroom making a nuisance of himself. In an attempt to improve the apartment's two air conditioners, he rendered both of them inoperable, and the New York humidity was suffocating. Owen was going to as many movies as he could—partly to keep cool, partly for "research" on his favourite actors, and partly just to get away from Max, whose episodes of confusion became more frequent. Even worse, he was losing his temper in a way that was quite new.

One August afternoon Mrs. Carlson, their neighbour from across the hall, rapped on the door and told Owen that she had just seen Max at the Pioneer grocery store. He was standing inside the doorway when she went in, and he was still there forty-five minutes later when she went out.

"I spoke to him both times," she said, "but I'm not sure he recognized me. He just said he was waiting for someone. I said, 'Owen?' But he just snapped at me and told me to go away."

Owen apologized on Max's behalf and dashed over to the grocery store. He found Max standing outside the place, unable to account for his afternoon and not at all certain who Owen might be. Owen managed to persuade him to come home, and when Max woke up after a two-hour nap he was his old self again, irritated that Owen was so frantic.

They lived in an area of Manhattan that was full of clinics and hospitals. That turned out to be lucky on another day, toward the end of summer, when Owen received a call from Bellevue. A kindly phlebotomist, an enormous Jamaican woman, had noticed Max on the corner of First Avenue and Twenty-ninth, repeatedly starting out across the street and then turning around and heading back. She had brought him to work, and the ID in his wallet had enabled her to call.

"He needs to have a full examination, child. They'll be wanting to do exams and scans and all kine a ting."

Max had done a perfect impression of her accent all the way home, this myna bird part of his character apparently undamaged.

"What if you hadn't had your wallet on you, Max? You could still be wandering around Manhattan like a homeless person."

"But I did have my wallet," Max said, suddenly red in the face. "I did have my wallet and I don't need you nagging at me like a harpy."

Owen tried not to be hurt by these sudden tempers. When Max refused yet again to be tested, Owen went to a pharmacy and had an ID bracelet made. To his surprise, Max didn't put up any protest about wearing it. But how could Owen go into residence at Juilliard next month if Max was wandering around Manhattan in a fog?

His episodes had seemed to be entirely random, but he developed another behaviour that occurred only in the evening. Just before suppertime, he would be sitting in his La-Z-Boy with a book in his lap or watching the news. Suddenly he would announce, "I want to go home."

The first time he said this, Owen felt a deep chill run through him.

"What are you talking about, Max? England?"

Max was staring in indignation at the room, as if someone had tried to pull a fast one.

"This isn't my home. I want to go home."

"Max, you are home."

"This is not where I live."

"It is, Max. This is your home. I'm Owen, your nephew, remember? We live together here in this apartment."

"That's fine for you to say, but I want to go home."

"Max, let's just watch the rest of the news, okay?"

After an hour or so Max would calm down, and when he had had his supper you would never know he had suffered a moment's confusion. Owen talked to his own doctor, who said it could be Alzheimer's, it could be a lot of things, but there was nothing that could be done unless his uncle came in for an exam.

It was Labor Day weekend when Owen came home one afternoon to find Max his old self again, whistling as he spread wigs and costumes over the dining table.

"Sit you down, nephew," Max said. "I would acquaint thee with a show of pure genius."

"No more shows, Max. Season's over." Owen went to the fridge in search of a snack.

"Bollocks," Max called after him. "That impudent wench robbed us blind, cost us at least three performances, and an untold price in peace of mind and security in my old age—should old age ever become a concern. I plan to make good my losses."

Owen selected a can of iced tea from the fridge and pulled out half a peach pie Max had made the previous weekend.

"Sometimes things don't go the way you planned," Owen said. "That's what you've always told me."

"Yes, and on such doleful occasions one must improvise. Which is why you need to look at this."

"You want a piece of pie?"

"What kind of question is that? Of course I want a piece of pie."

Owen cut two slices and brought them to the dining table.

Max was holding up a photograph of the Upper East Side—Madison Avenue, it looked like, but it could have been any one of a dozen corners in Manhattan, with its bank, its New York Sports Club, its Gap and Banana Republic.

"A bank," Max said, tapping a finger on the Chase sign. "A very handsome little bank, well framed for larceny and but lightly defended."

"Uh-huh," Owen said around a mouthful of pie. "You're going to rob a bank now?"

"A most excellent plan if you would but let me speak into the fearful hollow of thine ear."

"Max, it's a *bank,* and we don't rob banks. This is *New York,* and we never work in our hometown. Pookie is dead. Roscoe is laying low. It's time to retire while we're still alive. Let's not push it."

"Look at these." Max put on a green surgical cap and mask. "Dr. Abe Pfeffernan, oncologist," he said, tapping the nameplate on his chest. "Pfeffernan—you have to love the name. I have a set for you too. Unless—would you prefer to be a nurse? You're young enough. Elizabethan lads played women all the time. Test of a real actor if you can play a member of the opposite sex."

"Listen, Dr. Pfeffernan, you and I are specialists. Dinners only. Republicans only. Summers only. Even that was dangerous enough. Now you want to rob banks?"

"No, no, just this one. Look at these." He held two wigs aloft, one on each fist. "I've always wanted to play a New York Jew. Nothing obvious. Not the Hasidim, too easy. No, no. I want to do the classic New York Jewish professional. The sort of doctor, lawyer, dentist we all like to have—should we be in the dolorous circumstances that require such services. You could be a nurse, and I could do Ben."

Ben Levine was their neighbour down the hall, an English professor to whom Max had long ago taken a shine when he had referred to *Macbeth* as the first film noir.

"A little putty on the nose, some curls. The accent's easy, the manner . . ." He went into a series of shrugs and a mild New York accent. "What am I, a common thief? Of course not. I swear to you, Murray, I'm only thinking of your education, hand to God."

He held up a vast T-shirt decorated with the Nike swoosh. "Dr. Abe Pfeffernan, marathon man. See, this is where the genius comes in. The bank, you notice, is next door to a health club. I have cased the joint, as the saying goes. There is an exit from the health club, sans camera, that I will prepare ahead of time. We wear running gear under the scrubs. In one split second we change from medical professionals into sports fanatics. Central Park is a mere block away. You run there. Within sixty seconds you'll look like a hundred other people circling the reservoir like something out of Dante. I, meanwhile, will have stashed props, wigs and swag in a locker at the health club, where I shall proceed to hoist weights with the ease of a Titan."

"Max, it's the Upper East Side in broad daylight. Hundreds of people are going to see us."

"Thought of, dealt with." Max scooped up his pie and demolished it in three swift bites. He drank down most of Owen's iced tea. "Men's room downstairs," he said, brushing crumbs from his belly. "We exit the bank, head to the lav. There we dispose of the scrubs and exit severally, I to the health club, you to Central Park. They'll be looking for two doctors who don't exist."

"Max, it'll be broad daylight. The makeup and wigs are going to be totally obvious."

"We're talking about a microperformance, lad. A cameo of mere minutes."

"Please, Max. Let me take you to the doctor. You have no sense of reality anymore. It's nothing to be ashamed of, and there's probably some medication out there that could help straighten you out."

"My last doctor died of a heart attack at age forty-six. Shows how much they know."

"Max, I can't let you do this."

"Since when do you let or not let, you puppy? Look here . . ."

Max spread out more photographs on the table—pictures of the street intersection, the health club entrance, a nearby construction site, the chaos of cars. Max put his finger on the construction site. "The traffic is so bad on that block, owing to a convenient condominium tower currently heading skyward, that even when the constabulary is called, it is going to take them days—positive *days,* my boy—to make their entrance."

"I'm not going to discuss it," Owen said, taking the plates back into the kitchen. "You're being a lunatic."

"It's ambition, not lunacy. Unless he rob a bank or two, a thief is not a proper thief. Banks are where they keep the money. Willie Sutton said that."

"And if you had paid any attention to our criminal history tour," Owen said, coming back, "you would know that he was in prison when he said it. Max, you made me promise to keep you out of prison. I'm trying to do just that. Please forget about this."

"No. The show must go on whether you are in it or not. Your Uncle Max waits for no man."

"Jesus Christ, Max, I can't believe I'm even related to you."

"Fine, then, you ungrateful whelp," Max yelled. "You are not related to me."

Until the past few weeks, Owen had not seen Max lose his temper more than two or three times. But now the old man's face darkened and he brought his fist down hard on the dining table. Owen's can of iced tea hit the floor.

"Miserable stripling! You imagine any flesh and blood of mine would turn down an opportunity to make a quick quarter-million? Or quiver in fear before a security camera and some ill-paid minion in a blue uniform?"

An uneasiness crept into Owen's belly. "Max, what do you mean?"

"In brief? Thou art a chicken."

"About not being related to you. What did you mean by that?"

"Nothing. Spoke recklessly." Max was huffing still, but his colour was changing back to normal. "Heat of the moment."

"Max, answer me. What do you mean, I'm not related to you?"

"Nothing, boy. Nothing! Are you in or out?"

"Max, what did you mean?"

"Oh, fine, then, fine!" Max clamped his hands over his ears and let out a roar. "Hammer on my skull with your questions. Half drown me with repetition, repetition, repetition. If you will be told, you will be told: I am not your uncle. I am no blood relation to you whatsoever. Never was, never will be. There. Are you satisfied now?"

Owen was unable to speak for a few moments. When he finally did, he found himself stammering. "What are you saying? You're my grandfather's brother, right? My great-uncle. From Warwick. That's what you've always said."

Max unclamped his ears and sat back down, his roar having apparently deflated him. "I may have somewhat exaggerated."

"Oh."

"I—I hope you won't take this in the worst light."

"Max, just tell me the truth, will you?"

"Believe me, lad, with all my heart I wish I could say to you, with accuracy, that we are of one blood, but we are not. I am not your uncle, aunt or cousin thrice removed. I am not related to you in any way."

Owen sat down hard. He felt as if his insides had been scooped out.

"Max, I don't think you should say something like that just

because you're mad at me. Just because I don't want you to risk your life over another goddamn show . . ."

"No, boy, it's the truth." Max cleared a space and put his elbow on the table, leaning head to hand, shading his eyes. His voice was quieter than Owen had ever heard it. "I've wanted to tell you for a long time," he said. "A long, long time. But I could never—I could never come up with a satisfactory way to do it. It always seemed too soon, or not the right moment. But I knew you would have to be told."

"I don't get this at all," Owen said. He was staring at the floor as if the parquet squares would resolve themselves into an explanation. "If we're not related, why am I living with you, Max? Why did the courts give you custody? Why would you even ask to look after me? I just don't understand what the hell is going on here."

Max elaborately cleared his throat. "A ticklish question—no, no, I see the thing clearly now—a ticklish question indeed. Why indeed am I looking after you, a boy to whom I am no relation whatsoever—aside from loving caretaker, doting mentor, affectionate partner in crime?"

Now it was Owen's turn to yell. "Max, tell me what is going on! If you're not my uncle, who the fuck are you?"

"Calm yourself, lad. No good will come of yelling. I am—how to put this . . . I am. Well, to begin at the beginning . . ."

"Max, please."

"You remember the circumstances of your parents' untimely quitting of this world?"

"The car crash? They just happened to be in the wrong place at the wrong time. The police were chasing this guy, and—"

Owen gripped the table with both hands. The blood seemed to have drained from his head, and for the first time in his life he felt that he might actually faint.

"You're a bit pale, boy. Perhaps you'd better—"

"Oh my God." Owen clutched his forehead as if he could protect himself from the thought. "You're not my uncle."

"Easy, lad. Bound to be a bit of a shock at first."

"You're not related to me."

"Well, no." Max gripped Owen's shoulder and gave it a little shake. "Still your friend, though. Still your pal."

Owen took a deep breath. "You were the guy they were chasing? You were the—back when my parents were killed? You were the guy the cops were chasing?"

"Well, um, yes. I suppose I would have to say yes to that particular question."

"You were the guy they were chasing. I'm just—I can't—God, I can't deal with this. You're telling me you killed my mom and dad."

"No, no, no. Nothing of the sort. I was being pursued at high speed. A corporate banquet show gone awry. Bad timing. Bad casting. Doomed from the start, really, and the hounds were on my tail. Under the circumstances, I may have gone over the speed limit."

"'Speeds of up to a hundred and twenty miles an hour,' Max. I have the clippings."

"Don't belabour the point, boy. I've already admitted it, I was driving too fast. I made a sudden swoop to the right, and unfortunately the nearest driver thought it prudent to swerve to the left. Your parents, coming the other way, left the road and, well . . . the rest you know."

"They plowed into a utility pole."

"Gross misfortune."

"Misfortune!"

"Catastrophe, no question."

"You still don't think you did anything, do you. You still don't think it's your fault."

"It was thoughtless, reckless, hasty—"

"How about *stupid,* Max? How about *criminal?* How about *murderous?*"

"Stupid, I grant you. Criminal, yes. But murderous—no, my boy, not murderous. I didn't pull in front of your parents, some other car swerved into their lane. I was devastated by it. Racked with guilt. And yet I couldn't see that turning myself in would do any good. It would not resurrect them. It would not unbreak your heart."

"How did you even know about me?"

"I followed it in the papers. I read everything I could. Naturally, I was terrified of being caught and going to prison. But also, I was struck dumb by the profound coincidence of our having the same last name—as if we shared a ghastly destiny cooked up by some long-dead Greek. I decided to do everything in my power to make that destiny . . . less ghastly."

"Jesus, Max. Tell me you're making this up. Just because we have the same last name, you decide it's all right to come into my life and . . ."

"Not just that. My heart went out to you. I was appalled by your situation. I made inquiries at the social agencies and tracked you down. I had no plan, no chart, no map of the future. I just felt compelled to insert myself—discreetly, at this point, distantly—into your life. To make sure you were okay."

"Okay? You killed my fucking parents, Max. I was not okay."

"And when I heard that you would be made a ward of the state, that's when I decided to play the part of your long-lost uncle."

"You had pictures! Family photographs . . ."

"Lifted 'em from your house and made copies. That was no problem. Creating the paper trail, now, that was a challenge. The favours I had to call in! The arms I had to twist! Expensive, too. The signatures! But in the end the authorities bought it. I was your long-lost uncle Max, and as your nearest living relative I was granted temporary custody. Under supervision of the state. Eventually they were satisfied that I was looking after you properly, and—"

Owen leapt up from his chair. "You stole me!"

"No, lad. No. Sit down. I wanted to look after you. I wanted to do something to make up for what I'd done. Please, sit down."

"You stole me. Just like you steal everything else in your life."

"It was partly selfish, I grant you. I was a man of a certain age, I was alone, and I needed someone to love. And there you were. Love is, after all, a selfish sort of giving, don't you think?"

"You stole me. Just like you steal your identities, your jewels, your cars, your money. But I'm not an object, Max. I'm not a thing. Oh, God, I don't believe this."

Max got heavily to his feet, made a tentative move toward him, but Owen stepped back.

"I'm sorry, boy. I'm sorry for what I did long ago, and for what it did to your parents and to you. If I could undo it, I would. I would, so help me God. But I can't, and I couldn't, and so I did what seemed like the next best thing."

Owen started toward the kitchen, stopped. He started toward his bedroom, and stopped again. His mind wasn't working. He wanted to get away but didn't even seem to know how. His limbs lacked the skill.

Max came toward him—big, lumbering Max, clumsy as a bear.

"It doesn't change anything else, boy. To me, you could not be closer if you were fashioned from my own right arm. You are my boy, my lad, my prince, and I—"

Owen finally got his feet to work. He fled the apartment and punched the elevator button. Unable to stand still for even a minute, he ran down four flights of stairs and burst out of a side exit into the blinding grit of First Avenue.

TWENTY-SIX

OWEN DIDN'T GO HOME UNTIL LATE THAT NIGHT. He slipped quietly into his bedroom, packed a suitcase, and checked into a cheap hotel in midtown. He could have stayed with a school friend, but he didn't want to see or talk to anyone; he just wanted to be alone.

He spent the next few days wandering from Starbucks to Starbucks, bookstore to bookstore. He sat in Union Square feeding the squirrels, he visited the Central Park Zoo, he read magazines in the public library. He wasn't thinking; he wasn't able to think. His mind had seized up, locked itself around what Max had told him. Owen wasn't even sure if he was angry; he didn't know what he was feeling.

He would sit in the cool dark of the movie theatres taking in nothing of what was happening onscreen. His mind would not let go. And when he came out, the world seemed drained of colour, overexposed. The crowds, the noise, the traffic swirled around him and he hardly knew where he was.

He tried to separate the two essential facts that Max had revealed to him and weigh them one at a time. First, how bad was it that Max was not really his uncle? Did it alter the fact that he had raised him? Did it render everything else about their relationship false and empty?

And then the other, much worse: that Max had been the cause of his parents' deaths. His actions had led to all that tearing metal and twisted steel that had killed them both instantly. But obviously Max hadn't intended that outcome. He was just a criminal on the run, in a blind panic, heedless of everything except the spectre of prison looming before him.

Still Owen stayed away. After three days he moved into the dorm at Juilliard.

He felt a lot better once classes started. It was exciting to embark on a new life, and he found himself enthralled by all the books on the syllabus: critical works, texts on acting, playwrights he had never heard of. And he was fascinated by the other people in his class. They too had all earned raves for their performances in their drama club, and a lot of them had worked in theatre camps and small summer theatres while Owen had been busy robbing Republicans.

Owen was intimidated by some of them, they were so talented. While others, well, you had to wonder how they had ever passed the audition. The stage set his group was using consisted of leftovers from the previous semester, a living room suite that might have been new in the mid-seventies, cat-clawed and much stained. Halfway through the second week of school the instructor, Phil Major, was centre stage, analyzing the performance of a student named Jason who had mumbled his way through a Sam Shepard monologue. Then it was McKenzie's turn.

McKenzie was a knockout, with shapely cheekbones and wide-set eyes that made her look both innocent and wise. Everyone in her class wanted to recognize some speck of talent in such beauty, but when Phil gave her the go-ahead, she fell hard onto the couch and, in a manoeuvre straight out of World Wrestling Entertainment, pitched forward onto her knees, where she proceeded to claw at the carpet. She shrieked her lines at such volume that Owen covered his ears.

Phil clapped his hands twice, two sharp reports.

"Okay, McKenzie, thank you. Thank you," he said, in a silky tone that betrayed nothing of the horror he must have felt. "Well, that was certainly less restrained than Jason. But you have to keep in mind, this scene occurs early in the play, and if you start at that level of intensity you're going to have nowhere to go for later scenes. Remember, acting is never about losing control, even if your *character* is losing control. Okay. That's all we have time for today. Same time, same place, Thursday."

The students filed out of the auditorium, quieter than usual, subdued by the McKenzie Chernobyl.

"Owen, you heading to the caf?" It was Bobby Jaye who spoke. Bobby was all blond dreadlocks, an earnest Midwesterner with a skateboard under his arm.

"No, I'm gonna take a walk. I need a breather."

"Yeah, I know what you mean." Bobby looked around conspiratorially. "Man, that McKenzie really goes to eleven. I thought we were gonna have to call an ambulance."

"She may have given us a little too much."

"Oh, really, you think?"

Owen headed up Broadway to the Acropolis, one of the last old-style diners on the Upper West Side. Tuesday at four in the afternoon, the place was full of chattering high school students. Owen sat at the counter and ordered a Coke. The TV above the glassware was tuned to NY1, sound off, the mayor gassing on about something. Owen pulled out a used paperback copy of *Burn This*. He turned to Pale's opening speech, a fiendishly intricate rant that he was hoping to memorize by Thursday.

But all he could think about was Max. Here he was at Juilliard, immersed in theatre arts—it was ridiculous not to be discussing it all with Max. He pulled out his cellphone and set it on the counter beside the book, considering.

Dr. Abe Pfeffernan, a scholarly-looking man dressed in hospital scrubs, waited calmly in line with the other customers of the Chase branch at Sixty-eighth and Madison. He had a beaky nose, a slightly mournful expression, and a full head of curly salt-and-pepper hair bisected by the surgical mask he had pushed up there and forgotten.

The doctor chatted amiably with the lady behind him. They agreed that one of the problems with the prevalence of ATM machines was that when you eventually did require the services of a human teller, you faced a hideous lineup. And so *slow*. Invariably the person in front of you was there to refinance a mortgage or to exchange Ugandan shillings for Swiss francs; no one went to a teller for a simple withdrawal.

"Why don't you go ahead of me?" the doctor suggested. "You don't want to waste your entire afternoon here."

"Oh, no, no. That's all right."

"Please, I insist. I'm in no rush." He stepped aside so she could move up.

"Such a gentleman," she said, clutching her purse. "But surely you have to get back to the hospital?"

"You're very kind to think of it, but no. I'm only involved in research."

"Research whereabouts?"

"Over at Rockefeller."

"Oh, my, you must be a brilliant man. That's very prestigious."

"We have our victories now and again," Dr. Pfeffernan allowed with a small smile. "Failures, unfortunately, are more common."

"And what are you researching?"

"The old enemy, I'm afraid."

"Cancer?"

"And we'll conquer it," Dr. Pfeffernan swore, raising a palm above his head. "Hand to God. Someday, I swear, we're going to wipe it out."

"Oh, I hope so. My husband died of colorectal seven years ago. Irv Rosen? He was a pediatrician in a family practice, I don't suppose you ever met him."

"I never had the pleasure. I believe in a few more years we may be able to save people like your husband."

"Oh, you're just like him. He was totally dedicated, never wanted to retire, and always hoped for the best, even though some of his cases were heartbreaking."

"Pediatrics, yes. Such *tsoris*." Dr. Pffefernan placed a hand over his heart. "You see some real tragedies there."

Mrs. Rosen unsnapped her purse, pulled out a handkerchief, and dabbed at her eyes. "Well, Doctor. With people like you on the job, maybe someday there'll be a lot fewer of those tragedies."

"From your mouth to God's ear, Mrs. Rosen. I think the teller's ready for you."

"Well, it's been a pleasure, Dr. Pffefernan, you have a good day now. And good luck on your quest!"

When Max got to the counter, he met the inquiring gaze of a young black woman on the other side of the bulletproof glass.

"I need to open my safety deposit box," he said, handing her a piece of Pffefernan ID. "Can't go anywhere without a passport these days."

"Oh, you didn't need to wait in line for that, Doctor. You could have just got one of the managers to assist you. Wait there, I'll be right back."

She returned a moment later with another black woman. She wore a red dress and large gold earrings that gleamed against her skin.

"This is Miss Leary," the teller said. "She can help you."

"Dr. Pffefernan, you need to open your safety deposit box?"

"That's right. I rented it just a week or two ago."

"Come with me." She handed back his identification.

He followed her through a door into the back. A security guard was seated just inside.

Miss Leary showed him into the safety deposit room and inserted her key into the drawer. Max turned his key in the lock, pulled out the drawer, and set it on a table.

"There you go, Doctor. Is there anything else I can help you with?"

He pulled open the drawer and removed a snub-nosed auto-matic, pointing it at her.

"Don't be alarmed, my dear, but yes, I'm afraid there is."

The coffee shop was filling up. A man sitting next to Owen was explaining to his seven-year-old daughter what same-sex marriage meant.

"Well, you see, Megan, some girls like girls, so they marry girls. And some boys like boys, so they marry boys."

Owen picked up his cellphone from the counter and dialed home. No answer. He tried Max's mobile, but it switched him over immediately to voice mail. He didn't leave a message.

He was pulling out some change to pay his check when some-one said, "Hey, turn the sound up. Where's that happening?"

The TV screen showed the front of a Chase bank. The ban-ner said *LIVE: Upper East Side.*

"What's going on, Daddy?"

"Someone's robbing a bank," the man said.

"Why?"

"Because he wants their money."

"Will they give it to him?"

"If they do, he'll have to give it back. It belongs to other people."

According to the reporter on the scene, the robbery had begun barely twenty minutes ago, but the bank was already sur-rounded by police. A sweep of the camera showed snipers on the corners of buildings across the street. Helicopters hovered overhead. The amazing thing, the reporter said, was that the robber was a senior citizen, apparently a doctor, who was hold-ing a woman employee hostage.

"Hey, don't you want your change?" the counterman called out, but Owen was gone.

———

Lieutenant Nat Saperstein was hoping the hostage negotiation guys would get there soon, but word was they were hung up on the FDR. In the meantime it was his show, until such time as the SWAT team should get the go-ahead to take over. He had snipers on the roofs and an offensive football team of beefy guys blocking the only other exit. There was no way this scumbag was getting away, though why a doctor in his seventies or eighties suddenly gets it into his head to rob a bank, well, you have to wonder.

"Loo, we got a possible lever here."

Saperstein put down his binoculars and turned to see a uniform holding on to the arm of a young man, teenager really.

"Kid says the guy inside is his father."

"Oh yeah? You got some ID?"

"He's actually my uncle, but he adopted me. He's been losing it lately. He was talking about robbing a bank, but I never thought he was serious."

"Like I said, got some ID?"

Owen pulled out his wallet and showed him his driver's licence. "Please don't shoot him," he said. "He's not going to hurt anybody."

Saperstein looked from the licence photo to Owen and back again. "Maxwell? Good news, kid. It ain't your uncle in there."

"I'm telling you, it's him. I saw him on TV, through the front window when he was closing the blinds. He's not using his real name. He was going to make it something Jewish. He's always wanted to play a Jew."

"What are you, Ku Klux Klan? 'Play a Jew.' You think robbing banks is playing a Jew? Get this asshole outta here."

The uniform made a move to grab Owen again.

"Pfeffernan! Dr. Pfeffernan—that was the name he was gonna use."

The lieutenant's face changed now. He gestured at the uniform to let go of the kid. "Okay, son, you have my attention. Tell me more."

"His name is Magnus Maxwell—Max. He's British. A former actor. He likes to play different roles. He said he wanted to do an educated Jewish New Yorker, a doctor."

Saperstein looked him over. The kid looked sincere, and sincerely scared.

Owen went through his wallet and found an old photo of him and Max together at Niagara Falls. "This is him."

Saperstein looked at the photo, raised his eyebrows.

"He looks pretty different, kid."

"That's his theatrical training. He loves wigs and makeup, the whole deal. If you let me talk to him, I'm sure I can get him to come out."

"You're welcome to try." He keyed in a number on his cellphone and handed it to Owen.

An American voice answered, a New York voice. "You're trying my patience here, Lieutenant. How many times do I have to tell you: move your men back."

"Max," Owen said into the phone, "it's me. Owen. You have to give this up. You have to quit while you're ahead."

"I'm sorry, young man. You must have the wrong number." There was a click.

"He hung up on me," Owen said, handing the phone back.

"That's okay, kid, you did your best. Negotiation team'll be here in a—Hey, wait a second!"

Owen took off and ran straight through the crime scene tape. He was in the cordoned-off area, trying not to think of the snipers positioned above him. The front door was open; he was able to walk right in.

"Owen, me lad. What brings you here?"

The actual sight of Owen shook Max into dropping the American accent. He was in his surgical scrubs, seated in one of two executive chairs that had been pulled from offices. The other was occupied by a black woman with big gold earrings. A telephone on a long extension cord was on the floor between them.

"This is Miss Leary," Max said. "She's playing the role of hostage, though with a disappointing lack of conviction. I let the others go."

"Oh, you an Englishman now?" Miss Leary said. "Why don't you make up your mind who you are before you go robbing banks? You know this man?" she said to Owen. "Would you inform him, please, that his ass is in a world of trouble?"

"You have to let her go," Owen said. "There must be a hundred cops out there. Snipers. Helicopters. The works."

"Well, yes, that's the point," Max said. "If I let Miss Leary go, all those guns are very likely to go off."

"Max," Owen said, "the show is over. You're not getting out of this. The only question is how hard you want to make it on yourself. The sooner you let her go, the easier things will be."

"The sooner I'll be back in Sing Sing, you mean."

"Don't you talk trash to this boy when he's telling you the truth," Miss Leary said. "Mister, I get the feeling you a whole lot dumber than you look."

"Madam, can you not at least try to understand your role?" Max said. "Could we have some cowering, please? Some begging? Quivering?"

"The only person going to be begging around here, *Doctor*, is you when I get the chance to kick your fat ass."

"Casting problems," Max said to Owen. "Make an error in casting and no amount of good writing or good direction can make up for it. Look what I'm stuck with." He gestured at Miss Leary as if she had been delivered to his door by mistake.

"You think you in some kind of movie here? This my life we're talking about. Yours too, and this sensible young man's as well."

"Madam, you don't know him," Max said. "He's the least sensible person I've ever met. Wants to be an actor."

"Max," Owen said, "I told them you'd let her go, that you don't really want to hurt anyone."

"Thank you for that, Owen. That's very helpful. I do hope

your acting career takes off, because you're not what I'd call a first-class negotiator."

"Young man, would you tell this old party to undo this handcuff?" Miss Leary pulled up on her manacle, shaking it. "Believe it or not, I do not enjoy being held prisoner in my place of employment."

"You're not a real prisoner," Max said. "You're only playing one."

"Well, if that's the case, and we all just on a movie set, I'd like to go to my trailer now, please."

"Max, give me the key," Owen said.

Max went over to the window and peered out between the blinds. "The plan was good," he said. "I had backups and redundancies built in. For example, a change of clothes. Unfortunately, I forgot to bring them, and if you say I told you so, I shall smite you."

"Max, give me the key and let's get Miss Leary out of here. You can use me as a hostage."

The phone on the floor rang.

"Take a message," Max said. "Tell them I'm at the club."

Owen picked up the phone.

"Saperstein. What's the progress, kid?"

"Miss Leary will be coming out in a minute," Owen said. "Make sure no guns go off by accident."

"Nothing's going to happen by accident. You just send her out and we'll take care of her. But I'm warning you, do not try anything fancy. Anyone who makes any sudden moves when she comes out is going to get shot, you understand?"

"I understand."

Owen hung up. Max was back in his executive chair, rocking it.

"Max, give me the key."

"I'm ashamed to say I forgot it."

"Jesus Christ, Max. Do you hear how ridiculous that is? I told you you should be seeing a doctor, getting tests done, but no— you had to rob a goddamn bank. Fine, she can go out in the chair. It's got wheels. I'll push her out the door and they can come and get her."

"Actually, I was just kidding."

Max reached into the pocket of his scrubs and pulled out the tiny key. Owen undid the handcuff and Miss Leary stood up. Max, ever the gentleman, stood up as well.

"Get you gone, madam."

Miss Leary looked him up and down, hands on hips. "Mister, you are too smart to be pulling shit like this. You should be ashamed of yourself."

"Thank you for auditioning. Don't call us."

The woman folded her arms across her impressive chest and rested her weight on one cocked hip. "You a fool, and that's the truth."

"Madam, I said get you gone. Why do you linger?"

She pointed at Owen. "Frankly, I am concerned about this boy. I don't want you using him as some kind of bargaining chip."

"Oh, no, that's okay," Owen said. "I'll be all right."

"I don't think so, sugar. Why don't you come out with me?"

"Really. Max is my—" Owen looked over at Max. The old man gave him the slightest of New York shrugs, perhaps a last vestige of Dr. Pfeffernan. "Max is my uncle. The detective in charge out there knows the score. You just go ahead, Miss Leary, and I'll be fine. I'm sorry for your inconvenience."

"Inconvenience!" Miss Leary shook her head slowly back and forth. "Honey, you get out of this alive, got to be a job waiting for you in public relations. Inconvenience."

Owen held the door open for her.

Miss Leary turned for one last look at Max. "I hate to tell you this, sugar, but your old man on a one-way ticket to Crazytown," she said, and stepped out into the glare of Madison Avenue.

"Well, I hope you're pleased," Max said. "Now that we're rendered defenceless."

Owen watched as two cops in helmets and body armour jogged out to take Miss Leary by the arms and hustle her away.

The phone rang again.

"Good job, Owen," Saperstein said. "Now let's follow the same procedure with you and your uncle. You come out one at a time, him first. Hands in the air, understand?"

"Wait a minute. Why one at a time? I don't like that."

"One at a time because we don't want you to get hurt."

"Max isn't going to hurt me." Owen looked over at Max. "I'm more worried about you hurting him."

"I understand that, kid, but we have to handle this the safest way for all concerned. Soon as you get out, you lie down on the sidewalk, hands above your head."

"Me too?"

"You too. We have no way of knowing if he's passed you a weapon or not. It's not like you're a hundred percent hostage, is it? So, no sudden moves or someone's gonna get killed, understand?"

"I still don't like the one-at-a-time thing."

"Kid, your father, uncle or whatever he is, happens to be an armed bank robber who has taken hostages."

"But you just said I'm not really a hostage. Don't worry, I'll bring him out and no one needs to get hurt."

"Kid, one at a time, I'm telling you. Don't try anything else, or—"

Owen hung up and told Max what Saperstein had said.

"Thank you, my boy, but I believe they have the right idea. Better to go out one at a time."

"No, I'm not doing it that way," Owen said. "As long as I'm beside you, they're not going to shoot."

"I envy your certainty. No, the safest thing is for you to go out first, then me."

"We go out together, Max."

Max rubbed a hand across his hair, came across the surgical mask and pulled it off, studying it. "You know, from now on I'm going to devote more of my time to the sciences. I believe I have the makings of an excellent doctor."

"Well, you're going to have lots of time to study, so let's go."

Max reached out and closed a hand around Owen's forearm. "Listen, boy. About before . . ."

"I can't even think about that now, Max."

"I just want to be sure you understand. I never—"

"Max, please. Before they decide to throw tear gas in here and blast us to kingdom come."

"You're my boy, understand? Far as I'm concerned, no matter what else, you're my boy. Best part of my life. You know, when you first came to live with me, you were still very small. Sometimes I'd come home and you'd run to me and I'd hoist you in the air and spin you around, and you giggled like a magical sprite. A creature not of this earth, of finer stuff. Or you'd take hold of my leg and cling like a limpet. I'd have to hobble around the house with you hanging on my leg. An absolute monkey. I loved you like my own, lad. Love you like my own."

Still hanging on to Owen's arm, Max raised himself up out of his chair.

"Leave the gun," Owen said. "We don't want to give them any reason to shoot."

"Quite right, boy. Quite right." Max set the snub nose on the chair. "You know what? Why don't we have me sit in the chair and you wheel me out? Make a regal entrance."

"Max, you're not directing this, I am. We go out together, we lie face down on the sidewalk, hands above our heads. And no sudden moves or they'll kill you. All right?"

"Face down. No sudden moves. Roger that. Did you know that 'roger' used to mean *shtupping?* Samuel Pepys used to regularly roger the female members of his staff."

Owen tightened his grip on Max's arm as they reached the door. "Remember, there's going to be about a hundred guns pointed at us."

"Yes, yes. Tedious trolls."

Owen pushed open the door and the two of them stood arm in arm, blinking in the sunlight.

Someone, probably Saperstein, called over a megaphone, "Hands up, now."

They both put their hands in the air.

"Face down on the sidewalk. Now."

Owen started to kneel, saw Max wasn't moving, and stopped halfway.

"Max, no funny stuff. Just do what they say."

"Keep away from me, boy. They may shoot anyway, and I don't want you to get hurt."

The megaphone again: "Face down! Now!"

"Max, just lie down on the sidewalk. Please."

"Stop fussing, lad. I know how to hit my marks."

They both got down on their knees. Owen lay down and spread his hands over his head.

There was a pause. A murmur of activity went up among the squads of police.

Then Max said, "Sorry, lad. Can't go to prison again."

He pushed himself up and started to run—a hopeless manoeuvre, since he was long past the age of swift acceleration. He didn't get ten feet before a shot rang out, and he slammed against the plate glass of the bank before sliding down to the pavement. Owen crawled over to him. Max was slumped in a crooked seated position like a puppet from which the controlling hand has been withdrawn. In the sunlight, his makeup was obvious—the putty he had used to alter the shape of his nose, the sheen of glue at the edges of his added eyebrows.

Blood was pouring from the wound in Max's chest. Owen pressed a hand over it, and blood flowed hotly over his fingers. "You're gonna be okay."

Max was trying to say something.

"Don't talk, Max."

Max's voice was barely a whisper. His words emerged in a long, slow gasp, as if blown by a distant wind. "I have it," he said. "And soundly, too."

"Max, you're too old to play Mercutio," Owen said. "Be quiet now."

Four cops surrounded them, guns pointed, as two more cops frisked them.

Paramedics appeared, wheeling a gurney.

Max was trying to say something else. Owen leaned closer to hear.

"You guys have any brandy?" Owen said. "He wants some brandy."

The cops pulled Owen back. One of the medics felt Max's neck; his head had lolled to one side.

The paramedic glanced up at Owen. "This guy a physician?"

Owen shook his head. "Actor."

"Not anymore, kid."

TWENTY-SEVEN

MONK'S CASTLE ON SEVENTH STREET had always been Max's favourite pub, not just because they served Guinness and a healthy variety of British ales, but because they had no television, their sound system played only classical music, and—best of all—the bartender and waiters wore monks' robes complete with hoods, sandals and belts of knotted rope. Downstairs the place was all dark wood and stained glass, but the upstairs was a bright and lively space that the "monks" rented out for parties.

Max himself had held more than one celebration on the premises, so when it came time to choose a suitable venue for a memorial get-together, it had been the first place Owen thought of. The rafters were hung with huge posters of Max that he had had enlarged from his Photoshop files. Except for the presence of a jovial fat man in the foreground, they could have been used for a high school geography course. From the redwood forests of California to the rocky coast of Maine, from the badlands of the Dakotas to the boardwalks of New Orleans, Max had been there. In every photograph he was laughing, smiling or striking a pose, the camera his natural ally.

With the help of a schoolmate, Owen had dressed up a series of mannequins in a selection of Max's favourite costumes—Catholic priest, Saudi sheik, British major—and stood them up around the tavern with mugs of ale in their hands, like an exhibition of multicultural bon vivants. He had painstakingly gone through every contact in Max's tiny, pencil-smeared address books and sent out invitations with plenty of notice.

And now the place was crammed with villains of wildly divergent shapes and predilections, but they all had one thing in common: they had worked with Max at some point or other, and cherished the memory. There were many Owen didn't really know, who offered condolences and a funny story. There were lots of old guys, quite a few British accents, and there was Bobo Valentine, whose weight had doubled since Owen had seen him last and must now have been approaching metric tonnage. Sylvester Keech arrived in black silk Vietnamese pyjamas, being currently in love with a young chef at Indochine. Jimmy Coughlin came all the way from Dallas, tattoos and all, toting a case of single malt. And there was Ted "Brick" House, whose grey hair had unaccountably turned orange.

Best of all, Roscoe showed up and nearly broke Owen's heart by bursting into tears when he saw the photos. After a few snorts he pulled himself together enough to give a speech; Owen was too emotional to manage it himself.

"Max Maxwell was a great man," Roscoe told the crowd, "but a truly mediocre trivia player. His knowledge of geography was mostly restricted to the rivers of Warwickshire, his astronomy didn't go much farther than the Big Dipper, but his Shakespeare . . ." (Here Roscoe was interrupted by much cheering.) "His knowledge of Shakespeare delighted all of us who knew him, even if we didn't know Shakespeare."

He told several Max anecdotes that even Owen hadn't heard before, and finished up by saying, "Max loved three things, no, four things, no—wait, I can't count the things Max Maxwell loved, because he pretty much loved everything. He loved beer, he loved acting, he loved food, he loved Shakespeare, he loved thieving. But most of all—and way beyond all the others—he loved his one and only son, who organized this wonderful afternoon for us—Owen Maxwell."

Owen was barely able to smile and wave to the peculiar gang that swirled around him. He thanked Roscoe and went downstairs for a moment to pull himself together. The bar seemed pitch-dark after the noise and brightness upstairs. All of the booths were empty, except for one where a young couple talked in hushed tones. A monk came over to Owen, but he shook his head.

His breathing was just about back to normal when someone approached his booth from behind him.

"Is it okay if I join you?"

Light from one of the pub's stained glass lamps turned Sabrina's face shades of rose and royal blue. She was wearing jeans and a white shirt, and those two everyday items had never looked so good. She seemed a lot taller than Owen remembered.

He didn't reply, but she sat across from him in the booth anyway, setting her backpack on the floor. "I came to say I'm sorry."

"Don't you have someone else to fuck over? Personally, I'm not interested."

She placed her elbows on the table and leaned forward, dark hair cascading over one eye. "I'm sorry, Owen. I was raised by a criminal, same as you. Sometimes my moral compass goes out of whack, and I was hoping maybe you—you of all people— could understand how that might happen."

"You don't have a moral compass."

Owen looked over at the bar, trying to find something to focus on. Sabrina's voice was doing more to him than her words.

"The jewels, the cash, everything was just sitting there, Owen. It was a perfect opportunity, you have to admit. And— and I didn't know what I wanted."

"Money, Sabrina. It's called money. You sandbagged us, all right? I don't even care a hell of a lot about that, but I really fell for you. I actually believed you were starting to feel the same— don't know where I could've got that idea—and I really wasn't ready to get kicked in the gut by some half-smart slut who fucks her way into my confidence."

"I'm sorry, Owen."

"And worse than that, because of you, Max felt he had to make up what we lost, and that's what got him killed." This was not strictly true, but it felt good to say it.

Sabrina opened her backpack and drew out a smaller canvas bag. She put it on the table between them, and it made a clunk as she set it down.

"It's all here," she said. "I sold the Mustang. So this is everything I took, minus about three thousand I lost on the car."

"I don't want it. I don't want any of it."

"Maybe so, but I still have to give it back."

Owen kept staring at the words *in beer veritas* over the bar. He didn't want to look her in the face; her eyes would undo him. He looked away, surveying the other booths, the quiet couple, as if they were of great interest to him. An uninvited bagpiper had wandered in and one of the monks was gently urging him to turn around.

"The money, the jewellery, that's one thing," Sabrina said. "But I wanted to say, I'm sorry I hurt you. It wasn't what I wanted to do. I just—I guess I was in a kind of panic."

"Uh-huh."

"I was running from—well, you know what I was running from—and suddenly the idea of being in any kind of relationship scared me to death. Part of me figured this was a good way to make sure that wouldn't happen."

"Being an ice-cold bitch is pretty effective."

"Okay, I deserve that. But the truth is, I'm not cold, Owen. I was frightened, I was confused, and—"

"And badly brought up."

She reached out to touch him, but he pulled his arm away, feeling childish even as he did it.

"And badly brought up," she said. "But I want you to know, there hasn't been a single hour or a single day in the past couple of months I haven't thought about you. You saved my life at least once, maybe twice. And it's not like I got away unscathed."

Owen looked at her sharply. "What do you mean?"

"It doesn't matter. I'm not looking for sympathy, I'm just saying—if it makes you feel better, I've already paid dearly for what I did."

"I never wanted you to get hurt," Owen said, "even when I was pissed off at you."

She cupped a hand to her mouth and whispered, "Did I kill that guy?"

"Max finished him off. He would have killed us all."

She nodded, pursing her lips. "I've been hanging around Juilliard hoping to bump into you. I even saw you one day, but you were with a really good-looking girl, so I . . ."

"I think I need some fresh air."

Owen got up and walked outside. Traffic was getting noisy on the avenues, but Seventh Street was still relatively quiet. The bagpiper, kilt and all, blew a few raucous test notes through his instrument.

"So now you've found me," Owen said when Sabrina stepped out.

They were quiet for a couple of minutes, walking slowly toward Second Avenue. A woman with five tiny dogs on a single lead was just ahead of them, addressing her charges in crisp monosyllables. A slight breeze picked up, and suddenly Owen could smell Sabrina's hair. How could a fragrance, a mere sensation in his nose, have such power over him?

"I was sorry to hear about Max," she said. "Max was . . . Max was really something."

"He was very fond of you, too."

"Oh, sure. I bet."

That smile at last. It went through him just like the first time.

Sabrina tapped the canvas bag. "Max would take it back. You know he would."

That was true. Max would have taken it back, and Max would have forgiven her. It had never been in Max's character to hold a grudge, and, for a criminal, he was actually the most trusting of men.

"They didn't connect him to the . . . other things?"

"Nope. Far as they were concerned he was a wig salesman—a failed actor who suddenly snapped. Autopsy showed signs of senile dementia."

"Not such a failed actor, then. I'm glad you didn't get charged with anything, at least. Think you'll keep on the straight and narrow now?"

"Well, seeing as how everyone I've ever loved has been killed because of crime, yeah—I'd say I'm done with it." Owen suppressed the urge to ask about her own plans, but Sabrina answered as if she had heard the thought anyway.

"Right now I'm working in a restaurant while I figure out what to do next. I like the people I work with—they're all either actors or writers or artists, all completely devoted to something. But what I like best about them is they all have clear consciences. They're terrified about their careers, they're in a constant panic about making the rent, but none of them is getting up in the morning thinking, 'God, I did something really, really wrong. I'm a bad person.'"

"You don't know what's in their heads."

"I think I know them at least that well. Anyway, it's something I want to try out for a while. A clean conscience. I want to see how it feels."

They reached the corner of Second Avenue and Owen stopped. "I gotta get back."

She handed him the canvas bag, and he took it.

"What will you do with that stuff?"

"Way I feel right now, I'll probably mail it back to the people it came from."

"Really?"

"I don't know, Sabrina. I'm still feeling a little . . . uncertain, you know what I mean?"

When they were back outside Monk's Castle, the bagpiper was well into "Amazing Grace," marching slowly back and forth before the tavern. They watched him for a minute, then Sabrina said, "Have you ever walked along Forty-seventh Street?"

"The diamond district? Yeah, why?"

"Well, it just struck me, some of those places would be so easy to knock over, you know? It's amazing, the lack of security."

"Yeah, that's true. But Max was a firm believer in working out of town—until his final performance, anyway—so it was never an option."

"Right. Good policy."

"That's Max. Slow but steady." Owen put a dollar into the bagpiper's open jar, then jerked his thumb at the door. "I'm going back in."

"Okay. But I was thinking—a young couple, maybe scouting out wedding rings, could really get a good look at places like that. They could walk right in and who's going to suspect them?"

Owen shook his head. "Not interested."

"I know. It was just a fantasy."

"Then again," Owen said, sweeping his arm to include the street, the oblivious bagpiper, the entire vast immensity of New York City, "the whole damn thing is fantasy."

GILES BLUNT grew up in North Bay, Ontario. After spending more than twenty years in New York City, he now lives in Toronto. He has written scripts for *Law & Order*, *Street Legal* and *Night Heat*. He is the author of four Cardinal novels, including *Forty Words for Sorrow*, for which he won the British Crime Writers' Macallan Silver Dagger Award, and the most recent, *By the Time You Read This*, which was a *Globe and Mail* Best Book and was shortlisted for the Duncan Lawrie Dagger, the most prestigious crime fiction award in the world.